THE DEVIL'S GAME

The Hasting Sisters
Book One

Sandra Sookoo

ARE YOU SIGNED UP FOR DRAGONBLADE'S BLOG?

You'll get the latest news and information on exclusive giveaways, exclusive excerpts, coming releases, sales, free books, cover reveals and more.

Check out our complete list of authors, too!

No spam, no junk. That's a promise!

Sign Up Here

www.dragonbladepublishing.com

Dearest Reader;

Thank you for your support of a small press. At Dragonblade Publishing, we strive to bring you the highest quality Historical Romance from some of the best authors in the business. Without your support, there is no 'us', so we sincerely hope you adore these stories and find some new favorite authors along the way.

Happy Reading!

CEO, Dragonblade Publishing

Additional Dragonblade books by Author Sandra Sookoo

The Hasting Sisters Series
The Devil's Game (Book 1)

Willful Winterbournes Series
Romancing Miss Quill (Book 1)
Pursuing Mr. Mattingly (Book 2)
Courting Lady Yeardly (Book 3)
Guarding the Widow Pellingham (Book 4)
Bedeviling Major Kenton (Book 5)
Charming Miss Standish (Book 6)
Teasing Miss Atherby (Novella)

The Storme Brother Series
The Soul of a Storme (Book 1)
The Heart of a Storme (Book 2)
The Look of a Storme (Book 3)
The Sting of a Storme (Book 4)
The Touch of a Storme (Book 5)
The Fury of a Storme (Book 6)
Much Ado About a Storme (Novella)
A Storme's First Noelle (Novella)
A Storme's Christmas Legacy (Novella)

The Lyon's Den Series
The Lyon's Puzzle
The Lyon's Redemption

Dedication

To Allyson Leitner. I'm so glad you were hooked on my books after the very first one you read. Since then, you've become one of my greatest supporters, an ardent fan, and a dear friend. I hope you always have that joy of losing yourself in books.

CHAPTER ONE

January 15, 1817
Landover Manor
Bedfordshire, England

MISS AMELIA HASTING looked about the drawing room at her family, and a bout of bittersweet nostalgia assailed her. How much did she love the people filling this room?

At one and thirty, she'd had enough about fate mucking about in her life and leaving her nothing except disappointment, and since her family's future was in a rather shadowy place, taking her first paid position as a companion seemed the next logical step.

"I cannot believe this is the last time we will be together until most likely Easter or even May Day," she said after she took a sip of tea.

Anemic winter sunlight filtered into the room from the tall windows. The illumination gave the illusion of warmth, but the chill in the air suggested otherwise. As long as there were no major snowstorms, she would depart for London in two days.

Her mother's smile was a watery affair. Once upon a time, she was a dancer of some small acclaim, which was how she'd captured Mia's father's eye, but because he was a gentleman and a baron to boot, when he'd married her—a woman without blue-blood roots or a sterling reputation—it meant scandal and gossip would always follow.

"I will miss you girls so much, but I understand why you feel that you must do this." She bounced her misty gaze between Amelia and her sisters. "Your father and I appreciate your help. Don't we, Alan?" Then she patted her husband's knee with her free hand.

"It's the least the girls and I can do, and perhaps it will help Papa to pay the taxes on the property." That was only one of the worries the family struggled with currently, for the taxes hadn't been paid in forever, which meant her parents might lose the property, so she and two of her sisters had resorted to taking positions as paid companions to help with income.

Her father cleared his throat. When his gaze landed on Mia, he nodded, but a trace of confusion went through his eyes. That had been happening with more frequent regularity, and sometimes he forgot things which would once come easily to him. "I do—we do. Of course." His shrug was more helpless than anything else. "Things have gotten away from me."

"It's all right, Papa." Amelia offered him a smile she hoped conveyed confidence. "The girls and I don't mind."

Her mother huffed. "You should. I'd rather see my daughters married and living healthy, happy lives as you were raised." Then the huff became a sigh. "I would like to have grandchildren before your father's condition deteriorates."

"Please don't do this, Mama. Not right now," Mia said in a soft voice, for there was a note of failure in her mother's voice, and it resonated with the same that welled in her own chest.

Immediately, her sisters chimed in, and then excited chatter filled the air, which allowed her a chance to reflect on her family, and how much she would miss them.

Busying herself with refreshing her teacup, Amelia reflected on her life as it was now. Her mother's words had stabbed through her chest. She'd been engaged before, but the war took her fiancé before the relationship could mature into marriage. Due to the uncertainty surrounding the war, and how fleeting life was, she'd given herself to her fiancé before he shipped out. Unfortunately, fate had stepped in and handed her two disappointments. Not only had she not gotten pregnant from that coupling, but she'd also received news two months afterward that her man had been killed in the first battle he'd been sent to.

The laughter from her sisters pulled her back into the present moment, and she flashed a fond smile at all their blonde heads bobbing at something their mother had said.

Once she came out of mourning six years ago, she had made peace with the fact that she would go through the rest of her life as an unwanted and firmly on the shelf spinster with no prospects, so being a companion was what she'd told herself she would be.

But at least her sisters might have a chance at living their fairy tale lives.

"Well, this was all Mia's idea, Papa," her middle sister, Cora, said into a temporary silence. "Your man-of-affairs came around last month for Christmas, and during their talk, she found out about the taxes, then proceeded to set all of this in order."

Her father nodded and waved a shaking hand. "I always knew Mia had a head for business and numbers."

"Yes, well, unfortunately the rest of the world doesn't believe women can do anything except marry well, bear children, and keep a fine house," she said with a glance at her mother, who had the grace to blush. "I always thought I could be a wonderful estate manager if given the chance even though I'm female." That skill wasn't exactly something a lady brought up at dinner conversation lest it shock a hostess and turn men away.

Her sisters laughed, and one of them threw a linen napkin at her.

"That's not very ladylike," Cora said with a mock-frown and the shake of her head.

At nine and twenty, Cora had been jilted at the altar a few

years back, and though it had wounded her deeply, she'd tried her best to move on with her life, except suitors were scarce thanks to the war. It didn't matter, for there was no extra funding to provide for further trips to London or more Seasons to see if she might take.

This was their life.

Cora was a twin to Nora, who had agreed to stay at home to look after their parents when Amelia and Cora left for London. Gossip in the family beyond the immediate members held that Nora wasn't all there in her upper stories, for she had trouble speaking and could hardly hear as well, but since all the country doctors she'd been to couldn't understand why, they had proclaimed her deaf and dumb and practically said there was nothing anyone could do for her.

Yet Amelia wasn't so sure. Her sister was lovely, intelligent, clever, and resourceful. She would do great things in her future if someone believed in her. Thankfully, their parents refused to send her away to an asylum. That was a big part in giving her the confidence to discover the woman she could be.

Once this current crisis passed.

"A woman needn't be a lady merely because it's expected of her," this from Genevieve, the youngest true Hasting sister who'd been a hoyden most of her life. She was supposed to follow Amelia and Cora in finding a paid position, but as of yet, she hadn't done so. It was Mia's hope Gigi would eventually realize her responsibility to the family.

Their mother snorted. "A woman should *always* be a lady." Never once had she bowed down or buckled beneath the weight of the gossips throughout the *ton*. She had not let her past or her roots dictate who she should have been, and she'd taught that strength to her daughters. And it was appreciated.

"Perhaps that should be the Hasting sisters' motto," Gigi joked with a winsome smile that had no doubt broken countless hearts. "Always be a lady until something much more fun comes to light."

Everyone in the room chuckled, and again Mia smiled, for she would miss them terribly. Her sisters had never failed her; they were her best friends in life. Even the two sisters who her parents took in and essentially adopted when they were a pair of lost young ladies ten years before, when their whole genteel family had perished in a house fire. Now, the girls were four and twenty as well as three and twenty respectively. Anna suffered from the scars of that tragedy while Emmaline was terrified to leave the manor, so they both needed looking after, which required more coin than the already strained Hasting coffers could bear.

I will find a way to support my family because I owe them at least that.

Anna's lips twitched. She touched a hand to the side of her face. Her blonde hair was curly enough that if she arranged it well, the tresses could hide some of the puckered skin. "Sometimes I think being a lady is overrated and puts too much stress on us." Though she had never balked or complained that she'd never enjoyed a Season, Amelia wanted to succeed at life enough that she might be able to sponsor her with one.

Her sister nodded. "I would rather behave like Gigi and gain notice than spend my days hiding behind walls, but I'm simply not strong enough, and in that I've failed you all."

"None of us need to behave like Gigi to attract notice. If it's in fate's plan for us all to be wed, it will happen without us making fools of ourselves." Amelia tamped down the urge to point her gaze at the heavens. Such dramatics, but then she well remembered being that young once. "No one has failed. Not in any area of our lives."

"As long as you remember that too, Mia," her father said softly, in one of those rare moments when his eyes were clear and his voice strong. "You will be the savior of us all, but I refuse to let you toss aside your own life just to labor for coin."

She snorted. "I don't know that I'm a savior. Cora is becoming a companion as well, and both of these positions won't be forever. Neither will Genevieve's once she secures it." At least that was what she hoped, but the truth of the matter was, the salaries they would draw wouldn't be enough combined to save the family's finances. "We'll be back together for Christmas and then we can revisit our plans at that time."

"Of course we can." Cora nodded, but she exchanged a knowing glance with Amelia that said she largely doubted anything of the sort would happen.

Their mother sighed. She was still as thin as she'd been when she danced, for there was one painting of her from that period of time. Strands of silver were more numerous in her hair than the blonde was, but she could still command a room with her looks. "Perhaps you girls should tell us about your travel plans. I well remember the excitement found in London, and though I'd rather you not have to do this, I can't wait for you to have that too."

Amelia nodded. "I'm to be companion to nineteen-year-old Miss Millicent—Millie—

Featheringham. Apparently, she's headstrong and far too eager to talk with any man she makes eye contact with." A sigh escaped her. "I have a feeling she'll keep me on my toes, but I've had enough experience with four sisters that I can easily keep her in check."

Her father chuckled. "Mark my words, she'll try to evade your watch, just like Genevieve did."

"Oh, I recall the trouble Gigi gave us." Her sisters laughed, and a swath of sadness cut through her chest. "I'm confident I can take her in hand and steer her in the right direction. Her father wishes for her to marry a lofty title, and he has enough coin of his own to make that happen, especially if one of those men are in need of a fortune." It was unsavory business, but there was nothing for it. "I merely need to shield the flighty, brainless girl from the unsavory types and hope she'll fall in love."

Cora snorted with derision. "Love. Silly notion, that, and it means nothing."

"Oh, stop, dearest," their mother said as she reached out to clutch Cora's hand. "There is nothing wrong with wishing for love. It's glorious when you find the right one to share it with." Then she rested her gaze on Amelia. "You girls do not need to find work. You can still attract husbands and live your lives here in the country."

"And do what, Mama? Watch the manor fall to rack and ruin? See the coin dwindle and wonder what will become of everyone beneath this roof?" Mia shook her head. "No, it's a brave new world now. The war ended two years ago. Men are difficult to come by since many were decimated in battles. Cora and I will get our livings, bring some of that money home, and hopefully pay off the taxes so you and Papa will not need to worry where you'll spend your last years."

For the first time in the conversation, her sister Nora spoke, or rather fluttered her hands and made a few attempts at uttering words. She was an expert at reading lips. That was largely how she communicated. One merely needed to study her and spend time in her presence to understand. *I want to help too.*

With her chest tightening, Mia left her chair to sit next to her sister. She put her free arm about the girl's shoulders. "I have no doubts that you will help in your own way. Taking care of Mama and Papa is a good start, and I'll write as frequently as I can," she said into Nora's left ear, which was the only one she could hear anything out of.

Nora nodded, but worry clouded her eyes.

"If there is enough left over after the taxes are paid, I intend to find and hire you a tutor who can teach you the sign language of the Benedictine monks. We will all learn it and thereby help you to talk more effectively."

Thank you! Then Nora bussed her cheek, and she fluttered her hands in the way she'd developed over the years. *I love you.*

Tears filled Mia's eyes. "I love you too." She would miss her family so much.

"What of you, Cora? Who will you be responsible for?" Gigi wanted to know.

"She's an elderly lady supposedly well connected with the *ton*. Mrs. Bromington has been through a slew of companions already, so I don't know how long I'll hold the post." She shrugged. "But it's a start. If I don't find I fit, perhaps while in London, I can secure a position of a governess. I think I'd rather be lovely at teaching."

It was Anna's turn to joke. She waggled her eyebrows. "You could marry your charges' father if he were handsome enough."

"And rich enough," Gigi inserted, to much laughter throughout the room.

"While full coffers are grand, love is love," their mother reminded them and then looked at Mia again. "If you fall for your charge's father, marry him. At least your future will be secured."

It was unfortunate that the lot of women regardless of class in England—nay, most places in the world—was largely dependent upon the whims of a man. Unless a woman was independently wealthy, there was not much hope she could do anything by herself. Well, without gumption and stubbornness, that was, and thankfully, she had both in spades. Thanks to her parents. Still, Mia shivered. "I think not. I am completely capable of looking after myself, and in this way, I don't need to pay for room and board, which is expensive in Town. Besides, the captain isn't my ideal."

Gigi, being her rambunctious self, pounced on that. "Oh? Pray, tell us what your *ideal* man is, then."

Heat invaded Mia's cheeks. "I'm not certain, for they are only dreams, after all." When Nora clutched at her hand and encouraged her with a nod, she sighed. "I think, perhaps, I'd like him to be tall and dark, a little mysterious or naughty, depending. Someone who can stand on his own two feet, but he mustn't have vices or be cruel."

Another round of good-natured laughter went through the room.

"I remember you used to dream about such a man riding to your rescue, sweeping you onto the back of his horse, and carrying you away from everything here," Cora said with amusement in her eyes and a wide smile. "Is that still true?"

"Well, I don't know that I'd want the horse any longer, but what is so wrong with a Lochinvar type?"

Their father chuckled. "You always did read far too much. Filled your head with nonsense."

"I certainly don't think love is nonsense, Papa," Mia said with a slight frown. "It is merely a goal in life, but if that doesn't happen for me again, I won't bemoan the fact nor will I wring my hands like a Cassandra, and warn others from it."

"You should," Cora said with all amusement gone from her visage. "Men can't be trusted."

"Just because you were burned doesn't mean the rest of us will be," Gigi said with a toss of her head. "Men are simply too delicious to swear off."

Oh, dear. She would be a handful even now.

"Keep your hands to yourself while Cora and I are gone," Mia said with a stern look at her younger sister. "Mama and Papa don't need any more scandal, and you need to secure your own paying position to do your part."

Gigi huffed. "You are no fun at all. I'll wager you'll be quite the antidote in London." Then she pulled a face and her countenance cleared. "I did hear some gossip a couple of days ago while in the village."

"Oh? From whom?"

"One of my friends just returned from holidays in Town with her sister. She said that Viscount Wycliffe has returned to London, and what's more, he's looking for an heiress to wed."

"Who is Viscount Wycliffe?" Emmaline asked with round eyes and twin spots of color on her pale cheeks.

"Only the most handsome man," Gigi answered with a grin. "He's said to be wicked and a rake, that he takes a new woman into his bed each week, and that he's always avoided marriage. Until now."

Mia *did* point her gaze to the ceiling then. "He is a scoundrel, and any well-meaning mama or companion will steer young ladies well clear of such a man." She shook her head. "I'll be sure to keep Millie from his clutches, but to be honest, I rather doubt our paths will cross. We don't move in the same circles."

"Yes, but he needs a fortune, and your little Miss Feathering-ham has a large dowry," Gigi said with a giggle. "I'll wager he'll seek her out. Men with empty coffers can sniff out an heiress from miles away."

"Ha! Then he will be disappointed. She is not for him or to fix his wastrel ways. Millie deserves a good man for a husband."

"While I think your intentions to protect your young charge is admirable, just be careful, Amelia." Her mother frowned. "If you antagonize men like that in the *ton,* they will eat you up." She clutched her hands in her lap. "You aren't used to it and have enjoyed your life here more than in London when we had enough money for Seasons."

"Please don't worry, Mama. I am not afraid of men like that, nor am I cowed by them. If the viscount attempts to seduce Millie, I'll give him a dressing down and then continue on." She shrugged. "Times changes. *We* change. If we don't, everything is horrid. I *will* succeed in this. Just you wait and see."

If all went well, the Hasting family would return to good standing within the *beau monde,* and then all of her sisters would have a chance at living a fine life complete with romance if that was their wish.

For them, I will make this sacrifice.

CHAPTER TWO

January 22, 1817
Wycliffe House
Mayfair
London, England

A DESULTORY RAIN fell against the window glass as Nicholas Harcourt—Viscount Wycliffe—poured out measures of brandy into two matching crystal glasses at the sideboard. Though the drawing room was on the shadowy side despite the wealth of candles lit, there was no escaping the fact they were deep in the month of January.

"Foul evening," he said to his best friend Marcus Chapman, as he brought the brandy glasses to the grouping of Louis XIV furniture where Marcus sat. He handed one of the tumblers to the man, then dropped onto a low sofa that matched the chair. "Are you certain you wish to move on to the club after this?"

"That largely depends on how much entertainment you provide me tonight." Marcus raised his glass in salute before taking a sip. "And how much brandy I drink here."

With a snort, Nick settled more comfortably into the sofa. He rested an ankle on a knee. After a drink from his own cup, he sighed. "I don't know how entertaining I'll be, for it's becoming more and more apparent that I shall need to wed an heiress to improve my situation."

The whole of his adult life, he had avoided the parson's mousetrap; now because his father had been careless with coin, investments, wagers, and women, it was his responsibility to fix the Harcourt finances and restore the family name. Though his father had done his level best to make the Wycliffe title nearly unsavory, Nick himself hadn't been that much better now that he had it.

"You? Married?" The candlelight made Marcus' blond-brown hair glimmer. His lean, tall frame was dressed in the requisite dark evening clothes including a tailcoat, for they had planned to go out to White's tonight. "Considering you have followed directly in your sire's footsteps, I find that hard to believe."

"As do I." He peered into the depths of his brandy glass, but there were no answers there. "My parents were simply awful people as a couple, but I suspect my father especially would have been a horror on his own too." After a swallow of the liquor, he sighed. "At least I didn't marry only to fight like cats and dogs with my wife for twenty-five years. Those were horrible years."

He and his sister had endured the yelling, angry arguments between his parents during their more strenuous fights. During those times, objects in the house had become weapons as his mother and father sought to make their points. Those contretemps went on for years until his parents finally separated enough that the peace was kept, yet Nicholas and his sister Nancy had come out of those years with skewed views of what marriage and even love looked like. Quite frankly, it had hindered them in their adult lives to the point that they were both probably stunted. He'd never married, but he wasn't without women in his bed. More than was good for him, and never the same woman twice because he couldn't make himself form a lingering attachment or curate any sort of feelings for them past the urge for a physical release.

Though that might have been expected from him, his sister

had become obvious collateral damage from his parents' hatred. Nancy had married twice in the quest for love and acceptance. However, she lost the first man to war, but the second chose the severe scandal of divorce to rid himself of her and perhaps her inability to find closeness and affection. Were he and Nancy wrong or were they merely extremely broken?

For that matter, would they ever find what they were searching for in a mate? That remained to be seen.

"I suppose that is to the good. You'd no doubt make some poor woman's life miserable as a husband." Marcus tipped back the remainder of his glass and swallowed the contents in one gulp, wincing from the sting. "You aren't the marrying type, so why try?"

"I've no choice." After finishing his own drink, he sighed and set the glass on a small rose-inlaid table at his elbow. "Devlin Hall is in desperate need of repairs." The property in Oxfordshire had been sadly neglected for years, even before his father expired ten years ago, but Nicholas had done the best he could with what he had. Sadly, that wasn't enough. "So is the dear cottage in County Cork my mother left to me in her will." It was the one place in the world where he'd ever felt at peace.

One of Marcus' eyebrows rose in surprise. "When was the last time you visited Ireland?"

He shrugged. "It has been a few years, for I have stayed close to London in recent days." Why, he couldn't say. Perhaps it was ennui that kept him in Town or laziness or even boredom, for even the women he usually spent his time with couldn't fill the void that threatened to swallow him whole. "I need to go again, and soon, for my own sanity."

There were Irish roots on both sides of his family, and that was something he didn't openly brag upon when out and about, for public sentiment considered the Irish or Scottish peoples somehow less than the English. A ridiculous notion, that. But for the moment, there was no changing minds, especially in a nation recovering from war and one where immigrants were flooding into it yearly.

From a young age, he'd learned how to disguise the slight lilt in his voice, learned how to act like his English peers, affect the same attitudes and viewpoints, but as he'd aged, and especially after his mother died a handful of years back, not being true to himself had grown stale. Why couldn't he explore the man he wished to be, the man he *could* be if he wasn't held captive by worry and image?

"You should take the trip. It might give you a different perspective on life, my friend."

The sound of Marcus' voice yanked Nicholas out of his thoughts, but only enough for him to nod. "Indeed, I should, but I fear none of that will solve the problems I'm facing at the moment."

Ireland was where his parents had met, at a society event. Obviously, he was an English viscount while she'd been the daughter of an Irish lord of high standing. Perhaps that was another reason for the emotional vitriol and hatred in the marriage. Irish anger that went generations deep, and his mother had always been entirely too independent while his father had demanded obedience. Nicholas had admired her for that, and perhaps had been unconsciously looking for a woman with those qualities—steadfast, determined, strong, tart-mouthed, objective—someone he could rub along well with for more than a week. Sadly, English women came up lacking time and again.

Why was that?

The clinking of crystal against crystal brought him out of his thoughts. When he glanced up, he startled, for Marcus had gotten up and refilled both of their brandy glasses, and he'd completely missed it. "Perhaps travel wouldn't solve your problems, but it would help remove some of the sting from them." His friend offered him a glass, then set down one of the brandy bottles they'd both risked their lives to run through naval blockades during the war to smuggle into England. Currently, Nicholas' cellar contained countless bottles of the same, for there had been more than enough to go around. "In fact, why don't you relocate to Ireland for a while and ruminate? Life at the cottage would be much cheaper than here."

"True, and much more dull, but none of it would solve my current dilemma." Again, he peered into the depths of his brandy glass, but aside from the lovely tawny hue, nothing else was available.

Marcus was having none of his maudlin mood. "You mean you couldn't be without a woman for that long."

"There is that." Heat crept up the back of his neck. "However, I do need a fortune to infuse my coffers if I'm to remodel the hall, make repairs to tenant cottages, and purchase new farming equipment. To say nothing about bringing the cottage in Ireland up to more modern standards." He sighed, then took a large gulp of his liquor. Perhaps it was the brandy that gave him the courage to continue talking or perhaps he simply needed someone with a listening ear. "I have some ideas on how to rotate fields and use different types of cattle to regenerate the land that I believe will prove beneficial and quite lucrative in a few years." When his friend stared, Nick nodded and gave him a grin. "What? I've been studying farming and agriculture. It's quite fascinating and passes the time."

Marcus snorted. "More fascinating than smuggling?"

"Those were exciting days, I won't lie, but *this* has the potential to be so as well."

"I never thought I'd see the day when the wicked Viscount Wycliffe became dull enough to become a farmer." Amusement danced in his friend's green eyes. "Don't let the *beau monde* know or your appeal with the petticoat line will be downgraded and you won't be sought after. Your bed will remain empty, but never fear. Perhaps you can let a goat or a sheep sleep at the foot to keep you warm during the winter."

"Do shut up." But Nicholas shrugged. "I'm old, Marcus."

"You are nine and thirty. Hardly ancient, so stop trying to affect an air of tragedy," his friend said, with the same logic he always had when Nicholas assumed dramatics.

"I feel ancient some days, haven't felt vital since our smuggling days." He paused to take another sip of brandy and welcomed the burn in his throat. "Regardless, I need to change my life before I wreck it like my father did his." Was it truly him saying those words? "I need to make something of myself, for posterity, for children I'd like to have, so that someone—anyone—will remember me with admiration and fondness over the scandals and sin."

"I'll be damned." Marcus stared with raised eyebrows and a hanging lower jaw. "You're serious."

"I am." A sigh left his throat. "As stupid as it seems, I have grown weary of being a rake, of never remembering the names of the women I've had in my bed, of never truly connecting with them outside of a good fuck." And there had been a handful of memorable, spectacular bed partners, but none of that amounted to a decent life, an existence he could be proud of, that would make a name for himself outside of a scoundrel.

For long moments, Marcus rested a speculative gaze on him. The crackle of the fire behind a decorative metal screen filled the silence. Eventually, he stirred. "Who are you and what have you done with my best friend?" When Nick didn't answer, he sighed. "I don't know that I like this new responsible person you're leaning toward."

"Neither do I, but I cannot continue on as I have before. That life will likely kill me, and I'll be damned if I die of some disease contracted by a bedmate." Which was how his father met his demise. Died of the pox, and that was a particularly horrific way to leave this mortal coil.

"Or a faulty liver," his friend was quick to add, with a slight lift to his brandy glass.

"There is that." Heavily imbibing was yet another vice he either needed to curb or cut from his life completely if he were to make a respectable go of it. "At this point, I might as well become a vicar."

"Oh, that's rich." Marcus wiped at his streaming eyes, brought on by choking on a swallow of brandy. "You darkening the door of a church. Wouldn't that bring about the apocalypse?"

"You don't feel I'm capable of living a decent life?"

"I'm certain you could if you had enough motivation, but why would you wish to change your life so drastically? That would mean altering your personality as well, and at that point, you might as well be hiding." The man shrugged. "I don't like it."

"Neither do I, but how else am I to accomplish my goals? What I've been doing for years hasn't been working." He frowned, took another sip, let the liquor slide slowly down his throat. "I don't know how to explain it, but I feel as if I'm running out of time. Eventually, my looks, my body will fail me. I need to marry now before I lose teeth, or my stomach goes paunchy."

Marcus snorted. "As if that would be the end of the world. If you were ugly, there might be more women for the rest of us." When Nick didn't find that as amusing as his friend did, Marcus huffed. "Look, I understand. I do. None of us are immortal, and there is something compelling about having offspring to continue our lines, and I don't begrudge that for you, but don't change yourself so much that you are someone else entirely. Where is the appeal of that?" He met Nicholas' gaze with a raised eyebrow. "Most of us like you because of who you are. Bear that in mind as you embark on the next phase of your life."

What he said made sense. "I will."

"That being said, there are certain things you do that *are* beyond the pale, so perhaps work on those things but keep who you essentially are in the bargain." Marcus followed the statement with another sip of brandy.

Of course, the man with all the advice didn't go on to tell him which attributes were the most off-putting. *I suppose I'll have to puzzle that out for myself.* "So then we have come back around to my original complaint—I must wed, and marry an heiress in order to avoid my properties falling down around my ears."

The ghost of a grin curved his friend's mouth. "Soon enough

it will be Valentine's Day and the winter Season in London looks promising enough to yield a bevy of ladies hoping for an advantageous match." Marcus finished his brandy. "Perhaps you should make an effort to attend as many events as you've been invited to. That way you'll have a selection to choose from, but knowing fate, whichever of them are heiresses is bound to mean they're horse faced, but at least we can mourn the loss of your bachelorhood or celebrate your engagement in the same breath."

"Ah, then you assume you'll go with me?" He swallowed the remainder of his brandy, and though his throat burned slightly, it was damn fine liquor. At least that was something useful the French provided.

"Of course I will. We've no doubt been invited to the same social events, and what else have I got to do in the winter?"

There was that. At least it wasn't snowing. "I only hope the woman I must select for my bride," God, it hurt his throat just to utter that word aloud, "is compelling and moderately interesting, but more likely she'll have more bosom than brains." He rested his empty glass on the table at his elbow. "As long as she's an heiress, I can find stimulating conversation elsewhere."

God help him.

"Perhaps the chit will match your appetites in the bedroom."

"If I'm forced to marry a young girl, you already know she'll be untried. I don't know if I have the fortitude to take an innocent to my bed, even if we are wed." It was something he hadn't given much thought to before, but now that the very real possibility was staring at him in the face, he rather thought he might cast up his accounts. "Hysterics and tears don't encourage arousal."

"No, they do not, and I don't envy you the task ahead, but you'll somehow cock it up and take a mistress."

"Not immediately, and not until said wife gives me an heir." Though he wanted all that life could give, somehow, knowing himself and how he'd treat said wife, the idea rankled.

"There you go thinking again. Dangerous business." Marcus chuckled. "However, marry you must, and who knows? You might be fortunate and said woman might already be halfway in adoration for you. Your reputation always goes before you."

"Thank you for the reminder." Nicholas rolled his gaze to the ceiling. "Don't be stupid, Marcus. You know a wide segment of the female population in London hates me." Hadn't he had the scars to prove it?

"If that proves the case, I'll be certain to watch from the sidelines to mock you later. I suspect there are some who haven't heard of you or if they have, they're indifferent. Honestly, those women will be the ones who intrigue you the most, for you thrive on being wicked." When Nicholas would have interrupted, Marcus raised a hand. "Yet despite that, I'll wager against you and the fact you'll be ambivalent with your marriage vows or even take a mistress."

"Why? You know how I am."

"I do, but I've long suspected that is a shield, a wall you hide behind out of fear." When he lifted an eyebrow, Nicholas kept his own counsel. "Is it because deep down, you believe love is something to fight for? Do you believe that state is everything people laud it to be?"

"I… I couldn't say." Because he didn't know. Or didn't want to delve into his feelings on the subject.

"Ah." A knowing grin lit Marcus' face. "I think that's why you're so cynical about love and romance, but you're terrified about actually giving your heart to a woman, for that would mean you'd need to be vulnerable, and with the knowledge of your parents' marriage ingrained in your mind, you keep yourself aloof from any of it."

"Perhaps, or perhaps it's merely easier to bed them and leave them." No muss or fuss. And certainly, no tears or pain on his part… unless one of those women threw something at his head.

"True, except now you need a wife and an heir before you manage to off yourself or a scorned woman plunges a blade into your heart."

"Don't be an arse, Marcus." He refused to think upon anything that his friend had said in the event it might be true.

"As long as you aren't one as well, Wycliffe."

Nicholas heaved a sigh. "Here's hoping that the dismal month dedicated to love and romance won't be quite as dreadful as I assume it might be." If all went well, he could find an heiress, charm her, possibly seduce her, and then ask to pay his addresses to her so that come May Day, he could be wed.

And no doubt die of boredom shortly thereafter.

CHAPTER THREE

February 2, 1817
Featheringham House
Mayfair
London, England

M IA HAD BEEN a paid companion for all of nine days, and in
that time, she'd come to realize that Millie's father,
Captain Featheringham, had a taste for the expensive as well as
the garish, and all of the textiles as well as decorations came from
his importing and exporting business.

Gilt frames ensconced every painting in Featheringham
House. The legs and wooden details of all the furniture had been
painted gilt as well. Statues of Roman gods and goddesses
decorated nearly every room in the townhouse in some capacity.
Heavy, velvet draperies hung at all the windows. Accents on
much of the wallpaper had been done in gold paint, whether
those designs were vines, leaves, speckles, or in some cases, fish.
The floors were covered with plush Aubusson as well as Oriental
style rugs. All of that luxury oftentimes clashed with the different
styles and made the mind play tricks, but in the captain's mind, all
of that finery equated with wealth.

Unfortunately, none of that could give the owner elegance or class.

As she, Millie, and the captain paused in the entry hall to don outwear in preparation for going to a rout, Mia checked over her charge's appearance. "You are lovely tonight, Millie."

Perhaps dressed a tad too elegantly for her social status in a gown of rich vivid pink satin trimmed with golden embroidery and a rather lower neckline than the occasion demanded, there was no doubt that the brunette was a beautiful chit. Her dark brown hair had been arranged in a topknot that cascaded over one shoulder in sleek, bouncy curls. The tiara glittering with small rubies was out of place and over the top, but the captain had insisted his daughter sparkle like the gem she was. No doubt he wanted her to catch the notice of everyone at the rout, and so the ruby tiara remained, along with a matching necklace and bracelet.

The captain beamed as he donned a gray greatcoat. "Only the best for my girl. If you wish to attract someone of status, you have to look like you are already there."

"How clever of you," Mia murmured while hoping she'd schooled her expression into a mask of boredom instead of letting her shock show as she fastened the hooks of her plain black cloak with the blue satin lining. While the logic wasn't necessarily wrong, it was distasteful for a nineteen-year-old girl to assume she could land someone that high up on the social ladder as well as pull off the bejeweled look without having done anything to earn said jewels.

While the captain assisted his daughter in donning a rabbit fur-lined ivory cloak, he met Mia's eyes. "You remember that you have a specific purpose tonight, Miss Hasting?" Before she could answer, he rushed into the silence. "Find my girl an admirable match."

"There's no chance you'll let me forget, Captain," she said as she pulled on her kid gloves. Her only purpose for existing in this moment was to ferret out eligible men and steer Millie toward them. The higher on the social ladder the better, not to mention the richer the man was, the more likely the captain was to accept the match. "Never fear. By the time Easter arrives, she'll no doubt be on her way to a grand engagement. I'll also keep the unsavory men away, because the dowry on her head is sure to draw fortune hunters."

He beamed and then winked at his daughter, who blushed prettily. "I knew you were the woman for the job when I hired you, Miss Hasting, but we should be going now. Out to the carriage, ladies." As Millie went ahead of them out the front door, the captain waylaid Mia with a hand on her arm regardless of the butler, who lingered in the area. There was a light in the captain's eyes she didn't quite trust. "Once my girl is settled, perhaps you would let me court you. I could use a new wife once my girl leaves the nest, and there's no reason we cannot have a family of our own. You're not that long in the tooth."

Oh, be still my heart.

What woman wouldn't be flattered by such a compliment or a future? She couldn't keep the sarcasm from her thoughts while trying valiantly not to let her feelings show on her face. "Ah." The captain had a paunch and jowls and thinning hair. How revolting would it be to see him *sans* clothing? Or worse yet, have him climb on top of her to make said family? To be fair, she wasn't averse to physical affection or intercourse—she *had* been engaged after all—but if she *were* to marry, she'd hoped it was to a man thinner and perhaps with looks if fate was kind. Realizing he waited for an answer, she cleared her throat. "While I appreciate the offer, Captain Featheringham, I must decline. I rather don't believe I'll marry anyone again. Romance and love are best left for girls Millie's age."

"Understandable." The captain nodded with an expression of sympathy on his face. "Felt that way myself after my wife died, but keep the idea in mind, Miss Hasting. I won't rescind the offer any time soon." Then he bustled out of the house while putting his top hat upon his head.

"I rather hope you would," she whispered to the space where

he'd just vacated, much to the amusement of the butler as she, too, departed the house for the carriage waiting at the curb.

The rout, which was hosted by Earl and Countess Such and Such—Mia was terrible at remembering names or titles—but everything was glamourous and glittering. Wealth was on display everywhere she looked. Though she'd not grown up in poverty but on the outskirts of the *ton*, this level of excess was surprising to her, and for one moment, panic filled her chest. This wasn't her world; she didn't belong here. A bout of homesickness suddenly assailed her, which was the first time that had happened since she'd taken the position. All she wanted to do was go back home and hide away from everything.

Except, she remembered she wasn't here for herself. This wasn't an event for her to enjoy as a guest. She was here as a companion to Millie, to keep her out of scandal and find her an acceptable, wealthy match. Then she would move on to the next position. Whether that be to another young lady or an elderly lady like her sister Cora had done was anyone's guess, but she supposed she would take whatever opportunity came her way, for she was a widow and life stretched out before her.

It was a very liberating feeling.

With a smile, Mia turned toward her charge. "It looks to be a grand turnout tonight," she whispered as she glanced about the crowded drawing room.

"Oh, where do I start? It's maddening and I'm nearly frozen with the choices." Millie fairly vibrated with excitement and nerves beside her.

"Perhaps you should merely enjoy this first foray instead of going on the hunt immediately."

"But what if some other girl snaps up the good men before I get a look at them?" On and on she chattered about all the men she wanted to meet, because how could they possibly pass on a chance to vie for her affections? Her papa was rich, and he would spare no expense to see her launched and married.

With a hurried prayer for patience, Mia pressed her lips together. "There is more to life than coin," she reminded the girl. Millie was one of those young ladies who could have benefited largely from attending finishing school. She was a bit too raw, too exuberant for many of the English gentlemen circulating through the room. To say nothing of her general lack of refinement, which might put some of them off, especially the bluer their blood.

But the captain had been adamant his daughter was ready for society without all those extra fripperies, so here they were.

"Of course, Miss Hasting. There are men!" Her brown eyes glittered with excitement. "I cannot wait to get started."

Dear lord. "While this is true, those very men want nothing more from you than to get their hands beneath your skirting or put you into a compromising position, so you'll have to wed them." Whether they were a good match or not. "Which is why I'm here. To keep you on a good path and steer you away from scoundrels."

A huff escaped Millie. "You are a killjoy, Miss Hasting." The girl frowned at her as she raked her gaze up and down Mia's person. "If you made an effort at your appearance, you wouldn't be such a scare, for you *do* have pretty eyes and a lovely frame. I don't see why a man wouldn't take pity on you and ask to marry you."

Like father like daughter, apparently. Mia quelled the urge to point her gaze at the heavens. "Thank you for that compliment, but I'm not looking for romance at the moment. You are my first priority."

"Then encourage an affair." The girl shrugged but there was blatant pity in her eyes. "Perhaps some of your dour starch would fade if you were bedded. I'm told it makes all the difference in a woman's demeanor."

She couldn't help gawking at her charge. "That was out of turn, Millie." Heat filled her cheeks all the same. "I am *not* dour. I am merely out of patience with you for trying to always evade me. And don't deny it, for you've done so thrice since I arrived in

London."

The girl didn't even have the grace to appear embarrassed. "I can't help that you keep me from having fun because you can't fathom doing the same."

Oh, yes, Millie would be trouble. Perhaps it would be better to see her engaged, and sooner rather than later. "Your father hired me to keep you out of scandal. Like it or not, the both of us are stuck together." And she had the feeling the girl would try to slip away at the first opportunity. *I'll just have to be more clever.*

Millie huffed. "I'm going to ask Papa to exchange you for a better companion."

"You can try, but he knows I'm your best hope of landing a kind, decent man who will take care of you for the rest of your life. You want that over becoming some man's mistress, don't you?"

As she spoke, Mia constantly surveyed the inhabitants of the crowded drawing room. Captain Featheringham held court in one corner, no doubt boasting about his coffers and his eligible, innocent daughter. Truly, it was bad taste, but what could one expect from the *nouveau riche*?

"No, I want a husband! I'm quite certain once eligible men come to know me, the one I choose won't stray."

Good heavens. The girl certainly thought much of herself. "Then be smart and choose wisely. Don't accept the first offer that comes your way."

Snatches of laughter filtered through the air. The earl and his countess were in the opposite corner of Millie's father with their group of admirers. Everyone was chatting and laughing. The glitter of gems in the candlelight was exceptional; the gowns divine. Flutes of champagne and tumblers of brandy were plentiful, and footmen continuously circled with the alcohol on silver trays. So many scents competed for her notice that her nose was soon confused.

Then Millie's fidgeting recalled her attention. "What if no one finds me alluring?" Concern threaded through the girl's whisper.

"I'm quite certain that won't happen." The dowry on her head practically ensured that. "But the key is to be yourself, to talk about the things that interest you while finding someone who might share some of those interests." She patted Millie's arm. "Above all, don't put too much pressure on yourself. This is one event out of many over the course of the winter. You needn't decide the remainder of your life tonight."

Unexpected gratitude filtered over the girl's face. "Thank you for the advice. May I join Papa?"

"Of course." With the wave of her hand, Mia let Millie wander over to her father's side; she'd have the attention she wanted there if discerning men could overlook the popinjay that was the captain.

As she moved about the perimeter of the room, the attitude suddenly shifted. With a frown, she glanced at the door. Two striking men entered and were night and day different from each other. Both stood slightly under six feet. Both wore expertly tailored evening clothing and starched cravats manipulated into intricate knots. The blond man had chosen a waistcoat in sapphire silk while the raven-haired man's waistcoat was of dark red satin. While the blond man's expression held a note of expectation, the black-haired man's was a bit sardonic, as if he didn't wish to be there but knew he wouldn't leave alone.

Who are these two?

From her position near the wallflowers and other companions, Mia watched the dark-haired man fully enter the room. He moved as if the world had always altered itself to his whim. Slight silver glinted at his temples, yet he didn't appear that aged. In fact, he walked with a confidence that spoke of the fact he knew all eyes were on him. Further, he knew exactly what each person wanted from him. Whispers around her said he was the Viscount Wycliffe, the man her sisters had warned her about, and in that moment, she could believe the rumors. He was scandal, heat, and sin, and he *absolutely* had to be kept away from Millie. Just seeing him prowl through the shifting crowds made her catch her breath for a few seconds.

There was no doubt he had left devastated female hearts in his wake, and what was more, he was an expert at it.

With a tiny shake of her head, Mia removed her gaze from the newcomer and looked for her charge. Where *was* the girl? The group around her father had disbursed. Rugs were being rolled back and furniture shuttled to the sides or put into the corridor in preparation for some light dancing. Finally, she spotted Millie, and knots tightened in her belly. The silly girl was being plied with compliments and no doubt empty promises by Lord Wycliffe.

Drat, the man worked fast, but then, probably every man at the event knew Millie was an heiress, and her dowry alone would set them up for life. The captain had certainly seen to that. None of them would wish for someone else to steal the march on them.

Let's see if we can't thin the crowd a bit, separate the fortune hunters from the genuinely interested. With a huff, Mia joined them, took hold of the girl's arm, and reminded her she should be circulating through the room, completely ignoring the viscount. "There are plenty of men you haven't been introduced to yet. It's not fair that one should monopolize your time so soon."

"Oh, Miss Hasting, this is Lord Wycliffe. He's a viscount, and he says he's in the market for a wife. Isn't that fortuitous since I need a husband?" Her eyes rounded, and already there was an awestruck look in her eye. She wasn't as sophisticated as she wanted people to think if she was bowled over by meeting one viscount. Surely, she couldn't be as stupid as that to think he was her soulmate after conversing with him for two minutes.

"Not so fortuitous since you will find the same story on at least five other men's lips tonight." When she tried to steer the girl from him, Lord Wycliffe stepped into their path.

"No need to scurry away so soon." The timbre of his voice had shivers playing her spine, but it was the easy grin that had silly flutters moving through her lower belly. "We have only just met." He wasted no time in scooping up Mia's free hand and bringing the gloved fingers to his lips. "Good evening, Miss…?"

There was nothing for it. She couldn't ignore him at the moment. "Miss Hasting."

The sly fox grinned all the more as he kissed her middle knuckle, held her hand a fraction of a second too long before releasing her. "I'll wager you're the girl's companion, hmm?" He winked. "You have the look of a watch dog about you. Or perhaps a dragon."

Millie giggled, as if that were the funniest joke she'd ever heard. "Miss Hasting *is* my companion! Papa said she's to help me find a match." Another giggle, this one more hysterical than the first. "And keep me away from bounders." She sidled closer to the viscount. "Are *you* one of those, Lord Wycliffe?"

"I can assure you I'm not, Miss Featheringham." That easy grin was back in place, but Mia didn't like it by half. A girl without experience in anything would be taken in by his charm. "If your dragon will grant me permission, perhaps you will save me a dance tonight?"

"Oh, I would like that above all things!" Millie practically bounced in place, which only served to draw any male gazes in the vicinity to her full bosom on display from the inappropriate neckline of the gown. "Though I haven't done much dancing outside the schoolroom. Does that matter?"

"Not at all, my dear." He took up one of Millie's hands. "You are just so beautiful that I'm having a difficult time concentrating on anything else this evening."

Mia scoffed. Couldn't the man do better than that? If he was supposed to be a grand seducer of women, that comment was rather pedestrian. "Then might I suggest a pot of strong coffee, Lord Wycliffe? Perhaps that will clear your brain." She arched an eyebrow in challenge. "Meanwhile, Miss Featheringham has other people to talk with."

When a young man not much older than Millie drifted into their circle and stammered with a flushed face until he asked the girl to partner him in the country reel that was setting up, three pairs of eyes rested on Mia. Wishing to make things difficult for the viscount, she nodded. "You may go, Millie, and mind your manners but above all, enjoy yourself."

An annoyed huff came from the viscount.

The girl's smile was wide as she laid her fingers upon the young man's sleeve, and he led her to an open spot on the floor.

"You deliberately thwarted me from talking to the chit or even asking her to dance." Banked fury growled through the viscount's voice.

"It is what I'm being paid for." Mia ignored the awareness that prickled along her skin. It was nothing but the emotions of the moment and would fade. "Perhaps we should move to a more private spot if you wish to continue this discussion."

"Agreed." Though he narrowed his eyes, there was no mistaking the ire in those dark brown depths. As one, they moved to the side of the room out of the foot traffic and dancing. "You have no right to keep me away from the girl."

"No, I don't, but I do have a responsibility toward her to protect her from men of your ilk." Though they stood at a wall without the benefit of privacy, the crowds ensured they were jostled together. When his scent wafted to her nose, she was unexpectedly adrift on how delicious that was, like the air in winter just before the snow flew. Very crisp and clean with the veriest hint of mint.

"Men of my ilk?" he asked in a deceptively low voice. "What do you know of me, Miss Hasting?"

"I know enough that you are hunting an heiress and have no intentions of entering into a romance with Miss Featheringham."

"There is no crime in it."

"Perhaps not, but Millie deserves more from life than you, a man who will no doubt get her with child and then consign her to your country estate while you remain in Town, resuming your detestable life and forgetting you are wed." As hot anger rose in her chest, she crossed her arms beneath her breasts. It didn't escape her notice that his gaze dropped briefly to her décolletage.

She lowered her voice but gave no quarter. "So I will not allow you near my charge, and will do whatever it takes to keep you from defiling or even marrying her."

"Ah, there are the dragon's claws," he shot off in an equally low voice. Though annoyance still clung to him like a garment, his expression softened. "However, I'm not afraid of the chit's companion. You are merely an obstacle to my goal." The viscount took a step toward her, which compelled Mia to retreat until the wall at her back prevented further movement.

"You can try, but I'm just as determined to keep you away." Oh, he would be a challenge, but her sisters had tried her patience all her life, and he couldn't be worse than them.

"You are quite an interesting person, Miss Hasting." The man shifted his focus, and his whole demeanor changed. Gone was the annoyance to be replaced with overt charm and a grin that would have most women ready to swoon. "Perhaps if you were a few years younger, I'd try my fortune in pursuing you to dance with me."

"Ah, so then you assume I'll let down my guard if you ply me with flattery and flirting." She tsked her tongue and gave her head a shake. "I'm made of sterner stuff, my lord."

"So I can see." Slowly, oh so slowly, he raked his dark gaze up and down her body, and she swore she could feel that regard as if he'd physically caressed her. No one in the room seemed to pay them mind. "No longer young or with prospects, I'd imagine, but I wouldn't mind having you in my bed, teaching you a few things. At least then you won't die an innocent."

Such gall of the man! "You assume I have never been married, then."

"Have you?" When she didn't answer, for he didn't need to know anything about her, one of his black eyebrows—with a slight point at the arch—rose, and in that moment, he resembled the very devil. "I wonder if you'd scream when you hit release?"

Despite the gooseflesh that raced over her skin, the man had gone too far! "You overstep, my lord." Without thinking, she raised a hand and then quickly slapped his face. The sound of a kid glove hitting flesh was drowned out by the dance going on behind them, the buzz of conversation and laughter, as well as the vibrant notes coming from the pianoforte.

"Oh, my dear Miss Hasting, I have only just started." Shock etched through his expression as his eyes darkened to almost black as he held a hand to his reddening cheek. "You have won this round, but make no mistake, dragon. I know what I want, and your charge is an heiress with a king's ransom for a dowry." He leaned so close there was a hint of mint in the air as if he'd brushed his teeth before arriving at the rout. "I always get whatever—and whomever—I want."

Mia trembled where she stood, whether from his proximity or from reaction, she couldn't say. "Everyone is disappointed at some point in their life, Lord Wycliffe. Perhaps your reckoning has come, and you should adjust your attitude accordingly." Her hands shook so badly she fisted them in her skirting. "I bid you good evening, but it is time you went on your way."

"For now." With a nod and a lingering glance at her, he executed a mocking half-bow from the waist, then he easily slipped from the room. Seconds later, the man he'd arrived with followed.

Oh, dear heavens! It wasn't often a man burrowed beneath her skin to make her heated and angry, but this one had, and she wouldn't let it happen again. At least she had a purpose now, and that was to protect the flirting, far too impressionable and naïve Millie. The girl would *not* be the viscount's latest conquest, and neither did she deserve a life sentence leg-shackled to the man without love. *If he thinks he's clever, I am more so, and he will not win.*

CHAPTER FOUR

February 3, 1817
Wycliffe House
Mayfair
London, England

"Y ou had better be dying or on your way to Newgate for all the nerve you had in summoning me to your house at this hour, Wycliffe."

Nicholas grinned at the grousing in his friend's voice as Marcus entered the drawing room just as the carriage-style clock on the mantel chimed the two o'clock hour. "It is not so early in the day, and I did wait so as not to disturb your sleep since you don't rise until noon."

Not that he could fault the man. Most of the time, they were both out at either social events or their clubs until the early hours of the morning, so it was only natural they slept late. Especially if they'd taken a willing woman home.

The look Marcus shot him was quite laughable. "You can at least order me tea."

"Done." As Nicholas yanked at a brocade bellpull near the door, he grinned. They'd been friends since their Oxford days, and that friendship had only grown stronger as the years had progressed. When a footman came to the door, he ordered tea with plenty of edibles, then made his way across the room to drop into a chair near the fireplace. "Snowing yet?"

"No, thank God. I detest the winter." Marcus rubbed a hand along the side of his face. He leaned back against one of the decorative cushions on a low sofa and rested his weary gaze on Nick. "What the devil was so important you summoned me here posthaste?"

"I met the Featheringham chit last night."

"Yes, I know. I was there. Remember?" Confusion creased the other man's brow. "Surely that isn't the reason you were desperate to talk with me."

"It's not." In fact, he didn't quite know how to explain it to himself. "I also crossed verbal swords with her dragon of a companion."

"Well, that's not out of the realm of possibility. You didn't think the chit would be on her own, did you?"

"No, of course not." Nicholas paused as he sought out the appropriate words he needed to say. "Miss Hasting prevented me from talking to Miss Featheringham as well as dancing with her. To paraphrase the conversation, she said I wasn't good enough for her charge because I was a scoundrel."

Marcus snorted. "Well, you are a scoundrel, and that's putting things mildly."

"Truth, but that's beside the point. So I tried to change tactics thinking that if I employed flattery on her, she'd be more receptive to my possible courtship of the chit."

Amusement danced in his friend's eyes. "Oh, I'm quite certain that went well for you." Sarcasm fairly dripped from the words.

"It did not, and she slapped me. Hard. Right there in the drawing room in front of anyone who cared to watch." Such treatment had taken him by surprise, and he swore he could still feel the heat that had been left behind by the contact of her hand.

"What?"

"It's true."

"Yet that is tame compared to how women usually react to you after you've bedded them." Surprise reflected on Marcus' face. "I must have missed all the fun."

He huffed. "You'd no doubt decided to investigate the card room, but the woman gave me a proper dressing down that made my ears ring." Instead of being excited for the chase regarding the young chit with the fortune, oddly enough, he would rather pursue the ice-queen companion. "She was quite indifferent to me or my charm. And the violent reaction wasn't because of a bedding."

"Ah. So she has morals and better sense than to immediately fall to your overtures." A snicker escaped him. "You've never been presented with such a challenge before, and her refusal irks you."

"Well, of course it does." When the footman returned with a tea service on a service tray, Nicholas watched in silence as it was placed on the low table in front of them. Only when the young man departed did he continue speaking. "I'm not used to that, didn't know how to act following her slap." Slowly, he shook his head. "If anyone is in need of bedding, it's the cold Miss Hasting."

"What makes you think she doesn't already have someone in her life?"

He snorted. "Don't be a nodcock. She's a companion. Her life is empty, for what self-respecting man would let their woman take a paid position?"

"If she's not of the *beau monde* or quality, she would have need of making a living. There's no shame in it," Marcus said with a raised eyebrow.

"Also true."

"I can make some inquiries through a friend of mine who works at Whitehall."

"I would appreciate that." Though she was past the first and second blooms of youth, Miss Hasting's looks were still stunning. "There was an intensity about her eyes I am unable to evict from my mind." Eyes that had been sapphire blue with the thinnest darker blue ring around the irises. Eyes that held secrets and concerns he desperately needed to puzzle out. Eyes that portrayed a faint trace of vulnerability that called out to his own brokenness.

What maggot has gotten into my brain? Clearly, he needed more sleep.

While Marcus put edibles onto a small plate and poured out a cup of tea, he grinned. "The *companion* has caught your interest, then? If you are already babbling about a woman's eyes, that's a certain sign of trouble."

"You'd know if you'd seen them." With a shrug, he frowned. "Thus, my confusion and need to have you over." He leaned forward, poured a measure of tea into the second cup, and then sat back with the steaming beverage. "What should I do?"

"Why do anything? You need the fortune more than a distraction. Stay the course. Pay attention to Miss Featheringham until she's eating out of your hand, then propose to her. Those marriage contracts are as good as signed."

"Wed by May Day, hmm?"

"That was your original plan, yes? You want the coin more than the wife?"

"Nothing has changed." Yet he'd been taken by surprise by Miss Hasting. For more years than he could count, women had always thrown themselves at him, and if they didn't, if he poured on enough charm, sooner or later they would fall into his bed. "The companion's indifference rankles, though. I suppose I don't know how to act when women don't simper and flirt back with me."

"Are you certain she even knew who you were?" Obviously, Marcus wasn't as bothered as he regarding the animosity.

"Oh, she knew." And what was more, before she'd decided to thwart him in every direction last night, there had been a tiny gleam of curiosity in her blue eyes before it was lost beneath determination and annoyance. "However, she is quite serious about keeping her charge from unscrupulous suitors. It will be difficult to move past that defense. For anything."

That bothered him more than it should, for though he needed to make a good showing in front of Miss Featheringham simply because she was the heiress with an exorbitant dowry, he also wanted to knock Miss Hasting from her icy pedestal.

Why, though? She wasn't his usual style, and she certainly didn't dress as provocatively as the young girl—which was tasteless for her age—but she hadn't rigged herself out horribly. There was tailoring and skill in the gown she had worn, albeit a couple of years out of date, so did that mean she was part of the *beau monde*?

For long moments, Marcus stared at him as he ate his way through the plate of sandwiches and sweets. "All this angst after one meeting, and a quick one at that, which ended with her slapping you." One of his eyebrows rose. "I will say this. It's been an age since you were interested in a woman you couldn't immediately coerce into your bed, so that's new." Speculation ran rampant in his gaze. "*Why* do you wish to see her discomfited?"

Fair question. "I have no idea, but she has bedeviled me with one meeting, and I want to understand why." He drained his teacup. "I don't much care for this feeling." It made him question far too many things about his life.

"Perhaps you didn't find the young Miss Featheringham compelling enough and your eyes wandered?" When Nicholas didn't answer, Marcus put second helpings on his plate. "I've known you for years, and in all that time, you've been in the petticoat line, and the younger the better. Suddenly, a long in the tooth miss enters your gravitational pull, finds you lacking, and dismisses you, but now you've lost all sense of responsibility and want to pursue her?"

"Not pursue her necessarily." He sipped his tea while contemplating the flames in the fire. "Bed her, definitely. Introduce her to the world of carnal pleasure, absolutely. But dangle after her like a fool? Positively not."

Marcus shook his head. "What do you know of Miss Hasting?"

"Nothing. That is the bizarre thing. I only just met her last night when she swooped in and took the chit away. I have no idea who her people are, but don't ladies become companions if they've fallen onto reduced circumstances?"

"I cannot imagine anyone waking up of a morning and determining that's what they wish to do with their lives." An expression of distaste crossed Marcus' face. "Seems a damned waste of a life to me."

"Exactly, so then why am I suddenly fixated with a woman who has been broken down by society's foibles?" It was a conundrum to be sure. "She's not beautiful in the usual way, isn't young any longer, decent bosom if I had to hazard a guess if not hidden by a dull neckline, but not as generous as Miss Featheringham. Pretty enough hair if it wasn't pulled back so severely."

"Yet your whole life has come to a halt because of a woman's *eyes*?" A note of incredulity rang in his friend's voice. "I find that difficult to believe from you. Perhaps you were in your cups last night."

"You know I wasn't." Miss Hasting's reaction to him as a man was exactly what one of his greatest fears was—that he was unlovable and perhaps not redeemable, and quite possibly a failure in life.

"As I said before, I'll try to discover where she came from. In the meanwhile, why do you care what she thinks of you?"

"Again, I couldn't say." He frowned into the contents of his teacup. "Perhaps it's the novelty of the refusal."

Marcus poured tea into his cup. "If you decide to chase the companion, will you continue to show interest in the younger one?"

"Of course." As if there was even a question. "I need that fortune and I'd rather marry the chit, for she's more likely to bear children."

"Yet you don't truly want the wife, especially her."

Nicholas made a face. "I'll wager she doesn't have much in

the way of brains."

"Her dowry is the most you know about the girl, which is little more than what you know of Miss Hasting. If coin wasn't an object, which one would you chase?"

"That is not an option for me. I'm in need of a fortune, so there is no choice."

"Perhaps." Marcus popped a tiny seed cake into his mouth and chewed. "You could offer a *ménages à trois* and see what happens." His grin worked to further irritate Nick. "If you could handle two women at a time."

"The glory of having one woman in my bed is to put the whole of my concentration on her and her alone." Heat climbed the back of his neck, for all he could see in his mind's eye was Miss Hasting with her blonde hair unbound and flowing down about her shoulders as her gown slipped further and further down her lush body… "If you can't help this situation, then leave."

"I didn't wish to come to begin with." But Marcus remained unphased. He sipped his tea and watched Nick. "I can see you are almost obsessed with this woman, and since I'm curious as to what will come of this, I'll help you."

"How? Beyond inquiring as to Miss Hasting's history."

His friend shrugged. "I have a nephew around Millie's age. My sister is in Town with him for the winter Season as she wishes for him to gain some experience within society." He selected a small honey cake from the tray. "Perhaps we should introduce them, see how they get on. Then you can go on outings as a foursome without raising suspicion. The girl would have someone to hang about with, my nephew can keep her attention on him while you seduce the companion." One of his blond eyebrows lifted. "That *is* still your goal, right, other than marrying the chit for her coin?"

Was it? Though he'd said those things to Miss Hasting last night merely to provoke a reaction from her, did he truly want to bed her? He drained the contents of his teacup in one gulp. Finally, he nodded as heat rose up the back of his neck once more. "Yes, I believe so. Once I have Miss Hasting out of my blood, all will be well." At least he assumed so. "I'll court Miss Featheringham and then marry her. Then there will be no more need for the companion, so she can return home. Once the chit bears me an heir, I'll pack her off to my country estate and hopefully forget her."

Hadn't his father taught him well in that regard?

As Marcus finished the honey cake, he narrowed his gaze on Nick. "And then what? Pursue Miss Hasting? Ask her to be your mistress? That would be a lark, hmm? Impregnate the girl, but find entertainment and fulfillment with her companion, who is near twelve or so years her senior?"

"Interesting theory, my friend." Could he do such a thing with Miss Featheringham none the wiser? Would the companion even consent to it? "Though I'm not certain Miss Hasting would agree." He had the notion the cold Miss Hasting might be quite possessive once she found herself with the man she favored. There was that look, a certain air about her. Desire shivered down his spine and into his shaft. "If she did, she will be one of many I've had in my bed. No one special."

Yet if he *was* one for the silly notion of romance and love, she *might* be someone he'd try to woo. Good thing he didn't believe in such a state. Love was for foolish men who had nothing to recommend them and even less skill between the sheets. Romance was for daft men in fairy stories who stupidly gave away their hearts to women who didn't deserve those gifts.

A ridiculous notion, all of it.

"There *are* consequences from liaisons like that, Nick." A hard glint appeared in Marcus' eyes. "Enjoying a carnal relationship with a woman outside of marriage is one thing, especially if you take measures to avoid pregnancy. What if you have children with them both? Offspring from two women, children who might favor you in looks. What then?"

He shrugged. "I always thought I might have a chance at being a decent father but a horrid husband, and we both know

I'm an exceptional lover."

"Ha. I'd rather not think about you in the throes of passion." The other man made an expression of disgust. "None of that matters if you are married. There is every possibility such knowledge won't sit well with your young wife, even if she finds love with someone else. If her goal is to marry a title, she won't soon give that up to hide in obscurity in the country. She'll want everyone to know she's your viscountess, that she was the only woman in all of London who could bring you up to scratch, because she's different."

"Anyone can marry a titled gentleman."

"While that's true, only one of them can land you, even more so if that lady has coin."

"All of this is mere speculation. There is every possibility I won't have anything to do with either of these women. Surely there is more than one heiress in Town this time of year."

Yet he couldn't get Miss Hasting out of his damn mind.

Doubt lay reflected on Marcus' face. "Why do I have the feeling this is not going to end well for any of you? It's beyond folly, man. A bad Drury Lane production, really, that has the potential to make you bad *ton*."

"I cannot help what people will think or feel. I only care about what *I* want. You know that." It was how he'd always been. Sure, a small percentage of women despised him now, but he wasn't vying for their affections. And an even smaller percentage of men in London wished to see him dead for what he'd done to the women in their lives, but he wasn't a stranger to evasion, and there was always Ireland to retreat to until scandal died down. "What I want right now is to see the frosty Miss Hasting naked and discover what makes her fly."

There was no crime in it.

Much.

Marcus shook his head, but there was a trace of disappointment in his eyes. "Sooner or later, you will need to mature, Wycliffe. You'll find there is more to life than what you are chasing now. You'll eventually discover you're bored with the emptiness, the fleeting hint of feelings you hide from, the endless parade of women who don't give a damn about you. And that is when you will need to make a decision that will change the course of your life. For good or for ill, but you *will* change."

I'm nine and thirty. I rather doubt that.

By now, he was who he was, but his grin didn't feel as confident as it usually did. "Today is not that day. Now, if you'll excuse me, I need to visit the florist."

"What the devil for?"

"I'm going to send both Miss Featheringham and Miss Hasting different floral bouquets, but there will be something quite interesting in the dragon's offering, and I cannot wait to discover her reaction."

"Playing with fire, Wycliffe. Not a good idea." Marcus pushed to his feet. "I wish you well. At the very least, you're entertaining."

"And at the most?" he asked with a raised eyebrow as he, too, stood.

"Providing me with a benchmark for what I do not wish to become."

Later that night

"A PARCEL FOR you, my lord."

At the sound of his butler's voice, Nicholas glanced up from the book he was reading on new farming practices. "Thank you, Jennings." He accepted a small, plain wooden box from the other man's hands. "Quite late for the post."

"This came by special courier."

"Ah." Intriguing. After untying the plain twine, he then popped open the lid, and an unexpected laugh escaped him. "I'll be damned." The inside of the box was filled to the brim with rose petals and cut up stems and leaves from the flowers he'd sent

Miss Hasting.

"Will there be a reply, my lord?" the butler wanted to know.

"Not at this time. Thank you," he said with a grin, but there would definitely be a rebuttal tomorrow. Once the butler left the room, Nicholas upturned the contents of the box onto the top of a nearby table. At the bottom, pink tissue paper that had been wrapped about the flowers rested. A small ivory envelope lay half-buried in the mess of the bouquet. "Did you dress me down in a note, my dear Miss Hasting?"

A single card came out of the envelope. Beautiful, flowery script held his response.

> *Lord Wycliffe,*
>
> *Thank you for your floral gift. However, I do not require flattery, nor do I appreciate it from you, so I am returning it in a way surely even a simpleton such as yourself will understand.*
>
> *As for the silk stocking, it is fine enough that I didn't have the heart to destroy it, but if you possess the other one, I would be delighted to wear the pair, for stockings are a costly frippery, and I am, after all, a practical woman.*
>
> *I do not expect to hear from you personally again. As I have stated before, you are not for Miss Featheringham, and I certainly haven't asked you to bother me. I'm sure you have many women who would adore such empty offerings.*
>
> *Regards,*
> *Miss Hasting*

As Nick read the missive, his grin only grew wider. She was clever, and that practically guaranteed his interest. Flipping the note atop the mess on the table, he hooted with laughter as he rubbed a hand along the side of his face. His heartbeat accelerated while awareness prickled over his skin. "Ah, Miss Hasting, you haven't asked me to bother you, but the pursuit is on all the same." He couldn't wait for tomorrow.

Never had he felt as alive as he did in this moment.

Damn her eyes.

CHAPTER FIVE

February 4, 1817
Featheringham House
Mayfair
London, England

Mia frowned at her reflection in the small compact mirror she kept in her reticule while her charge blathered on about all the men she'd met at the rout. Currently, they were readying to go out visiting the shops and then perhaps stop by the lending library, though Millie would be incredibly bored during that leg of their outing. Why she felt compelled to check her appearance was beyond her, for she knew what she looked like: blonde hair in a plain knot at the back of her head, plain navy day dress of a light wool blend done in a military style, but her eyes were lively and the hue arresting if one were inclined to notice.

Which no one would because she was a companion, and that rendered one invisible.

"Yes, you made quite the sensation the other night, which is all to the good as long as you manage to bring a decent man up to scratch."

The girl blew out a huff that ruffled the curls on her forehead as she peered once more into the cheval glass in her rooms.

Today she'd chosen a gown of pale pink cotton that featured two flounces at the hem and a ruffle about the bodice. A silly design, but appropriate for a girl her age. "How dull, Miss Hasting. I want a man interested in me who is a bit dangerous and exciting. Who is a worldly sort, who will enter into scandal at any second."

"Scandal will not help you reach your goals." Millie had just described Viscount Wycliffe perfectly though she didn't know it, and the fact that Mia thought him exciting made her question her own ability to be a companion. "And neither will flirting with men of his ilk." The sooner she found the girl a decent, stable man of good connections, the better.

"Truly, you are no fun, Miss Hasting."

"No, I suppose I am not."

"Have you ever been excited or even happy? Something more than the dull creature you've become?" Knowing Millie, there was no vitriol behind the words. It was simply an inquiry.

"A few times, but then fate mucked about in my life and forced me to reconsider many things." Reminding herself she made a living to help her family, Mia snapped the compact closed before returning it to her reticule. However, she couldn't help a satisfied smile, for her mind bounced to the note she'd had couriered along with the box of butchered flowers the viscount had sent her. If he didn't understand her refusal, he was little smarter than a dunce, but it had been quite amusing all the same, and something much needed to break up the monotony of listening to Millie.

The butler appeared in the doorway and softly cleared his throat. "I realize you are readying to go out. However, there are a couple of gentlemen who wish to call upon Miss Featheringham. They are waiting in the gold parlor."

Knots of anxiety twisted in Mia's stomach. "Who are they?"

"Lord Wycliffe and a Mr. Marsden."

"Oh!" Millie bounced off her vanity chair and snatched up her gloves. "Lord Wycliffe is here! After he sent the flowers from yesterday, he must be nearly caught!" She was all sunshine and smiles.

"Ah." This didn't bode well, for Mia knew a man such as the viscount wouldn't have thrown his hat over the windmill for a chit like Millie. "Tell the gentlemen we are not accepting callers just now, for we have errands."

"No!" Millie stamped a foot. Her eyes flashed. "You are *not* in charge here, Miss Hasting, and your first priority is to find me a titled husband. A man with a title is downstairs." She glared. "And he's handsome as sin to boot. Why shouldn't we entertain him?"

Oh, there were a multitude of reasons, but she blew out an annoyed breath, for Captain Featheringham would be displeased she'd turned away a perfectly eligible man. It didn't matter said man only wanted Millie for her coin, but that was beside the point. She glanced at the butler, who shrugged with an expression of slight distaste. Clearly, being in the employ of the captain was a strain on everyone involved.

"Fine." She released a huff of frustration. "Tell Lord Wycliffe we shall be down directly." Once the butler departed, she turned to Millie and leveled a serious stare at the girl. "You *will* behave with decorum this afternoon.

"As if I have a choice with you around." She pinched her cheeks. "Don't dawdle, Miss Hasting. I wonder if he has plans."

God help us both if he does.

The moment they entered the parlor—and in the typical Featheringham style it was garishly decorated with touches of gold—both men stood in greeting. Of course the viscount was dressed in the first stare of fashion beneath the dark greatcoat with his hair artfully arranged. The sky-blue satin of his waistcoat provided a lovely pop of color for the winter afternoon. Mischief reflected in those dark brown eyes.

"Good afternoon, Miss Featheringham, Miss Hasting," he greeted, and the timbre of his voice sent a few flutters through Mia's lower belly. "I hope you don't mind me calling, for I found I couldn't evict you from my mind." Though he glanced at Millie, there was no doubt his words were meant for her.

Mia fought off a blush. She ignored him in favor of focusing on the young man, who appeared to be a few years older than Millie. "Good afternoon."

He ducked his head while a ruddy flush rose up his neck and over his collar. "Hullo. I'm, uh, Mr. Marsden." When he offered Millie a posey of purple flowers, the girl exclaimed with enthusiasm, as if it were the best present she'd ever received.

"Thank you." She promptly pinned the flowers to her waist.

Together, the men were trying far too hard to impress the girl, and that didn't please Mia. She frowned. "The captain is busy with business today, if that is why you're here."

"We are not here to visit with him," the viscount said as he clasped his hands behind his back.

Mr. Marsden nodded. "Lord Wycliffe said it would be all right if I accompanied him today."

"Of course it is all right!" A demure smile graced Millie's lips that was directly opposite her attitude. "I'm Miss Featheringham, but *why* are you both here today if not to see Papa?"

The viscount softly cleared his throat to return everyone's attention to him. "We called to see if Miss Featheringham would enjoy going driving. Since there is no rain in the offing and there is a bit of weak sunshine, it could be a delightful outing." Again, though he looked at Millie, his words were directed at Mia. "Incidentally, Mr. Marsden is the nephew of my best friend, Marcus, so he comes from good stock."

His subtle interest in her was disconcerting. "We already had plans for the day." The fact that he was here made her suspicious, especially after the flowers from yesterday.

Millie huffed. "But we can easily reschedule them to go out with you." She bounced her gaze between the two men. "The chill in the air means I can wear my fur-lined pelisse and muff, as well as my new bonnet."

Good heavens. Mia stopped short of rolling her eyes to the ceiling. It was the height of bad form to discuss one's clothing in mixed company. "Since Miss Featheringham apparently doesn't mind changing plans, I suppose she can go driving, as long as I come with her as chaperone, of course."

"Of course." A slow grin snaked across the viscount's face. "Propriety must be observed at all times." Then he affected an expression of disappointment. "Unfortunately, both Mr. Marsden and I have only two-seater curricles, so if you wish to keep an eye on your charge, you'll have to let me drive you." One of his eyebrows rose when she offered a soft protest. "There is no need to worry, Miss Hasting. We'll follow along behind them. Perhaps stop for a sweet somewhere along the way. There is a French chocolate shop not far from Rotten Row."

"That sounds marvelous!" Millie enthused as she made cow eyes at the younger man. "I've never ridden in a curricle."

Hot annoyance speared through Mia's chest. She curled one hand into a fist, hidden by her skirting. Oh, he thought he was so clever, and he'd probably planned this ever since yesterday. However, she *did* appreciate that Millie's attention might be deflected from the wicked viscount. Perhaps this would prove a good idea after all. "Fine. We'll go." But she reluctantly agreed, for it would head off pouting from Millie.

"Lovely!" The girl bounced on her feet as if she were a small child. "Then let us not waste another moment." She smiled at the young man. "I need to don my outerwear."

As Mr. Marsden followed Millie from the room, Mia narrowed her eyes on the viscount. "This is your doing," she accused in an angry whisper while moving swiftly to the door.

"Of course it is." Never once did he sound repentant.

She huffed with annoyance, especially when he easily kept pace with her in the corridor.

"For the next hour or so, I have you all to myself, Miss Hasting." His grin was this side of wicked and made her feel both queer and excited. When he leaned into her, the warmth of him called out to her. "I appreciated your note from yesterday, but not how you destroyed the bouquet I picked out for you."

"I didn't ask you to send those flowers to me."

"In the event you wondered," he whispered as she donned her outerwear while the young people went out the front door, "I brought the second stocking so you can have the pair. Perhaps you'll wear them the next time I see you."

Dear heavens, the man is shameless! Heat infused her cheeks. Of course, she *had* teased him about the stockings in her note, so this was her fault, but still. He could have been a gentleman. Not knowing what else to do, Mia ignored him. She jammed her bonnet on her head and tied the ribbons with more force than necessary beneath her chin.

"If you need help in donning them, I'm available to assist. It is one skill I'm quite competent at. Of course, I'm more likely to divest a woman of that article of clothing…"

Another round of heat slapped her cheeks. "I'm quite capable of putting on stockings," she hissed at him as she drew on her kid gloves.

His face lit up in delight. "Ah, then you'll accept the gift?" He tugged the hosiery from a pocket of his greatcoat.

Why was she so unfortunate as to have the viscount bedevil her? Almost drowning in clouds of hot embarrassment, Mia yanked the stocking from his hand and stuffed it into her reticule. "Behave, Lord Wycliffe."

"Where is the fun in that?" he purred into her ear as they both left the house. His clean, crisp, wintery scent wafted about her to add to her confusion.

"Not everything needs to be for your entertainment." She frowned when Mr. Marsden assisted Millie up and into his tall curricle with the large wooden wheels. Another similar vehicle waited behind that one. Wycliffe's pair of horses were well-matched, dappled gray mares while Mr. Marsden's were bay and had slightly different markings. Both vehicles were open and sporting. Easily, she could envision the men racing them illegally through the streets. Not quite as tall as the old-fashioned high perch phaetons, but only just.

"Pardon the familiarity, Miss Hasting." Before she could

puzzle out what he meant, the viscount put his hands to her waist and assisted her up into the vehicle, chuckling when she uttered a tiny squeal of surprise. When she settled onto the well sprung bench, he vaulted up beside her, his sleeve brushing hers. "All ready, Marsden?" he called to the younger man.

"Quite, my lord," the man called back. Shortly afterward, his vehicle sprang into motion while Wycliffe eased his out onto the street with a smoother motion.

If interacting with the viscount in a parlor or drawing room had been disconcerting, sitting in a vehicle so close to him was even more so. Since the bench wasn't that wide, her arm was layered against his, and each time he moved to manipulate the reins, he jostled her, which set off another avalanche of shivers down her spine as well as flutters through her belly. Eventually, and after several silent moments had passed, Mia began to relax enough to enjoy the outing and not sit as rigidly beside him. This was an experience she wouldn't soon forget.

Then the quiet grew stifling, and she had to break it. "By the way, Miss Featheringham was thrilled with the flowers you sent. The lilies were gorgeous. It was a lovely gesture."

He snorted. "I'm glad someone was grateful for the floral offering." The viscount gave her a sneaking glance. "It was quite the shock to see little bits of flowers laying in that box."

"I'll wager it was." She smiled softly. "I'm not in London to have men flirt with me. I am a companion. Nothing more."

"Just because you are a companion doesn't mean you are invisible." He kept his gaze on the road in front of them. "You do yourself a disservice if that is what you think."

Her chest tightened as shock went through her from his observation. "It doesn't matter what I think. I am here for Millie only."

"That's too bad, because that slight longing at the backs of your eyes when you think no one is looking says that you should be courted and plied with gifts and flattery." Silence brewed between them, for what could she say? The social life wasn't hers any longer. Then he spoke again. "The fact of the matter is that your charge is an heiress, and from the enthusiasm she showed last night as well as when she met young Marsden, it would be better she found herself engaged rather sooner than later."

"What you say has merit and it is something I've thought about since taking this position. She'll be trouble." Damn his eyes. "However, I don't believe you are the appropriate man for her."

A muscle in his jaw ticced. Had she hit upon a truth? "Due to my reputation?"

"A bit, and there is your age. You are twenty years her senior." That alone was worrisome. "However, answer me this. Do you truly wish to align yourself with a girl who has no ambition or goals, who is quite materialistic and wants nothing more from a man than a title?" Why did she ask him that? She didn't care what the viscount wanted out of life, did she?

"Not very flattering to say about your charge."

"I am only telling the truth, and it isn't anything everyone else won't see as time goes on."

He shrugged. "These things would make us well matched."

"Poppycock," she said beneath her breath. "It would be a shallow marriage at best and eventually the both of you would be miserable." As she spoke, Mia watched him as he drove, and was thankful for the shallow brim on the bonnet that allowed her to see nearly everything around her. It was impressive how he handled the ribbons, how he guided the horses without using force, how his muscled thigh looked encased in dove gray breeches when the greatcoat slipped open and her gaze dropped to that appendage, how solid and strong he felt beside her.

He is not for you, Mia, and is an annoying acquaintance, nothing more.

"Perhaps that is all there is for me at this point—a shallow marriage with a wife who doesn't show me affection."

What was this, then? Mia frowned. "Why would you say that?" It was an interesting peek into his private world, and one she didn't think he showed to many people.

When he shrugged, his arm brushed hers. Tingles danced up her limb. "I'm nine and thirty with nothing to show for it except nearly empty coffers and a crumbling estate in the northern Hampshire countryside."

"Then I'm sad for you." Was he only telling her about himself so she'd lower her guard? That only made her more wary. Mia kept her focus on the curricle ahead of them to distract her from the man beside her. It seemed as if Millie was having a gay time chattering to the young Mr. Marsden, who was somewhat less skilled at guiding his horseflesh than the viscount. She couldn't let the viscount's statement go unanswered. "Yet you are so desperate for funding you would take on someone like Millie into the deal?"

"If I wish to modernize my properties and incorporate new farming practices, I need that influx of coin."

"Interesting." Despite herself, Mia was definitely that. She stared at him with slight shock. "You... care about that sort of thing?" Never would she have thought that about him.

Ruddy color rose above his cravat and collar. "In the past few years, yes. I've done extensive reading on the subject and would like to put some of those ideas into practice for the betterment of everyone involved." His grin was genuine this time. "However, if this truth starts to circulate through the *ton*, some of my charm will be tarnished. Rakes aren't supposed to be interested in that sort of thing."

"No, I don't suppose they are. Neither should they admit to enjoying books."

"That as well," he said with a half-grin that sent shivers of awareness tripping over her skin.

"Ah, but those things would make you vastly more interest-ing."

Unexpectedly, he chuckled, and that rich sound did odd things to her belly. "I don't believe you've been in Town long enough to know how the *beau monde* works. Book learning and talents in farming practices are not what they value." Another round of silence grew between them as he guided his curricle through light traffic and kept Mr. Marsden's vehicle in sight. "Speaking of which, you talk as if you have intimate knowledge about this world *and* you knew who I was. Are you of the *ton?*"

Well, drat. Remaining nameless and invisible as a companion was rapidly coming to an end. There was no sense in lying. He could undoubtedly discover her lineage anyway. "I am the oldest daughter of Baron Landover. We have, uh, fallen upon difficult times recently." He didn't need to know about her father's deteriorating mental state or anything about the rest of her family. Besides, she didn't trust him. "I wished to help so I took a paying position."

"Let me guess. Either health issues have put the family into a downward spiral, financial issues have prevented upkeep or tax paying, or there has been a scandal that soured the family reputation?"

Mia refused to answer, even if he came perilously close to the truth. She didn't want him that close, and she certainly couldn't afford to be vulnerable before this man.

"Ah, I see. You don't trust me and have already said too much." Lord Wycliffe turned his head, met her gaze, and again offered a slight grin. "You and I have known hardship, which is something Miss Featheringham doesn't have."

"She is young yet." Then she pressed her lips together. He didn't need more information.

"What happens once Miss Featheringham is matched and married? You move on to yet another position and watch it occur again? Never finding such for yourself? Never having a home or family of your own?"

Oh, the man was too astute for his own good! Remembering not to let him lull her into complacency, Mia huffed and kept her focus on Millie. "I am long past the age where I moon about and dream of love or romance, for I had that once and fate took it away. Being a companion is my life now."

"You were married?" Surprise littered his voice.

"Almost. Engaged not even a year before he died in the war."

"How interesting."

"Why?"

"I cannot see you as someone's wife."

Confusion furrowed her brow. "Why?" When had she become the world's dullest parrot?

He offered another grin. "You are far too dour, cold, and stiff to let a man into your bed. The fact you almost married indicates you weren't always thus."

Heat burned through her cheeks. "Much more of that will earn you a second slap, my lord." Why did he rub her the wrong way?

"Fair enough, but you didn't deny the claim." They rode in silence for a bit while he navigated traffic in order to keep Mr. Marsden's curricle in sight. "You won't dip your toe in those waters then?"

"I rather doubt it. If I did, the man would need to be extremely convincing or do something I wouldn't expect or never had before." She swallowed hard around the sudden wad of emotions in her throat. "Since we both know men are shallow beings, I'm confident I'll remain an unwanted spinster."

His soft chuckle had a butterfly ballet going in her belly. "There are ways to change that, my dear Miss Hasting. I would be happy to help in that regard."

"Argh!" Just like that, the serious conversation between them was over and he had returned to the rake he'd always been. "I have no time for such teasing, Lord Wycliffe. Millie has all my attention." Had she done the girl a disservice by consenting to this drive?

"How terribly depressing for you. However, if Miss Featheringham has a lovely time this afternoon, perhaps you should consider another outing for all of us."

That was… odd. She half turned toward him, which was a mistake for she could now peer into his face more easily. "If you wish to pay your addresses to her, why bring along another man for her to set her sights upon?"

"Ah, logic. I expected nothing less from you, dragon." The viscount snorted with apparent amusement. "Percy is nothing, has nothing. Barely came out of Cambridge by the skin of his teeth. Should have been studying at a medical college as his mother wished, but that is not where his interests lie. He has no ambitions as far as I can tell, beyond oil painting, but he has a good heart."

"It is odd you care."

He shrugged. "I am a complicated man."

Unfortunately, that was true, and it tugged at her to keep digging. "Mr. Marsden also has no title, so Millie won't let him pursue her after a few outings, I'll wager. Neither will her father."

"Time will tell, Miss Hasting. For the moment, he serves a purpose for me."

Did he use all the people around him for his pleasure? She crossed her arms beneath her breasts and faced the front again. "Well played, my lord." Another swatch of annoyance cut through her chest. Having Mr. Marsden here meant Millie's attention was on the young man as a distraction and the viscount had neatly trapped her—Mia. "How silly of me to think you might be genuine for half a second. Must you always have an ulterior motive?"

"When it suits me, and a man can be both genuine and rakish at the same time."

She scoffed. "Only in a devil's game it seems."

"Indeed, and it helps you are clever."

They rode in silence until he pulled to one side of the curb behind Mr. Marsden's curricle. A row of shops lined a street located off Rotten Row, one of which was a tea café and another a chocolate shop. Her stomach suddenly rumbled with unladylike loudness, for she hadn't eaten much at breakfast.

"Obviously, you are in need of sustenance." He winked. "And I am good at anticipating a woman's needs."

"Do stop, my lord. Relentless pursuit grows dull after a

while."

"We shall see." The viscount hopped down from the vehicle, then came around to her side. "Come." He handed her out of the curricle but did it in such a way that she had no choice but to slide down his body in a scandalous fashion that provided many more thrills than it should have.

When her feet found purchase on the ground, Lord Wycliffe didn't release her. She had no choice but to rest both of her hands on his hard chest as he stared down at her. Since it was an hour before the traditional fashionable hour, there wasn't much traffic, and they were blocked from the chocolate shop by the horses and the side of the curricle. Millie was busy exiting her own curricle, for the young man was quite awkward about the whole business. "Thank you for the assistance, my lord."

"Oh, we are not quite finished with our conversation, Miss Hasting," he said in a barely audible whisper.

"I think we are." As Mia went to move away from the viscount, he cupped the side of her neck, brushed his gloved thumb along her chin, tilted her head slightly backward, and then claimed her lips with his.

Oh, dear. Shock held her captive, and surprise kept her feet rooted to the street as she froze and stared up at him. Of course she'd been kissed before by her fiancé, but there was something about the effortless movement of this man's mouth on hers, the way his lips cradled hers, the warmth of his body as he pressed her against the side of the vehicle that gave her pause… and lit tiny fires in her blood. Something she'd assumed long dead came flickering back to life, and it both excited and terrified her.

In truth, the kiss only lasted a few seconds before he pulled away, with that same wicked grin curving his mouth. "We should catch up. Percy and dear Millie are almost at the door to the shop, and as much as I like the boy, he is too green about Town to secure a decent table." He tossed a boy a coin as the urchin took the reins, then he offered her his arm, crooked at the elbow. "I look forward to furthering our conversation this afternoon."

Not knowing what else to do, Mia rested her gloved fingers upon his sleeve as her mind reeled. He'd kissed her in public and she'd done nothing to prevent it.

That will not happen again.

CHAPTER SIX

A S LUCK WOULD have it, there were no large tables available inside the chocolate shop, but there were two small tables, which Nicholas promptly secured. He ushered Miss Hasting to the one near the front window while Percy and Miss Feathering-ham took the table closer to the center of the room.

The low buzz of conversation and laughter drowned out Miss Hasting's protests at being so far from her charge. As he seated himself next to her, which earned him a narrow-eyed glare, he grinned. Was she out of sorts from the situation or because he'd dared to kiss her? That surprise and shock he'd glimpsed in her expressive blue eyes earlier told him all he'd needed to know about her brief engagement: her ill-fated fiancé hadn't known how to kiss, and it was a good bet that he hadn't known what to do between the sheets either.

"Nothing will happen between your charge and Mr. Marsden while we are ensconced in a chocolate shop, Miss Hasting." When he peered at her, the weak February sunlight enhanced the blue hues in her eyes. "Besides, there are far too many witnesses. What could possibly occur?" Well, he had a few ideas he couldn't wait to employ upon the companion, but he didn't wish to tip his hand just yet.

"It is the unknown that worries me, especially where you are concerned."

"Ah, but there you are wrong, for I'm not concerned at all." At least not about Marcus' nephew and her young charge. When woman wearing a pinafore-style apron over her dress came to their table, he winked. "How are you today, Miss Twixbury?" She was the daughter of the proprietress, and someone he saw on a regular basis, since this was one of his favorite stops in London, and often when he came, it was by himself with only a book as company.

Another truth he didn't want as general knowledge. It was hardly a club, was it?

"Well enough, Lord Wycliffe." She looked questionably at Miss Hasting, but then rested the whole of her attention on him. "The usual?"

"Uh, no. Today we'll have tea, a variety of pastries, a set of your finest French chocolates and caramels, as well as two cups of drinking chocolate, which need to be brought out midway through the meal." When she nodded, he gestured at Percy's table. "Put their order on my bill. Thank you."

"As you wish, my lord." As she moved to take the order from Percy's table, Nicholas grinned at his companion of the afternoon.

"What shall we converse upon now, I wonder?"

One of Miss Hasting's eyebrows rose in question. "Firstly, I wish to know how often you dine here and secondly, what your standing order is." Curiosity threaded through her voice as she unfastened her cloak and let it drape over the back of her chair.

Well, damn. He didn't think she would have felt the need to inquire, but the woman was clever and intelligent, which pushed his admiration up a few notches. When choosing women to take to his bed, what was between their ears wasn't his first priority, but sitting here with the companion, he was slowly realizing it should have been. Verbally crossing swords with her was quite exhilarating.

"Uh…" Ignoring the urge to tug at the knot of his cravat as heat swept up his neck, Nicholas met her demanding gaze. "I come here once a week by myself, and I use that time to indulge in a fiction novel. In that time, I order a pot of coffee, two Parisian eclairs, and a box of four bonbons."

"Bonbons?" Surprise propelled the word into the air.

"Yes." Perhaps this truth would help her thaw. "I give those treats to my housekeeper, for she has a sweet tooth." Yet another truth that would completely change the way the *ton* looked at him.

"How interesting." She tugged her gloves from her fingers. "And in not keeping with the persona you show the world." Slowly, her expression softened. "Why are you so afraid of letting your true self shine through?"

If he wasn't careful, she would ferret out all his secrets, and then what advantage would he have? "I am not of a mind to delve into the motivations for why I do what I do. Today is for something else entirely."

"That is disappointing, for you might have potential if you would be honest with yourself." Once more, her luscious lips turned downward in a frown.

"The afternoon is not yet over."

Nothing else was said, for a waiter came to the table and arranged the tea and edibles Nick had ordered on the small, cozy tabletop. Once he departed, Miss Hasting went ahead and poured out a cup of tea for him. As their fingers brushed at the hand off, subtle heat twisted up his arm and prickled the hairs. Soon enough, she'd poured out her own cup and then added a tiny splash of cream.

Not wishing to become lost in his thoughts or give her the same opportunity, he slid a silver, oval-shaped plate of chocolates toward her. "These are for you." There were five of the confections arranged on the plate, each more stunningly decorated than the last. "You may indulge all you want, for I have had them plenty of times before."

"What are they?"

"Soft vanilla caramel enrobed in bittersweet chocolate. The

others are chocolate ganache covered with a less bitter chocolate." He leaned forward. "Chocolate is the next best thing to intercourse a person can experience. Some people who eat the confections swear they are the closest thing to a physical release as they've found."

"Ha!" Miss Hasting's eyes widened with disbelief. Slowly, she lowered her teacup. "I rather doubt that."

He gestured toward the pieces. "Try them for yourself." Then because he felt slightly guilty for leaving Percy to his own devices with Miss Featheringham, he glanced at the table where the young people sat. The two of them had their heads together and seemed to be talking quite seriously about something.

"I'm not of a mind for sweets." She pushed the plate back at him and then contemplated the savory sandwiches that had come out with the tea.

"You'll miss out on some of the best confections found in London, though." With the urge to bedevil her front and center, Nicholas scooted his chair closer until his leg brushed hers and the outside of his thigh pressed into hers. A tiny inhalation of breath on her part betrayed the fact she wasn't indifferent to him, and that bolstered his confidence. "Throughout the history of Western civilization, chocolate has been reputed as used for aphrodisiacal purposes. Though I do feel sorry for those fellows in the East if they've shunned the use of the stuff."

"Ah." It was a noncommittal response, but as she laid her teacup into its saucer on the table, the light of interest sparked in her eyes.

"So the stories go." He pulled the plate toward them, took one of the sweets and held it between his thumb and forefinger. "Some historians have linked chocolate and bed sport." Would she slap his face for the effrontery? As her eyes slightly narrowed in displeasure, he rushed onward, that's how certain he was this would hook her. "The Mayans used the beans of the cacao pod as a way to pay for prostitutes in the early version of brothels." Discussing such things in front of a lady wasn't well done of him, but then, he *was* a rake. To further convince her, Nick took a bite of the confection. Sweet with vanilla and the bittersweet notes of the chocolate, the treat melted in his mouth as he chewed. Once he swallowed, he grinned. "If you're interested, the rate was eight beans per woman."

"That is an insult to women." She eyed the remaining chocolates but didn't make a move to take one. "Especially if the woman in question needs to constantly stroke an ego like yours or suffer your immense arrogance."

Damn how he was coming to adore her tart mouth. Dropping his voice, he said, "That isn't the only thing of large size." When she gasped and a faint blush stained her cheeks, he winked. "But I heartily agree. Women are worth much more than that, nor should they be used in such a fashion."

She snorted. "Yet you do so with alarming regularity in your life."

Heat went up the back of his neck. "Yes, well, we all have our faults."

"You far more than others, apparently." She traced the edge of her teacup. "By all means, try and convince me you aren't vying for the title of worst man in London."

Suddenly, he wished to do just that, but didn't want to take the time wondering why. "Perhaps you'll see why presently." He popped the rest of the confection in his mouth, chewed, and then swallowed it. "Women, once aroused and primed for coitus are so much more valuable than mere vessels for a man's prick, especially if their hearts are engaged during such an intimate act."

She didn't appear convinced. "If you think that, then why are you a rake?"

"Why indeed. Perhaps we will discuss just that at a later date in a more private setting." Nicholas sipped his tea as maudlin emotions welled in his chest. Now was not the time to examine his existence. "We can learn much from history. Men in the Mayan culture should have kept their women steeped in piles of beans. That's how valuable such women are." Daring much, he slid the toe of his boot along the back of her calf.

Rosy color bloomed in her cheeks, but she scooted her chair a tiny bit away from his, annoyance clear in her expression. "Somehow, I'm not convinced you are anything more than a man who uses women for many things."

That aggravation amused him, and he wanted nothing more than to see her undone… or at the very least bothered. "Mmm, of course I can't help what you think of me, but it makes me want to try harder to convince you otherwise, for you are quite a discerning lady."

A huff of exasperation escaped as she shook her head. "I've told you before, flirting and flattery won't work on me." When Miss Hasting cast a glance to her charge's table, cool relief twisted down his spine, for her eyes, the times her focus was on him, had the power to pick at his soul.

"What about suggestive talk?" As unobtrusively as he could, Nicholas moved his chair close to hers once more as he plucked a watercress sandwich from the tray. "I am quite good at that." As he spoke, he trailed the fingers of his free hand along the top of her thigh beneath the table.

Almost immediately, she smacked his hand and the color in her cheeks deepened. "I rather think you know that is a waste of time as well your highly impertinent touches."

He couldn't help his chuckle. "When it comes to women, my dear dragon, the frostier they are, the hotter they burn, and you are fairly ripe for the plucking." While she sputtered, he leisurely consumed the sandwich as if he had nothing better to do.

"You know nothing about me," she hissed in a whisper, and as confusion rose in her eyes, she took refuge behind her teacup.

"Perhaps we should test that theory, hmm?" Nicholas paused in his seduction attempt as the proprietor's daughter brought two porcelain cups of drinking chocolate to the table. "Thank you." He nodded at the woman. "This is exactly what I need in the moment."

"You're a wily one, Lord Wycliffe." She flicked her gaze to

Miss Hasting. "I wouldn't trust him by half."

The dragon nodded, and in all earnestness said, "I absolutely do not." Once the woman moved on to speak with other diners, the companion turned her head to meet his gaze. Damn but he wished she had removed her bonnet, for the sun would have brought out strands of gold in her tresses. "Are you trying to use chocolate's effects on me?" Suspicion warred with amusement in her eyes.

"Only you can say since you think evil lurks in shadows. I merely wanted you to try the drinking chocolate here. It is quite lovely and not nearly as bitter as what you might find at home."

She snorted. "It has been an age since we were allowed luxuries such as this."

"Then by all means indulge." He didn't need chocolate to do the job his words would. As she sipped the rich, fragrant drink, he moved his leg so that it caressed hers. Heat jumped between them. A wash of pink color stained her cheeks. Awareness hardened his shaft. "Chocolate, especially the melted variety, is pleasurable on the tongue and the senses. It envelopes a person, warms them throughout the body, fires the brain with feelings of goodwill and…"

"And?" Anticipation flooded her voice as she hung on his words with the cup hovering midway between the table and her lips.

"It puts them in mind of other… scandals one can find when one is somewhat undressed." He left it at that. At least her mind would be primed.

"Ah. All of that aside, it smells heavenly." She sipped from the mug and a sigh escaped her once she tasted the beverage. "This is marvelous. So velvety."

"Yes," he fairly purred. One step closer to having her to himself. "Imagine chocolate is like the finest silk. Feel the coolness of the soft fabric as it caresses your skin." Ever so briefly he touched her hand. No one in the shop was paying them the slightest attention. "Imagine that rich warmth if one were to perhaps drizzle the concoction over a lover's sensitive skin." Once more filled with daring, Nicholas turned her hand over on the table. He lightly drew small circles on her palm, grinning when she gave in to a shiver. Then he lowered his voice, being sure to infuse suggestion into that whisper. "Imagine your lover licking that thick, sweet, sticky, melted chocolate from the pale slope of your breast, perhaps swirling his tongue around and around your pebbled nipple, teasing that aching peak and coaxing a moan from your perfect lips." As her eyes drifted closed, Nicholas grinned. "He might then drizzle a rich, forbidden path of the melted goodness down your naked, quivering body, then, as a gentleman, he would lick your skin clean, leaving no part of you unattended."

"Oh, dear." Miss Hasting drew in a shuddering breath as her fingers gripped the mug's handle so tight that her knuckles whitened.

"Indeed." Continuing to caress her palm, Nick leaned his head closer to her, daring to let the warmth of his breath slip over her nape. "Imagine your lover's wet tongue going into illicit places, discovering your secrets, unlocking your pleasure points, all the while whisking that sinful chocolate from your skin."

Her eyes popped open, and her eyes had darkened. "What then?"

Ah, yes, well and truly hooked. Was the ice around her thawing? He couldn't contain his grin. How surprising was her appetite for play, at least through her imagination. Would she be as interested if he were to truly make such an overture?

After glancing about the crowded shop to make certain no one paid them attention, he continued his verbal seduction. "That lucky man who will have you oh-so-needy beneath him might employ an artist's brush to liquid chocolate. He might paint a heart upon your navel, perhaps write endearments along your belly for the reward of licking and sucking away his handiwork until your skin was once more pristine, then he would blow over the skin he'd just dampened and watch the gooseflesh race in that wake." The trouble with trying to seduce a difficult subject was that his words would oftentimes affect him as well. Already, his shaft pressed painfully against the front of his breeches, but there was nothing to be done about that.

"I… All of that merely to bed someone? Isn't it a perfunctory act?"

"You have been cheated from that part of life, my dear Miss Hasting." If he could raise the dead, he'd bring her fiancé back to life and take him to task for not fully appreciating this woman. "Half the fun of coitus is to bring one's partner to the heights of insanity during arousal." Again, he leaned close to her, and the subtle scent of apple blossoms teased his nose. Innocent but somehow highly erotic on her. "Seeing how many times his partner can fly without him ever penetrating her body."

"Oh!" Her hand shook. A bit of the drinking chocolate sloshed over the cup's rim, and she quickly set it down. "What would he do then?" The breathlessness of her tone pleased him.

"So many things, I suppose, but he might abandon his chocolate artistry in order to kiss you senseless." Would she notice his slip in the narrative to make it about her? While he spoke, Nicholas continued to draw circles on her palm, and when he moved his hand slightly to brush the pad of his thumb along the pulse point on the inside of her wrist, she uttered a quick, barely audible gasp. So responsive just to a pedestrian touch as this. What would she be like in his bed? "Once you were properly aroused, he would once more proceed to explore every inch of your skin with tongue, teeth, and fingers until you begged him to send you flying again."

Her eyelids fluttered as her cheeks colored. "Who is this knowledgeable lover? I have never been treated to such things as you speak about, so you are either lying or wildly exaggerating."

In time she would discover he was neither. "I would have no idea, for you have kept men at arm's length after the death of your fiancé. Isn't that true?" Would that they were not in a public place. He desperately wished to kiss those slightly parted lips, see the raw pleasure she felt as it scudded through her expressive eyes. "Only you can choose to let a man so close, and perhaps it wouldn't be such a terrible experience as you believe."

Her hand beneath his trembled. "It's frightening to open my heart only to perhaps have it broken again and find myself more alone than when I started."

The truth threading through that statement pressed in on him to rile his own demons, for that was one of his own fears. Not wishing to delve that deep into his life, Nicholas shifted his position on his chair to accommodate his erection. "Perhaps you should weigh being alone against taking a lover who would make you forget about those things."

Is that why he did what he did?

"It is a risk," she said in a barely audible whisper.

"All lovely things in life are," he answered in a matching tone.

A shuddering sigh issued from her. "Is chocolate always this sensual?" Her pupils were dilated, a sure sign of arousal, and he wanted nothing more than to spirit her from the shop and into the first semi-private area he could find to make good on that momentum.

"Sometimes. Most people don't wish to explore that side of it. To them, sweets are merely sweets, and they cannot imagine chocolate having any other uses or meanings." He took his hand from hers to once more let it wander upon her thigh beneath the poor shield of the table. Slowly, ever so slowly, he traced his index finger closer to the vee of her thighs. "Perhaps life has beaten them down until they have no more curiosity or adventure. Which sort of woman are you, Miss Hasting?"

"Oh!" Unfortunately, his lost companion came back to herself with a tiny shake of her head. Her eyes widened, the desire fading, and she quickly batted his hand from her person. "I… I am the kind of woman who knows exactly what she must do, and if that means denying things that might benefit her own life, so be it. Family is the most important thing."

How… disappointing. He'd been so close to convincing her.

"Not always, Miss Hasting. Not always." With a frown, Nicholas contemplated the remainder of the tea service. Might as well tuck into the meal, since nothing would come of the failed seduction attempt.

"It seems Millie is enjoying herself."

At least someone is. With a flick of his gaze, he glanced at the table in question and then cringed. "The boy is far too green." Percy laughed too loud, had the manners of a mountain goat as he ate through the tray of sweets on their table. What the hell had Marcus' sister taught him? He frowned, knowing he needed to give the young man some pointers, but it was equally apparent that the young Miss Featheringham was taken with him, for she watched him as if he were an Adonis. So then why was the companion such a difficult endeavor?

"Whatever Mr. Marsden is saying to Millie, it seems to have fascinated her," Miss Hasting whispered but worry etched the smooth porcelain skin of her brow.

Nick snorted. "More likely she's merely enamored to be in a man's company without you next to her."

"As long as she doesn't become infatuated with him."

Was the woman against all men, or was it him she took vast exception to? Annoyance stabbed through his chest. "Why, because he's not good enough for her?"

She turned her head and met his gaze, but the only emotion he could read was concern. "No, because I don't want her to settle on the first man who is kind or attentive to her. That would be a mistake and might not be what she needs for her life."

Ah. Interesting. Here was the chance to gain insight into the companion's life. "Is that what happened to you? That you might have married the wrong man?"

A faint blush moved through her cheeks. "That is none of your concern."

"Oh?" His flagging confidence bolstered, and again he leaned toward her. "I wonder if you enjoyed the act of intercourse with said man, then?" Did she crave the touch of a man even now after his teasing words, but was too skilled in hiding her own needs due to familial obligation?

"You overstep, my lord." Frost had entered her voice as she reverted to the formal.

"We are merely conversing, Miss Hasting." As he refreshed the tea in his cup, his curiosity grew, so he pressed onward. "Is that why you are concerned for your charge? Because you gave away everything and received little in return?" When she didn't answer, he grinned. "You and your fiancé indulged in scandal. There is no shame in that."

"Perhaps not." She frowned at her plate. "He went off to war and died in the first bout of fighting he saw. That was seven years ago." The delicate muscles in her throat worked with a hard swallow. "I was four years older than Millie is now. Yes, it was a more confusing, stressful time, but that didn't excuse the consequences."

What was this, then? "You have a child." It wasn't a question.

"No." The word sounded pulled from a tight throat. She didn't look at him. "At the time I was devastated. I'm glad now, for I would have brought disgrace upon my family. When they weren't as… reduced as they are now, with reputations hanging by a thread to respectability."

"Ah." Once more they were alike, and that had unexpectedly formed a bond between them. "I am sorry life didn't go as you thought. I well know that feeling."

One of her blonde eyebrows rose. "Will you share your story?"

"Not just yet." She wasn't an innocent. One obstacle removed, but he hated that unknown man, who'd been the first to introduce her to the carnal world. Yet, from the way she'd acted at the rout and when he'd kissed her and just now when he'd talked about chocolate and scandal, Nick wasn't entirely certain the man had done anything correctly or even for her pleasure. Had he rushed the coupling? Made it only about him getting off? A slow grin curved his mouth. The chase had become that much more interesting. Wishing to form some sort of closeness with her to help further his cause, he brushed her arm with his. "We needn't be enemies."

"Ha." Miss Hasting snorted in apparent derision. "There is *every* reason for us to remain so. You are after Millie."

Ah yes. Couldn't forget about the heiress. "True, but that doesn't mean you and I should remain frosty toward each other." What would help to endear him to her? "Please call me Nicholas, or Nick if you must." He unbent enough to infuse a bit of the native lilt into his voice.

Her eyes rounded. "You are Irish?"

"Don't tell anyone. From both sides of the family, but I was raised to forget that ancestry as a matter of course and survival." He tamped down the urge to reveal anything else about himself. Trust was an issue. For good reason. And though he desired this woman, he didn't know if he could absolutely trust her.

"What a lovely tidbit, and if we *were* friends, I'd ask you to tell me more, but since we are indeed enemies, I'll leave my comment there." For long moments she held his gaze. "I'm Amelia… Mia really."

"What?" He scoffed. "Why the devil would you want such a beautiful name destroyed with a shortened moniker?"

A lovely blush colored her cheeks. "Do stop, my lord. We are not that close."

"Mmm, perhaps not, but give me a week and reassess things then." He nodded at the young people. "Apparently, they're ready to move on." There was no choice but to stand. When Amelia sighed, he held out a hand and assisted her to her feet. "I shall be escorting you home now, for we cannot linger here." He left enough coins on the table to cover their meal plus what the young people had ordered, with enough to tip the establishment. When he caught Amelia looking at the largesse, he couldn't help but grin. Perhaps he'd impressed her.

"That is all to the good. Millie has a musicale evening to attend tonight and should be rested for that."

"Ugh." He pulled a face. "Sounds ghastly."

For the first time in his company, she offered a genuine smile, and it completely transformed her face, so much so that he stared. "It does, rather, and will no doubt be a travesty, but it's what she wants to do."

"Better you than me. Will I see you tomorrow?"

"I don't know. Will you? Or will you suddenly go blind, Lord Wycliffe, while Millie and I are at the British Museum?"

Ah, she'd let their destination for the morrow slip. Did that mean she wanted him to meet her there? How very interesting.

When he chuckled, her grin remained. "We are adversaries. *You* want Millie for her money; *I* don't want you to have her. Therefore, we are locked in an endless battle."

He gave her a half-bow from the waist, then gathered his greatcoat while she did the same with her pelisse and gloves. "At least I have a worthy opponent." More intense awareness of her shivered along his shaft as he donned his top hat. "I *will* see you— and her—tomorrow in some capacity. And I do hope you wear the stockings. They'll suit you, I think."

Amusement sparkled in her eyes. "If they do, you will never know."

Oh, that's where she was wrong, for he *would* see those legs and that figure soon. It was only a matter of time before he found the keys that would unlock her frosty demeanor.

CHAPTER SEVEN

February 5, 1817
Montague House
Great Russell Street
London, England

MIA FROWNED UP at the façade of Montague House where the British Museum was housed. A late seventeenth-century mansion, its clean, brick walls hosted three stories, and the whole edifice was stuffed full of antiquities, many not on display and hadn't been for years, destined to languish in dusty storage rooms on rickety shelves.

While she was excited to tour the museum and the displays contained therein, she wasn't best pleased to see Lord Wycliffe exit his closed carriage along with Mr. Marsden, which meant she would be stuck with the viscount all afternoon. It wouldn't have been an issue if yesterday afternoon hadn't happened.

I cannot think about that now.

Ignoring him for the moment, she continued to stare at the outside of the mansion, for contemplating the building was much safer than thinking about Lord Wycliffe… Nicholas and his beautiful Irish brogue that wove seamlessly through his voice. Even his name conjured up wild imaginings she could ill afford.

Redoubling her efforts, Mia concentrated on the mansion that she'd visited countless times with her father when their coffers had been full and there had been funding for Seasons and her whole family was able to come to Town for a few months.

It was doubtful the artifacts and relics locked away in storerooms would ever see the light of day, and most likely the museum would sell them to private collectors once deemed no longer "interesting" to the museum itself. The loss of that knowledge from both scholars and the public alike was devastating in the quest to piece together history from around the world.

"Oh, look, Miss Hasting. Mr. Marsden has accompanied Lord Wycliffe again today." Excitement threaded through Millie's voice. Her breath clouded about her head, for it was chilly enough, and if the temperatures dropped too much lower, they'd have snow. Yet the girl, in her miniscule wisdom, had chosen to wear a day dress of thin cotton that was wildly inappropriate for the weather regardless of her green brocade pelisse and matching bonnet.

"I see them both." Mia detested the fact she felt a twinge of fascination that the viscount would once more bedevil her day. "It's too bad you and I won't be able to tour the museum ourselves." Perhaps then she could have tried to talk sense into the girl, for she'd been quite the flirt at the musicale evening last night.

Then there was the problem of the viscount. After his nonsense from yesterday at the chocolate shop, she was far too sure she didn't want Millie to end up in his clutches. Quite frankly, his alleged skill in the bedroom as well as his intelligence that he tried to hide would both be wasted on the girl. However, Mia was reasonably certain she didn't want to fall for his silver-tongued flattery either. Yet he continued to pay her too much attention that bordered on the scandalous. Due to his words regarding chocolate and pleasure, the images he'd put into her mind, and his illicit caresses yesterday, she'd nearly forgotten herself and would have eaten out of his hand like an adoring puppy.

Thankfully, she'd come to her senses before she'd fallen beneath his spell.

But that didn't mean she hadn't dreamed about the dratted man last night, had even woken from a particularly vivid dream of the two of them together drenched in sweat.

Not that he would ever know that. It would feed his ego.

"That sounds like a dreadfully dull time, Miss Hasting, for you have been quite the grump of late." Millie smoothed her gloved hands down the front of her pelisse. "You would like Mr. Marsden if you would come to know him," she said to her as they waited for the men to complete their approach.

"*You* have known him one day. I am reserving judgment, but it is my duty to remind you that your father wishes you to encourage and marry a man with a title and social standing."

The girl huffed. "As if that means anything to me."

"It did two days ago. You wanted a title or nothing."

Millie snapped her fingers. "A woman is entitled to change her mind, and I'm not certain a man with a title will make me happy."

Well, this would prove to be a dire little problem if she didn't nip it in the bud. "Perhaps I'll bring up the conundrum with your father over dinner tonight. He'll no doubt reiterate his plans for you." There was only one person in this world Millie respected, and it was the captain.

"Pish posh, Miss Hasting. He'll do whatever I want, and at the moment, I do not fancy tripping through the museum after you and Lord Wycliffe. The pair of you are just so... old! The viscount has nothing interesting to say when he tries to talk to me, and the only thing you do is scold and lecture."

Nothing humbled one faster than an assessment from a younger person. "Ah, well, apologies for continuing to cling to life despite my age in order to embarrass you," Mia shot off and didn't even try to keep the sarcasm from her voice. "I'll pass along your displeasure to Lord Wycliffe and perhaps he'll research topics that might interest you for next time."

"That would be lovely, thank you." Of course, everything Mia had just said went sailing over the girl's head to dissipate into the ether. Clearly, she didn't understand the nuances of the English language.

Then there was no more time for conversation. The viscount and Mr. Marsden were upon them. Greetings went around their little group and shortly afterward, Mia and Millie were escorted up the stairs and into the building.

"I cannot believe you decided to wriggle your way into this outing like an unwanted worm on the pavement," she said beneath her breath to the viscount as they strolled through the entry hall.

Lord Wycliffe chuckled, and the sound released hundreds of butterflies in her belly. "I did warn you yesterday I *would* see you again today." The dratted man moved his head closer to hers and whispered, "Did you wear the stockings?"

Heat went through her cheeks. "Once more, you have overstepped, my lord," she whispered back. Absolutely not would she admit to having donned the hosiery he'd given her, nor would she tell him how luxurious the fine silk was against her skin or how delicate the embroidery. Truthfully, it was one of the most expensive things she owned.

"What will it take for you to say my Christian name?" he asked in the same low voice as they followed Millie and Mr. Marsden while they made their way to the admission desk.

"Perhaps you should do something unexpected for a rake." Mia shrugged. "I imagine I'll be so shocked that your name might accidentally tumble out of my mouth."

"You never disappoint, Miss Hasting." With a slight grin curving his lips, Nicholas went past the younger couple, and as he engaged in the rather arduous task of obtaining admission from a grim-faced clerk who sat behind a high counter, Mia couldn't help but admire his form, for he hadn't worn a greatcoat, or if he had, he'd left it in his carriage.

The taut lines of his backside encased in fawn-colored breeches nearly left her breathless until she reminded herself she had no interest in him, but she couldn't help but admire the width of his shoulders, set off to perfection in the jacket of bottle green superfine. Once he'd procured the tickets and turned toward them, his waistcoat of brown brocade called her attention to his flat abdomen.

Why did she suddenly wish to divest him of those clothes merely for a look at his nude frame? *What is wrong with me?* Obviously, she was much too intelligent to lust after one such as the viscount. In fact, she didn't need any man in her life, for they were nothing but trouble.

He held the tickets up and fanned the papers in his hand so they could all see. "Shall we begin our tour of the museum?"

Millie, always far too bold for the situation, came toward him and plucked two tickets from his collection. "Or you could let Mr. Marsden and I tour on our own while the two of you do the same."

Concern rose in Mia's chest. "I don't think that is a good idea." The girl simply didn't need to be alone in the young man's company, for the captain would dress them both down if she continued to lead an untitled man along.

To Mr. Marsden's credit, he'd put space between him and Millie and kept his gaze cast downward. Perhaps the viscount had told him to behave himself. "I promise to ensure Miss Feather-ingham will see the most popular sites and practice decorum."

For her or him?

"It is a museum, Miss Hasting. With other patrons filling each exhibit hall. There is no place for them to fall into scandal." The viscount's grin widened, and a hint of wicked intention danced in his dark eyes. "Besides, we might enjoy the offerings more ourselves without huffs of boredom or rolled eyes from the young people."

"And it's not as if we would ever be far from your location, Miss Hasting," Millie reminded her. "You are always in the way, preventing me from having any fun."

If she didn't firmly know her place before, that statement would have done it. Finally, Mia sighed. "Fine. Go explore, but meet us at Elgin's marbles at three o'clock." That was two hours from now. "If even a hint of scandal reaches my ears, I will consign you to the house and only let you out for select events in the evenings, your father's displeasure be damned."

Something had to be done to curb Millie's potential wild ways.

With a wave, Millie fairly pulled the hapless Mr. Marsden toward the grand marble staircase, and they soon blended in with the crowds.

"I rather adore that forceful side of you, dragon," the viscount purred next to her as he offered his crooked arm. "I also enjoy seeing your claws bared at someone other than myself. For obvious reasons."

What was it about him that made her want to grin or even laugh from his wit? She shouldn't enjoy his company so much, and the fact that she did sent annoyance into her chest. "Perhaps we should begin our tour if we have a hope of keeping the rest of our party in sight." And because she couldn't ignore him any longer, Mia rested her fingers on his sleeve.

"I rather think those two will do everything they can to avoid our watchful eyes," he said as he resituated her hand into the crook of his elbow. "Take heart, though. There is no place they can hide for a kiss, and I rather doubt it's on dear Percy's mind. Not after the lecture I gave him yesterday."

"That's rich. You telling another man how to be a gentleman." The thought amused her far more than it should have, and strolling beside him toward the marble staircase was rather lovely, for it had been an age since she'd had either in her life.

"I can be admirable when needed." On the way up the staircase, they were forced close together to accommodate the ebb and flow of the crowds. One such time, he put his lips to the shell of her ear. "There will be a couple of small tokens of affection waiting at the Featheringham home for your return later this afternoon."

"Oh?" She'd rather die than affect any sort of reaction in front of him, but it was rather lovely to be given gifts, even from him.

"Yes." When he put a hand to the small of her back and guided her up the rest of the way, curious warmth spread through her being. "Yours is a silver handled mirror. Each time you peer into it, I want you to look at your eyes and know they are your best feature and are capable of driving men to their knees if you harness that power just right."

"That was kind of you." Hoping he didn't see the blush in her cheeks, Mia tipped her head up to meet his gaze. "Though, once again, I'll caution you to stop sending me gifts. I am not trying to attract anyone."

"Don't worry. I also sent Miss Featheringham a gift as well." He waggled his eyebrows. "A book of poems, though I doubt very much she will read it. In which case she will undoubtedly give it to you, so therefore you will receive two gifts. From me." With a wink, he guided her across the floor. "And when you come to the offering on page thirty-two, I hope you'll have me in mind."

"Whyever for?" Truly, the man perplexed her.

"Some of the poems are of an erotic nature."

Oh, dear heavens. "I truly hope Millie doesn't read that book." She didn't know what the book's content was but there was already heavy heat in her cheeks.

"I'm quite confident she won't. The girl will take one look at it, discover it's poetry, of all things, and then toss it." His grin put her in mind of wicked things. "But you have a more discerning spirit and enjoy things that stretch the mind. I cannot wait to hear your thoughts."

At this point, Mia was out of patience with her impromptu companion, so as they came abreast of the Reading Room, she said, "If you would like, you can enjoy the respite here. I won't mind, and I know you enjoy reading as well as books." She gave him what she hoped was an encouraging smile. "If I could, I would adore seeing the inside of that hallowed space, but I am barred due to being a woman."

"Which assumes that many members of the fairer sex are not intelligent enough to read." The viscount frowned as they passed the double doors. "There are many lovely books inside that space, and spending time there is quite tempting, but I can go there whenever I'd like. Right now, I would rather spend the time in your company, Amelia."

The way he said her Christian name prompted a mad rush of flutters in her lower belly. She didn't want to like him, wanted to continually push him away, but the more time she spent in his company, the more he was endearing himself to her.

With a sigh and knowing he wouldn't go anywhere for the time being, Mia nodded. "Very well. Let us go ahead and move to the Egyptian gallery." Located on the third floor, they made a loop and returned to the grand staircase.

On the landing at that floor, three rather imposing and freakishly lifelike giraffes kept watch, stuffed within an inch of their former lives and looking for all the world as if they'd just stepped off an African savanna.

"It seems as if their eyes are following me," she said in low whisper as gooseflesh raced over her skin and left her feeling uneasy.

"Though they *are* disconcerting here, I still would like to meet one in person."

"As would I." Both fascinated and repelled by the creatures— so seemingly alert in death and with dark, long-lashed eyes that followed her every movement—she glided closer, determined to study them, and imagine what it might be like to visit the plains and basins and see such beasts in their natural habitat. Would she ever meet such a dream? In her current situation as a companion, most likely not unless the family she worked with decided to travel.

As they toured through the Egyptian wing, Nicholas once more managed to surprise her by keeping up a commentary on various items. How he knew about the artifacts, she couldn't say, but perhaps the museum was a place he visited often. Mia listened to the pleasant timbre of his voice with half an ear as she perused the cases and shelves. There were so many things to look at and read about, also so many items that had been miscatalogued or had other erroneous information displayed on the placards. That she remembered from visiting with her father over the years.

"It is quite a terrible crime no one is accountable when these things go on display." She waved a hand to a plaque where a set of funerary jars had been labeled as from the era of Ramesses II, when they were clearly from the time of Seti I. Certain stylistic markings and paint colors made the difference. "How are people supposed to learn about proper history when the men in charge of teaching are nodcocks?"

Nicholas frowned while staring at a mummified cat taken from a merchant's tomb. "I quite agree with you." He glanced at her with an amused grin. "Your annoyance must be stirred if you've resorted to using such language, my dear Miss Hasting."

A quick stab of heat infused her cheeks as she passed a giant bust of Ramesses II. "In this case, I believe it was needed." In the attempt to forget the lack of detail throughout the gallery, Mia sent a glance about the immediate area. The displays she'd seen years ago during the last time she'd come with her father remained, and they made her smile. A few things had been removed, no doubt consigned into storage rooms. New items and artifacts had been added, crammed between others with no sense of flow, design, or chronological history of moving along a timeline of Egypt. With each new mistake, her annoyance rose. "Where is the outrage for what the museum has become?"

"Calm yourself, dragon. I am just as annoyed at the miscategoriztions as you, but nothing will come from it unless the director involves himself."

"Which he won't." Which was too bad because it would have made touring the exhibits better for everyone involved.

"It is difficult to ignore."

His grin helped to diffuse her ire. "How have you become so familiar with the museum?

"My father enjoyed coming here when he was in Town. I was the only one of his daughters who shared his love of old things, so he brought me every chance he could. Together we learned about history—correct history—and then discussed world events afterward." She sighed. "I miss that."

"You could have that again. Just soften yourself, lower your ideals and let men pay you their addresses. Once funding has been infused into your father's coffers, he could come to Town again."

She snorted as she wandered up and down the tight rows and shelves of artifacts, funerary accessories, jewelry, and scraps of pottery. Elongated shadows bounced and moved before her, eerie in the silence. "That would assume I'd make such a sacrifice."

"But you told me family meant everything."

"It does, but I will not marry a man merely to save my family, for I'd be trapped with the man, and if we didn't suit, my life would be horrid."

"Fair point… unless the man in question brought excitement or scandal with him. Then your life would become something else entirely." His gaze was intense as he looked at her before he turned away to examine a recent addition—a collection of necklaces and chest plates done in gold, turquoise, and lapis lazuli. "But that would mean you would have to extend trust to someone. Do you have it in you to do that?"

"I'm not certain," she said in a whisper while she moved on to another collection behind glass. "Losing my fiancé took much out of me. Seeing my family struggle with the various things they do is exhausting and heartbreaking." Resting a gloved palm on the glass, she sighed, and her breath left a spot of fog behind. "There is only so much I can bear before I'll break."

What a ninny I am to admit such to him and leave myself vulnerable.

Three mummies were inside the case, displayed with the

same haphazard precision as everything else. It was too much effort to put forth further annoyance. Slowly, Nicholas joined her. "How lovely that they've made the decision to put out a few more mummies. The last time I was here, there was talk the museum didn't want anything else to do with such things."

She snorted. "Well, mummies are quite abundant in London. Everyone who visits Egypt brings back a few."

"I was at an unwrapping party a couple of years ago." The viscount peered into the exhibit and then shuddered. "It wasn't as exciting as it sounds. Mostly, the resins smelled vile, scraps of wrappings littered the floor, brittle bones broke far too easily, and the two mummies on display that night had been robbed in antiquity of anything that might have been valuable." When he shivered, Mia did too.

"That sounds terrible." One of the mummies retained a shock of brownish-black hair and a mouthful of missing teeth that managed to look macabre in death instead of serene or at peace. "What do you suppose this man was like during his life?"

"It's difficult to say since we don't know what he was surrounded by in death or even where he fell in the social network of ancient Egypt." The viscount shifted closer to her. "I would like to believe he lived each day to its fullest."

"By spending time bedeviling some poor priest's daughter?"

His chuckle echoed eerily in the gallery. "Or perhaps he set his sights a tad higher than that by pursuing a pharaoh's daughter."

"Is that what you would have done?"

"If I could get away with it, I suppose. Unless the cold sandalmaker's daughter intrigued me by keeping every other man at arm's length."

"Have you always been like this?"

"Like what?"

Mia huffed in frustration. "Always on the prowl, always chasing women."

"My dear Amelia, being with women is what makes life

worth living." As he stared at her, some of the cocky confidence left his expression to be replaced with a longing that resonated with something deep inside her. "However, eventually that sort of life begins to grow stale."

"Yet you freely admitted you're seeking marriage only for the coin." Unless that was another lie?

A flush slowly rose up his neck. "While it's no secret I need a rapid infusion of cash, there are times when I'd like the companionship as well."

For long moments she held his gaze as the crowds shifted inside the gallery. "I'm not certain how much of that you will find with Millie. The girl is a curiosity unto herself, and she only alights long enough to change her clothes before she's off again, visiting someone new." Now more than ever, Mia knew the two were wrong for each other. "Since she is young and she enjoys flirting for men's attention, I'm not certain she'll remain faithful."

Perhaps it wasn't well done of her to speak thusly about her charge, but it was the truth.

"That is a possibility, but then, you already know the chit doesn't fascinate me." He appeared to want to say something else, but instead, the viscount shook his head, perhaps to clear his thoughts, and grinned. "Come. We have lingered here a long time. I'd like to have enough time to explore Elgin's marbles before meeting with your charge."

Though he managed to always key her up when she was in his presence, somehow, she was a bit deflated, for he hadn't put much effort into teasing her as he'd done yesterday. "Have you seen the marbles before?"

"Oh, yes, many times." His hand drifted again to the small of her back as they navigated the crowded corridors and peered at a few more exhibits along the way.

Due to the crowds, they were obliged to wait their turn at each sculpture, but Mia didn't care. This exhibit was one of her favorites, and she always wondered what it would have been like to travel the world, take away valuable works from their countries of origin, only to bring them back to England and promptly sell them for a profit to the museum. Not very gentlemanly of Elgin, but then, over the centuries, the English had been essentially raping other cultures at the altar of art.

And greed.

At the third sculpture, Mia sighed. "For years, I've thought it would be lovely to travel the world and learn from studying different people, to see how they live, work, and love, to understand how it differs from the ancient cultures in those lands. See the wonderous art and sculptures and paintings, to perhaps enjoy warm temperatures and sunshine in Greece or even Rome." As she spoke, she longingly traced the marble with her gloved hands.

"I understand what you mean. There have been many times I've daydreamed about being in Rome for Christmas or lounging in an outdoor café in Athens in the shadow of the Parthenon." The viscount clasped his hands behind his back. "But they are dreams that have no feet without coin, I'm afraid."

"Which is another reason why you adore reading, I'll wager. You can go anywhere you'd like without cost, especially if you utilize lending libraries." Bit by bit, she was coming to piece together the holes in his story he didn't tell anyone else, and in that picture, he wasn't the rake he portrayed to the *ton*. Why hide who he was?

"Exactly. The volumes in the Reading Room here are quite exquisite." He gave her a sheepish glance. "Reading brings knowledge and knowledge breeds power."

"You wish to lord that over everyone?"

"Not at all. I wish to use that knowledge to eventually combat and annoy the men currently in charge." He shrugged. "England will undergo severe changes, and soon. I wish to be on the right side of history."

She gawked at him, for the fact he even cared about anything beyond himself shocked her. Not knowing what to say, Mia returned her attention to the marble sculpture. "I thought I might be adventurous in my life, especially since I don't have children, but alas, I don't possess a fortune. Like you, traveling anywhere past Bath or even Brighton is out of the question." A ball of unshed tears climbed her throat. "It was why I didn't have more Seasons and had to settle for a private in the military with nothing to recommend him."

"We can only do the best we can with what we have." The empathy in his voice was as comforting as that drinking chocolate from yesterday.

A gasp escaped her as she realized what she'd said. It made her sound ungrateful. "I didn't mean that. He was a lovely man, of course, but—"

"—but not your ideal," he finished in a soft voice. "Not someone who could help you meet your goals, your dreams. Not the man to keep the special secrets of your heart."

Understanding reflected in his eyes. "Yes, but then, perhaps fate has something better in store for me." For long moments, they stared at each other, and she teetered. The crowds around them disappeared, and the only person she saw was the viscount. Slowly, she leaned toward him. They were drawing closer, damn his eyes, but it suddenly didn't seem the horror that it was three days ago. "Though I couldn't begin to puzzle out what that could be." For it *would not* be with this man.

It couldn't. She wouldn't let it.

Eventually, the viscount sprang away from her, only to crash into a man behind him. After apologizing, he cleared his throat. "Do you see Miss Featheringham or Percy?"

"Oh." Mia shook her head to clear the haze that had filled her mind. She glanced about the room containing the exhibit. "No." Slight alarm rose in her chest.

"No need to panic yet. They probably wandered off."

A near hysterical laugh escaped her throat. "Since we're both so old and dull we couldn't possibly hold their attention?"

He snorted with laughter. "Well, there is that."

"I hope they aren't trying to steal kisses." The captain

wouldn't be best pleased with her for allowing Millie's attention to wander onto a no-name boy.

"That's all to the good, isn't it? That means there would be no time for anything else, especially since we're on the hunt of them." Yet worry etched through his expression.

"Perhaps." She assumed the concern stemmed from the fact he didn't want Millie's head turned away from him. More foolish was she to have temporarily forgotten why she was even in his company.

"Let us backtrack and then we'll move downstairs."

Twenty minutes later, they found the missing young people on the ground floor, indulging in glasses of lemonade from a vendor.

"Where the devil have you been?" Annoyance wove through the viscount's voice as he prepared to take the unfortunate Mr. Marsden to task. "Miss Hasting was worried sick."

Millie huffed and pointed her gaze to the ceiling. "We were bored waiting for you at the marbles as we'd said, but now you're here." She brightened and fixed her gaze on Nicholas. "Perhaps we should go for tea or visit the menagerie at the Tower." Then she glanced at Mr. Marsden. He colored and glanced everywhere but at her.

"As if you should be rewarded for bad behavior?" Nicholas shoved a hand through his hair, upsetting the dark locks as he peered out the closest window. "It's raining. I don't fancy driving the cattle through the muck."

Of course that made sense. Mia chose that moment to step in before the conversation could grow heated. "I think we should return home, Miss Featheringham. You need to be rested for the dinner party your father is throwing on your behalf tonight." She refused to meet Nick's eyes for fear she might laugh at the absurdity of everything. It was all a dance and the players shallow and tasteless. "Think of the men you might meet."

"Right." The girl brightened, but not overly much, yet her gaze lingered on the viscount far too long for respectability. What game did she play now? "Will we see you tomorrow, Lord Wycliffe?"

"I couldn't begin to say, Miss Featheringham, for I am not a fortune teller, but perhaps there are gifts at your home to soothe the disappointment." A grin flirted with his sensuous lips, and for one second, Mia dropped her focus to his mouth.

What would a proper kiss from him feel like?

"Fine. I suppose that is acceptable." At least Millie was mollified and wouldn't have a fit of temper while in public.

Mia couldn't help but tease the viscount. "Spoiling her won't help."

"Don't forget, there is something there for you, dragon," he said softly under his breath as he shepherded the party toward the front doors. "Perhaps you'll be reminded of the chocolate shop and how I put you at sixes and sevens."

Heat slapped at her cheeks. "She blushed. Enough of that, my lord." Teasing was dangerous when they weren't alone.

He put his head near hers. "Nicholas." The warmth of his breath skated over her cheek.

She huffed. "Nicholas." Why was he impossible? "If you'd like to take part in the Reading Room, please do so. I can tell your driver our address, and it might be a good thing to introduce Mr. Marsden to, to give him more Town bronze."

"Very true." His expression brightened. "Go on, then. At least it will keep him away from Miss Featheringham." When she cocked an eyebrow in question, he nodded. "Oh, I've noticed the mutual interest and it's concerning."

The muscles in her belly knotted. "No doubt it is, since you now have competition for her hand. Not that you've tried hard to win it since you've given over most of your time to me."

"There are those claws again." The maddening man grinned and merely winked. "Good afternoon, Amelia. I have no doubts we shall see each other soon."

"Good afternoon, Nicholas." Then she proceeded out the doors to re-route the young Mr. Marsden.

Lord Wycliffe might be a rake and a wicked one at that, but he certainly made her days more interesting... when he wasn't flirting with her.

CHAPTER EIGHT

February 6, 1817

NICHOLAS FUSSED WITH the knot of his cravat. He'd tied it three times already, and he still wasn't pleased with the results.

"If I may, my lord?" His valet—an older man who'd filled the same position for Nick's father—stood by, watching from slightly behind him. With his gray hair and his kind eyes, he was a link to the past, a time gone by that would never come again.

"Well, Barnes, if you think you can do better, go ahead. It's a slippery piece of fabric tonight." Why the devil couldn't he get the knot right?

"The key is to not overthink the problem." The valet moved in front of Nicholas, and with a few twists and tucks, manipulated the cravat into what looked like a masterpiece. "When one clears the mind and focuses on mundane chores, that's when one finds the answers one seeks."

"Perhaps." When Barnes stood off to one side, Nicholas peered into the cheval glass. "I like the design."

"Thank you. It was a favorite of your father's."

"Let me ask you something." He dropped into one of the comfortable chairs in the dressing room and took a boot in his hand. "You were with Father the whole time he held the title, weren't you?"

"I was." Barnes removed a jacket of sapphire superfine from the clothespress. "What would you like to know?"

"From an early age, both my sister and I knew our parents hated each other. Did Father ever love my mother?" Why the devil was it important to bring up such a subject now?

"It would be an assumption on my part to say either way, my lord. Their union was arranged by their parents, and for a time, I did think they might make a go of it." He offered a soft smile. "There were moments of peace, stretches of life where they rubbed along well enough."

"What happened?" Nick tugged on one of the recently polished boots.

"Let's just say your father's penchant for lightskirts got in the way of what could have been a tidy little romance. This began a couple of years after your sister was born." The valet shrugged, then folded the jacket over one arm. "I think that particular vice proved too strong or addicting for him to overcome, and not even a romance with his wife could help."

For long moments, Nicholas remained silent as he donned the second boot. Finally, he asked, "Do you think I'll follow in his footsteps?"

"That is also not for me to say." Barnes peered into his face, but there was kindness and a sense of hope in his expression that tightened Nick's chest. "Is there a particular lady in your life you might be interested in for marriage? A lady for whom you might change your life?"

Was there? It was no secret to people within the *ton* he was in need of a fortune and a wife, but had that knowledge also crept to his staff? If that were so, he couldn't lie. "I must marry. There are needs of my holdings that require coin."

"That isn't what I meant, my lord."

"Oh?" He met the other man's gaze in the cheval glass.

The valet nodded. "Putting all of that aside—for that is where your father made his first missteps I believe—do you have a notion of marrying a woman because she fascinates you, because you can honestly see a future with her, perhaps enjoy an abiding friendship and trust with said woman?"

"I am not certain at this point." Immediately, his mind jumped to Amelia. There was no question that he was interested in her, beguiled by her due to her frosty nature and her penchant for holding herself above his charm and teasing. He couldn't deny that he desired her for no other reason than to teach her a few lessons within the carnal world, to ensure she never forgot him in that regard, but was she his ideal in a marriage partner, especially knowing her family struggled financially and she would bring nothing to a union? "No, I'm not certain at all."

Barnes frowned. "In my experience, once a woman has gotten into your head and invaded your thoughts, she's worth the pursuit."

"Perhaps, but we both know life isn't that simple."

"It is not." The valet shrugged. "However, consider this. Wouldn't you rather pass the remainder of your life in comfort and happiness instead of strife and resentment?" He held out the jacket, and while Nicholas slipped his arms into the sleeves, he continued. "I believe that is where your father went wrong. He was forever chasing something elusive he assumed would bring him happiness, when he had a chance of that with what he already had."

"And in the end, he was left with nothing, died from a disease given to him from one of those empty liaisons, with no one around who loved him." For Nicholas' mother had been on holiday on the Continent with his sister at the time that his sire had expired. As for Nick, he'd been aware of his father's failing health, but he couldn't summon enough interest in traveling to the country to see him before he expired, had thought it was merely a ploy on his father's part to bring him home from London.

"He did, indeed. I was with him at the last, so he wasn't quite alone." A trace of sadness entered Barnes' voice as he brushed a piece of lint from a shoulder of the jacket. "Some of his last words were to look after you. As he faced death, your father was racked with concern that his bad habits had rubbed off on you and that he'd led by horrid example."

A lump of emotion lodged in Nicholas' throat. He attempted to swallow it down and ignore it. "That is what came to pass." Did he regret it? Difficult to say. If asked a week ago, he would have roundly said no. Now, he wasn't certain… of anything.

"But you aren't so far gone that you can't change, my lord. Learn from his mistakes and use that knowledge to correct the things in your life you aren't satisfied with." One of the valet's gray eyebrows rose. "Finding happiness—beyond contentment— is a rare occurrence in our world, but when it happens? Best hold onto it with both hands, for it might not come your way again."

"I shall bear that in mind." At the last second, Nick turned away before the older man could see the emotion he struggled with. Even more surprising was the fact he hadn't taken stock of his life at any point before now, and that rankled. The only thing different had been meeting Miss Hasting.

Once I bed her, she'll leave my blood and my mind, and then I can resume my plans.

"If you are for outdoor entertainments this afternoon, have a care, my lord. The rain has ceased for now, but I don't like the look of those clouds."

The sound of his valet's voice wrenched him from his thoughts. "Thank you. I'll make certain the visit isn't a long one. With luck, I should be at the club by dinner." For he required a much-needed talk with Marcus.

"Very good, my lord. Enjoy the afternoon."

"Thank you, Barnes." There was some sort of a curiosity exhibition in Hyde Park that had been going on all week when the weather permitted. He would escort Miss Featheringham and her companion there, and since Mr. Marsden had another engagement that prevented him from joining, there probably wouldn't be time for Nicholas to further Miss Hasting's acquaintance.

But I can strive to make her jealous, and if it takes, I'll know her interest has been snared. That would make the seduction even easier, for he had a feeling they were both sitting on a powder keg of sorts from the tension that brewed between them.

Providing the companion consented to the outing at all. She was quite stubborn, but damn if that wasn't one of the things he admired about her.

AN HOUR LATER Nicholas alighted from his closed carriage and then immediately turned and handed Miss Featheringham down, followed by Amelia. It was interesting to note he felt absolutely no reaction when he briefly held the chit's hand compared to when he held Miss Hasting's, then was forced to relinquish his hold as soon as she was out of the vehicle.

"Come, Miss Featheringham. I'm told there is a bear in this exhibition as well as a few exotic birds from the far-flung Amazonian rainforest. Quite the menagerie, really." When he offered the girl his crooked arm, she huffed and put her hand in his elbow as if she were granting him a huge concession. "I'm even told there is a mermaid on display." Though how that could be, he couldn't imagine.

"I rather doubt that is possible, Lord Wycliffe," came Amelia's logical reply as she butted into the conversation. Her commitment to staying at true north amused him, and oddly enough, he craved her being a moral compass.

"I believe he was addressing me, Miss Hasting. You're the companion, remember?" Annoyance threaded through Millie's voice, and the pout she affected wasn't attractive. "Where is Mr. Marsden this afternoon?"

"I am not privy to his schedule, but suffice it to say, I'm sure he'll be free for our next meeting." Did she truly prefer the young pup's company over his? *I have a blooming title! Isn't that what she should be chasing?* "Though I will endeavor to prove an entertaining escort for you." With a nod at the man collecting entry fees, he gave over the appropriate coins for the three of them to attend.

"Oh. I'd looked forward to continuing a discussion he and I had started yesterday, but I suppose you'll do just as well, since all the men Papa invited to dinner were dusty old lords even older than you." She glanced over her shoulder at Amelia. "Perhaps now I can discover why you think Lord Wycliffe is so frustrating, Miss Hasting."

The companion huffed, which made Nicholas tamp down the urge to grin. If nothing else, the outing would be amusing. "Pick a reason, Miss Featheringham. Then you'll know the same frustration."

Surprisingly, the girl wrapped her hand about his arm and fairly clung to him as they set out down one of the paths. "Well, I think he's lovely and he smells delicious. It rather helps a courtship when the man doesn't stink like garlic or sweat." She simpered up at him, and he did not find that charming at all. It was rather like staring into the face of a porcelain doll. Pretty, of course, but the eyes weren't animated, nor did they contain secrets or a soul like Amelia's. "And I won't mind his suggestive talk like you object to."

"You are more than welcome to listen as much as you want, but I am only doing what my position demands, and I will still be here, watching to make certain you aren't indulging in scandal— or keeping you from it." Slight annoyance lingered in her voice. Was she jealous that he'd chosen her charge over her? Perhaps he could use that feeling to his advantage later.

"What is the purpose of being alive if one cannot indulge in something fun and exciting every once in a while?" There was a decided whine in the young lady's voice that somehow set his teeth on edge.

"To a certain extent, I agree with you, Miss Featheringham."

More than ever, he remembered Amelia's comment about spending the rest of his life with one such as Millie. It was beginning to sound like a ghastly endeavor. However, he was committed to escorting the young woman about the exhibition this afternoon, yet he remained fully conscious of Amelia's presence as she walked behind them.

All too soon, they reached the part of the park where the exhibition was being held. Contained to a flat strip of ground about a quarter mile long and flanked by wooded areas on both sides, there was a surprising crowd that moved through the area. Tents and booths were set up on either side of the walking path. Here and there, vendor handcarts rested where guests could buy beverages or foods designed to be partaken as one walked. Savory and sweet scents competed for notice in the air, while barkers called patrons' attention to the various tents and small stages.

As they stood at a cage that housed the colorful parrots he'd spoken of, he frowned. "Imagine being in that hot, steamy rainforest, perhaps lost in the foliage and undergrowth while searching for these very birds knowing people in England had never seen their like before," Nicholas said as the birds strutted and preened in front of the gathering crowd. "Or rather, imagine yourself bedding down in a tent or around a fire, praying that jungle cats and rodents are afraid of the flames and that you will survive through the night."

Millie snorted. "I'd rather not, thank you." She gave into a shiver. "I do not enjoy bugs or being dirty, and I'll wager the Amazon isn't as tame as Hyde Park."

"Not adventurous, then?" How very disappointing. It meant if he were to wed the girl, the whole of their union would draw out before him as a study in boredom.

"I don't know why anyone would wish to venture out of England." The young miss shrugged. "Why cannot people be satisfied with where they are?"

"Why indeed." He slid his gaze to Amelia, who stood at his other side, and when she didn't quite stop rolling her eyes heavenward, he bit down on a snicker. "What of you, Miss Hasting? If you had the chance, would you travel?" He already knew she would, thanks to their conversation from yesterday at the museum.

"I would be delighted to see everything that was different from England."

Millie snorted. "Too bad you're in reduced circumstances without prospects. I doubt you can afford Bath."

While Nicholas narrowed his eyes at the audacity of the chit's assessment spoken aloud, even if it were true, he watched the blush march across Amelia's face. "Circumstances can and often do change," he said in a low voice that could have been a response to either of them.

Amelia nodded but turned her head away so he couldn't see her face. "I sincerely hope you find a husband who indulges you, Millie," she said, and there was a slight note of ire in that tone.

"I'm sure I will, for I'm quite extraordinary," the girl rejoined, then she moved away from the bird cage and on toward the next exhibit.

Again, he looked at Amelia and their gazes briefly connected. "I'm sorry," he mouthed, for he wanted to make it plain that he did not share the young woman's viewpoints.

She shrugged. "It is nothing, but it reminds me of my place in life." That tiny waver in her voice cut through his chest. "There is no shame in it."

"No, perhaps not."

"You should catch up to Millie, since courting her is the whole reason we are here." Then she made a shooing motion with her hand.

"Right." Then he frowned. "Yet you've told me a few times before it is your duty to keep me from the girl."

"Oh, I still intend to do just so, but that doesn't mean you cannot lead her on a bit, since that is what she's probably doing to you." It was the faint smile that gave him the strength to resume touring the exhibition with the chit.

After three more cages and visiting tents, it was readily obvious that compared to Amelia, engaging Millie in intellectual conversation on any topic proved near impossible. She didn't know about the things he did. Had no idea about the poets or composers or novelists he spoke of, had absolutely no dreams beyond marrying a man who could lift her status and give her visibility within the *ton*. And dash it, she didn't smell like Amelia, neither did she possess the sarcastic wit of the dragon, neither did she rebuff his attempts at flirting. Since there was no challenge in it, he wildly curbed doing such with the girl.

She was as dull as he'd feared.

Midway through the tour, Miss Featheringham saw a group of girls she recognized, and he gladly let her go off to talk with them. "Miss Hasting and I will wait for you at the food carts in a half hour or so."

Millie huffed. "I am not a child, Lord Wycliffe. I am more than capable of doing what I want with whomever I wish."

"No doubt you are." He was too tired to argue with her. Once she'd left, Amelia came abreast of him. "What?"

A string of laughter escaped her. "Oh, it's highly amusing you have nothing in common with Millie."

"It's disturbing, is what it is. Additionally, she makes me extremely aware of my age. I feel as ancient as a mummy in her presence." He didn't mind admitting that to her, for he suspected she, above all others, would understand.

"At least she hasn't hurt your feelings yet with careless words." She gave him a rueful glance while shrugging. "Are you prepared for a lifetime of her behavior, or will you cart her off to the country, so you don't need to interact with her unless on holidays?"

"Ha!" He'd missed verbally sparring with her. "I shudder to think about any of it."

"Good for you." One of her eyebrows rose in surprise. "What of your need for a fortune?"

"Honestly? I don't know. Perhaps it's more of a matter of

closing my eyes and just jumping off the ledge and hoping life won't be as horrid as I suspect." God, what a dismal prospect.

"You poor thing. Sacrificing yourself all for funding. A gilded prison to be sure." She led the way toward a glass window set into wood, and inside the alleged tank was the much-lauded mermaid. "Do you suppose she is real?"

"No." Nicholas snorted. Though the woman inside the "tank" looked as if she were swimming, her legs were obviously covered by a fabric tail no matter that the designer had attempted to hide the fact with scales, fins, and other ornamentation. "For that matter, I rather doubt she's in the water, for there is something not quite… right with the whole picture. Something about how her hair is flowing."

"Do you not believe in the unknown, then?"

"I believe in things I can see with my own eyes." He tapped on the glass, and up close, it became more apparent there was water behind the glass, which meant there was another panel of glass behind that encasing the few inches of water.

"What of how you feel?" Of course Amelia would persist. "Are you ever led by your heart? For surely you haven't been logical in making past decisions."

He couldn't help his grin, for she wouldn't let him gloss over anything. "I don't know that my heart has ever been that engaged for me to pay attention to it."

"Then you have missed part of the point of living, my lord." Amelia moved toward the next tent where a two-headed goat pranced inside a wooden pen. "And it is not always about the excitement, as Millie has suggested."

There was something to be considered in her words. "Can I assume that you have followed your heart a time or two?"

"I have." She frowned at the goat. "That is even what led me to London as a companion. You do what you must for those you love and care about."

"Would that I could believe you." God, the goat was ugly, yet in its way, there was something oddly beautiful about the animal, which got along with all the other goats in the pen and wasn't treated differently. "Outside of my sister, I don't know that anyone has ever truly cared about me, or me them."

"You have a sister?"

"Yes. I see her a couple of times a year, usually at Easter and the Christmastide holidays, but I fear she is as damaged emotionally as I am, due to our parents." He put his hand to the small of her back and led her away from the goat pen toward the next tent. "My parents' marriage was fraught with arguments and resentment, and then later as my sister and I grew, hate had been invited into the union before my mother eventually left to permanently reside at Wycliffe Hall in the country."

"That sounds like a horrid way to live and go through the years." When she touched his elbow, he nearly vaulted out of his skin. "My experience in childhood and early adulthood was much different, for my parents have always loved each other. Still do to this day, even as my father's mind is in decline and my mother's strength is failing. They were there for me and my sisters throughout the whole of our lives. They will be there for each other until the last." Her voice broke a bit just then, and tugged at his chest.

"I cannot even imagine what such support and love feels like." He stared at the black bear on a lead without fully seeing the animal. "Due to how my family is, I assumed every family was like that too."

"And you were no doubt taught to keep a stiff upper lip, never let anyone see you show emotion. You were a future viscount so you could do whatever you wished." She glanced up at him, and their gazes met beneath the shallow brim of her bonnet.

"I was. Father detested if I reacted to anything. In his opinion, Englishmen should be stoic."

"Except when it came to bed partners?" she asked in a soft voice.

It was amazing and somewhat frightening how well she knew

him. "Well, coitus and the people involved in that is rather a different subject than daily living with people one is related to." Though the subject matter was exhausting, talking about it with her made him feel slightly lighter than he had in years, yet he refused to pause and reflect why that was. "But there are times when I hope to marry, wish to do better than my parents merely to say it can be done in a titled household. So that I know I'm not like him in every way..." How did she pull such admissions from him?

"It's an admirable goal, and one that surprises me from you." Amelia kept her focus on the bear as it went through a collection of antics its trainer demanded. "For a long time, it was my dream to marry a man and enjoy a marriage as happy and seamless as what my parents had." She sighed. "I'm not naïve enough to think they never fought or disagreed, and while we saw that to an extent, we saw the love and kindness along the way as well."

"Why did you give up on that dream?" Nicholas could hardly force the words from his tight throat.

"Life, my lord." Her smile was faint and a bit wobbly in the chin. "Fate had other plans for me."

"And now? Do you still dream of being married?"

For long moments, she held his gaze. "Every once in a while, but I don't know if I want the staid responsibility my parents had."

"What is it you *do* want?" he asked in a barely audible whisper as he turned toward her.

"Love. It's the same as anyone in the world wants. To be loved by the one person who complements me. I don't want a man who dominates or bullies. Neither do I want a man who would allow me to boss him." Hope danced in the blue, blue depths of her eyes. "But there is nothing without love, respect, trust, and support. Everything else can be managed if one has that, but those things are merely a dream, after all."

As she talked, Amelia had moved away from the bear exhibit, Nicholas' thoughts had shifted, coalesced, and a couple of new possibilities opened before him, illuminated where they'd been dark before. The way she'd spoken of her parents and their love had made him long for exactly that for his own life, made him want to change the whole of his existence in order to gain that life.

"Don't toss it aside, for everyone should have at least one dream to motivate them." There was nothing for it; he wanted her, and he wanted her immediately, but he would settle for a kiss until such time that he could bed her. After a quick glance about the area, he spied a pathway that contained a set of stone steps. "Come with me."

"Where? Why?" Confusion echoed what flitted over her face.

"Away from people," Nicholas said, and daring much, he caught her gloved hand, tugged her away from the exhibition and along the intersecting path. Perhaps too recklessly he flew down the steps, pulled her with him, and once the gravel path resumed, he led her onward. He might be a fool, but in this moment, he didn't care as he pulled her off the path and didn't stop until they were well into the wooded area, hidden by evergreens and winter dead foliage that still clung to shrubberies and trees. With her drab brown pelisse, she would blend in perfectly.

"What are you doing, Nicholas? Have you gone mad?"

"Apparently." Never had he been more certain of anything in his life, but he knew he had to kiss her. Seconds later, he snaked a hand about her nape and dragged her into his arms. When Amelia continued to protest, he cut off her words by swiftly claiming her lips with his. He'd wanted to do that since the first one, but now he was afforded more time to savor it.

At first, she planted her palms to his chest and pushed him away, but there was dark desire in her eyes that said she was as interested in the embrace as he was. For the space of a few ragged heartbeats, she stared at him, possibly weighing the consequences against wants, then the slight nod of her head gave him all the permission he needed. With a grunt of victory, he encouraged her against him once more, settled her into his embrace, and this time set out to kiss her senseless.

Dear God, it was as satisfying as he thought! The heat of her seeped through her clothing and transferred to his hands regardless of his gloves, into his body as he gathered her closer. The faint apple blossom scent of her filtered into his nose and fed his hunger, and still he moved over her lips, determined to draw the kiss out and explore for as long as she'd let him.

"Hellfire, woman, you tempt me beyond all reason," Nicholas said as he dragged his lips down the column of her throat, and the satiny skin urged him onward. He caressed his fingers along the inside of her wrist beneath her sleeve, traced her palm through the kid of her glove, danced those digits up her arm to cup her cheek. "So damned beautiful, and don't let anyone convince you differently."

Why the devil had he said that? He wasn't courting this woman.

Was he?

"Yes, indeed, you are quite mad, unless you are in your cups, but you certainly don't act like it." Her whispered words drifted across his chin, and the heat of them added fuel to the fires in his blood.

"Sober as a saint, I'm afraid." He bent his head, kissed the hollow of her throat behind the undone top fastening of her pelisse where her pulse rapidly fluttered, licked at the life force that surged through her veins, and when she gasped, he moved to her lips, kissing her without pressure, merely teasing little nips to build her arousal and perhaps tug a response from her.

"Insanity, then. Not a good look for you." A sigh shuddered from her, but then she lifted on her toes to return his kisses. Her decided lack of skill only built the lust building within him.

"Does it matter in this moment?" He kissed her lips, dared to deepen the embrace to find out how far her experience went.

Amelia was hesitant in returning the overture, but when he remained patient, nibbling at the corners of her mouth, moving over her lips as if he had all the time in the world, tracing those two pieces of flesh with the tip of his tongue, she sighed, followed his lead, and he continued with more insistence, fencing with her tongue, sparring with her as they did with words. With a moan, she looped her arms about his shoulders and gave herself over fully to the embrace.

Surrendered to him, which was quite unlike the woman he'd come to know, but the action spoke volumes.

And he was lost.

With a groan, Nicholas backed up against a bit of tumbled brickwork hidden amidst the foliage and covered with moss. How could she be so inexperienced yet represent a siren at the same time? His hardened member pressed insistently against the front of his breeches, pulsing in time to the rush of blood through his veins. Needing so much more, he kissed a path along the side of her neck, undid the fasteners of her pelisse, then followed the line of her bodice with his lips and tongue. When she murmured something unintelligible, he rested a palm on the broken wall, drew his other hand up her side to cup a breast, and when she didn't slap his face, he teased the beaded nipple with the pad of his thumb.

"Oh!" A surprised moan followed the breathy exclamation, and when he kissed her lips, she sighed. The mewling sounds she made at the back of her throat when he continued his fondling tugged at him, fueling the flames of his own need.

Had her fiancé never teased or stimulated her?

Spurred on by that thought, Nicholas grinned against her impossibly soft lips as she curled the fingers of one hand into the lapel of his greatcoat. "You were made for pleasure, Amelia." His pleasure, hers—theirs together, but she was definitely a creature who craved physical contact and affection.

Daring to move forward, he cupped both of her breasts. The plump globes tempted him, her body called out to his, the way she held her kiss-swollen lips slightly parted with her eyes gently closed left him gasping with a need that went deeper than wanting to bury his shaft into her heat. She pulled him closer, so he dipped his head and took a tight bud into his mouth, teased it with his tongue. The scrape of the fabric of her dress provided an interesting texture and added another layer of heat to the desire circling through his body. What would that nipple feel like against his tongue? How did she wish to be pleasured?

"Heavens…" She furrowed her fingers through his hair, holding him to her breast as she wriggled from his attention. "Nicholas." His name from her lips was the most pleasing invocation and worked to further see him undone. "I never knew I could feel such things, merely from a kiss."

He snorted. "This is slightly more than a kiss, dragon." Yet he wanted so much more from her. With her.

"Whatever it is, I feel oddly… free."

Well, damn. As if she'd given him permission, he encouraged her leg upward to wrap around his waist while he gathered her skirting enough so that he could slip a hand beneath the layers of fabric. Dear God, he wanted to touch her, feel her heat, make her come—

"No." The sound of her voice interrupted his thoughts and movements. Apparently, she was finished giving him liberties. "That is quite enough, Lord Wycliffe." Amelia pulled violently away from him with a heaving chest and the fingertips of one gloved hand hovering at her lips. "You need to evict the idea of seducing me from your mind. It won't happen. It *cannot* happen."

"I don't see why not. We are obviously suited for a coupling." Why the hell did he say such a thing?

"That matters not." Yet confusion sprang into her eyes. "I am a companion. You are a peer. I am to remain invisible for the remainder of my tenure in London." By increments, her chin went up, and he caught a tiny trace of regret in her expression before she banished all emotion from her face. "Do you understand?"

Without giving him time to respond, she gave him a wide berth and then tramped out of the woods while dusting off her clothing. The crunch of gravel beneath the soles of her half-boots was the final testament to her retreat.

"Damn." The woman was a spitfire. Nicholas lingered at the small folly, for he suffered with a cockstand that needed to calm. Kissing the hell out of her hadn't helped put the companion from his blood. If anything, she'd set fire to it and was slowly burning him from the inside out. He wanted her more now than ever, especially since her spirit and mind matched the lush figure she somehow hid beneath her drab clothing.

What am I to do now?

By the time he found her, Amelia had joined Millie, and the pair of them were enjoying food from various vendor carts. They both eyed him askance as he approached.

"Where have you been, Lord Wycliffe?" Millie demanded as she licked crumbs from her fingers.

"Oh, you know men like him. He was probably out chasing yet another woman," Amelia said with teasing in her eyes, but she maintained space between them.

"Ah, well, that is good, isn't it? At least there is someone out there who doesn't mind his age and how often he's dipped his wick, as they say." The chit stared at him as if she couldn't puzzle him out. "Perhaps you aren't the catch I thought."

"Thank you for that." Though he'd finally found his voice, it was riddled with annoyance and sarcasm, but since he'd been thwarted carnally as well as conversationally with Amelia by Millie's very presence, he was well on his way to a rotten mood.

Doing a horrid job of tamping down a grin, Amelia held out a hand. "Would you like the rest of this beef pie? It's quite tasty."

"I do not. Thank you. My appetite has fled." At least for food. Wanting to devour her had only doubled, and now she held all the power. Did she know that?

"Then perhaps we should see the rest of the exhibition. Oddly, I'm feeling quite refreshed."

Damn it all. She *knew*.

The girl frowned. "I have a megrim, Miss Hasting, and wish to go home to bed."

Nicholas nodded. "I have pressing business that cannot wait."

"Are you certain, my lord?" Apparently, Amelia wasn't quite done teasing him as Millie pulled ahead of them, retreating up the path toward the front of the exhibition. "I'm certain you had the same intent as Miss Featheringham but with much different results, hmm?" She gazed at him with a secretive grin that had the power to drive him slowly insane.

"Actually, I *am* rather out of sorts and don't wish to be in *any* woman's company at the moment." At least that was the truth.

"Now you have time to clean yourself up for a club or a society event this evening." Amusement danced in her eyes. "I doubt you've been with a member of the demimonde for a week. The *ton* might begin to think there was something wrong with your prowess."

"Perish the thought," he bit out in a barely audible whisper, but the laugh he uttered was a dismal, mocking affair. "Do shut up, Miss Hasting."

CHAPTER NINE

February 7, 1817

"MR. CHAPMAN IS here to see you."

Nicholas frowned as he glanced up from his book to see Jennings at the door to his sitting room, where he was supposed to be dressing for the afternoon. The last person he wished to see was his best friend, especially after being at White's with him last night, but there was nothing for it. "Send him up. No doubt his visit will be brief. I am on my way out in any event."

"Very well."

Once the butler departed, he snapped the book closed, tossed it on the chair he'd just vacated, and then donned the shirt Barnes had laid out for him after styling his hair. Marcus arrived just as Nicholas was tying off the laces of his green brocade waistcoat.

"Why are you here?" he asked as soon as his friend came into the room.

"Why are *you* so grumpy?" Marcus questioned instead. There was a knowing grin on his face that Nicholas didn't dare inquire about for fear it would be about the reason for the rotten mood.

"There is a particularly important session in the Lords tonight, and quite frankly, I'm not looking forward to arguing with the bullheaded men who oppose any sort of change or progress." That was but one facet for his foul temper.

"I imagine that wears on a person after a while." Marcus sat on the arm of the chair Nick had previously lounged in. "Better you than me, though."

"Yes, I'm sure being the fourth son of an earl does have at least that advantage." With no responsibilities and not even a courtesy title—and never wanting to create a lordship for himself as was his right—Marcus enjoyed a good bit of freedom that Nick had always been envious of.

"You know I spend my days in decent work."

"Yes, I know." His friend owned one of the premier tailor establishments in London. In fact, the Regent was an occasional customer. Though he was of the *beau monde*, circumstances demanded that he find a living, and he happened to be good with a needle as well as dressing a man to advantage, but very few people in London knew that. "Forgive me. I'm out of sorts, and I don't want to spend my night with the Lords." Quite frankly, all he wanted was to seek out Miss Hasting and kiss her again until she consented to take him into her bed. That's how he wished to spend those precious hours.

"Understandable."

"And it's raining besides."

"What difference does that make?"

"There will be no chance of escorting Miss Featheringham through an outdoor venue or even taking her on a drive."

"Ah, which means you won't have the chance to try and steal another kiss from Miss Hasting." The dratted man chuckled. Humor sparkled in his eyes. "The companion has infiltrated your blood and is now affecting your thoughts. You're nearly obsessed with her. Why don't you bed her so we can all move on to other things?"

"Don't you think I would have done exactly that if I could? Unfortunately, Miss Hasting is proving difficult and stubborn."

Marcus cringed. "The worst sort of woman. Why do you

bother with the pursuit?"

Why indeed. "Those traits—among others—make her deliciously fascinating." Another truth. Why the devil was he suddenly speaking them over the last few days? "Much more so than the girl." He shivered. "Truly, Miss Featheringham has got fluff for brains."

"That is practically a given since her father is offering a king's ransom to rid himself of her." For long moments Marcus watched while Nicholas finished his toilette. "Perhaps you're merely delirious or slightly deranged from not having a courtesan in your bed for a bit." One of his friend's eyebrows rose. "Have you?"

"Not since I met the companion." That alone was cause for concern. Even worse was the fact when he'd met Marcus at the club last night, the betting book was filled with entries wagering that he'd land the Featheringham chit and would marry her by Easter, while other entries stated dates of when he'd bed the companion and ruin her life. Both wagers infuriated him, though just last week he was doing the same by wagering against other people within the *ton* and their indiscretions. "What is happening to me, Marcus?"

A snort issued from his friend. "If you don't know, you're a nodcock, but I'm not going to tell you, for I wish to see how this will play out."

He huffed. "You've wagered against me." It wasn't a question.

Marcus shrugged. "I have laid down a couple of wagers, so either way you fall, I'll collect."

"I'm *so* glad I have a supportive friend." Sarcasm weighed heavily in the statement. "None of that answers the question of why you are here."

"Right." His friend nodded. "I came by to see if my nephew was here."

"Is he missing?"

"Apparently. My sister came round about an hour ago saying she couldn't find Percy and thought he and I had plans. Which we did not, so I assumed he was with you." Concern shadowed Marcus' eyes. "I can't imagine he's suddenly found a club to join or a wealthy chum to go about Town with."

"Interesting, but no. I haven't seen him since the last time I was out with him." He rooted about in a drawer for a pair of kid gloves. "If he does call, though, I'll be certain to send him home."

"Thank you." Marcus eased to his feet. "Where are you off to?"

"Honestly, I don't know. My mind is unsettled and—"

"Your neglected prick is demanding vengeance?" his friend asked with a raised eyebrow.

"Do shut up." Heat spread over his neck. "But yes."

"Then seek out the delectable Miss Hasting, trifle with her, take care of your needs, and then resume the responsibility of your life." He shrugged. "Once she's finally out of your system, you can concentrate on the heiress or return to prowling society events with me."

"Right." Nicholas nodded. Life had suddenly turned far too complicated, and more than ever, he wished to retreat to the cottage in Ireland merely for peace and to try and sort out his thoughts, to be honest with himself and confront some of the demons he struggled with.

"Well, I won't keep you, but I do wish you luck. You seem like a man determined."

"Thank you, and if I see Percy, I'll escort him personally to your house."

"I appreciate it." His friend frowned. "I suspect we've rather set things in motion that we didn't expect when we brought him on as a distraction."

"Indeed, and I'm afraid if the scandal escalates, Miss Hasting will be caught in the middle." Then she would blame him, and her fury would once more be unleased on him.

"Let us not rush fences, friend."

Nicholas said nothing as he left his rooms with Marcus.

Why had life suddenly become so complicated?

THE ANNOYANCE HADN'T faded by the time he'd gained his closed carriage. He had no particular destination in mind, merely wished to drive hoping that would help order his thoughts, but nothing soothed his frazzled nerves or fractured thoughts. Above all, he wanted to see Amelia, but that would mean calling at the Featheringham house and he didn't wish to spend time with Millie.

As the carriage slowly moved through the Mayfair streets and the traffic therein, he peered out the window. Through the rain-speckled glass, he spied a woman in a black cloak with the hood over her head, hurrying over the pavement, and there was an air of panic in her expression, but what was more, he recognized her.

Rapping on the roof, he demanded the driver stop, then he rolled down the window glass. The carriage pulled over to the side of the road. "Amelia!" When she didn't immediately respond to his hail, he tried again. "Miss Hasting!"

Finally, she looked his way, and when she realized it was him, she narrowed her eyes but came toward the carriage. "Go away, my lord. I have no time for you at the moment."

"What are you doing out in the rain and chill? It's too foul for anyone to walk about, and you'll be drenched soon if you aren't already."

When she huffed, her breath clouded about her head. "It's no concern of yours, now if you'll excuse me?"

"No." He shoved open the door and then put down the steps. "You'll catch your death, so tell me why."

She sighed again as the rain continued to come down. "Millie slipped out of the house without my knowledge. I have no idea when she left or where she is, but I've been unable to locate the girl. So I set out thinking she might be with friends."

"Hell's bells." Was she with Marcus' nephew? "Percy is missing as well."

"Well, drat." Worry clouded her eyes. "Do you think they're together?"

"It's a good possibility." This could be a sticky wicket he hadn't anticipated and might put an end to him calling upon the chit and thereby seeing the companion. Shoved that worry from his mind for fate had handed him the opportunity he'd been waiting for. "Come out of the rain. I'll drive you around and we'll keep an eye out for them."

For the space of a few heartbeats, she stood outside but was wavering. "Perhaps you're right. I can cover more ground in a vehicle, and it will be lovely to not have to walk in the rain."

"Most definitely." Nicholas could hardly believe his good fortune as he extended a hand to her, assisted her up the steps, and then tugged her into the carriage. As she settled on the bench opposite his, he rapped on the roof once more. Quickly, he pulled up the steps and folded them. "Rob, drive about Mayfair and then go toward Hyde Park. We're looking for a young couple, and the girl is wearing…" He glanced at Amelia. Quickly, she told him of Millie's outfit. "She's wearing a pink frock with a green brocade pelisse and bonnet with a pink ribbon."

"Of course, my lord." As soon as the door was closed, the driver urged the horses into motion and the carriage lurched forward.

"Afterward, we will return to Mayfair and drop Miss Hasting back at the Featheringham house. Perhaps the girl might have come back by then."

"I'll shout if I see them, my lord."

With his heartbeat accelerating, Nicholas turned his attention fully to Amelia. A slow grin curved his lips. How could it not? Today *would* be the day he taught her a few things, and perhaps if he was fortunate, he'd know what it felt like to bury his shaft deep into her heat. It would make the day better, clear his mind, and then he could fully concentrate on the pursuit of the chit. Then if he secured Miss Featheringham's hand, marriage contracts could be drawn up and funds transferred so he could bring order to the rest of his life.

She stared at him with a heady mixture of wariness and expectation. "Why do you look at me like that?"

"Like what, my dear dragon?" Seconds later, he joined her on the bench. It wasn't the one directly beneath the driver, which was a good thing, for he fully intended to see her come undone.

"As if you wish to eat me up."

"Mmm, now that is quite a temptation." Daring much, Nicholas slowly undid each of the fasteners. "The cloak is drenched. You'll catch your death if you remain in it for too much longer." With exaggerated movements, he removed the garment from her head and shoulders, letting it fall unheeded to the floorboards. "You are shivering." The silly thing hadn't worn a pelisse beneath the cloak, and neither was the fabric of her plum-colored dress thick enough for the February chill.

"I didn't give thought to my wardrobe; I merely wanted to find Millie before she does something she might regret." Another shiver racked her shoulders. "As much trouble as the girl is, she shouldn't be allowed to destroy her life or her chances."

"You are a good person." The tiny catch in her voice had his chest tightening as he tugged the gloves from his hands and let them tumble to the floor with her cloak. "She certainly is committed to causing a sensation. What will her father say when he discovers her clandestine activities?"

"He will be livid at her or at me, and if it is with me, no doubt I'll lose my position." When she glanced over her shoulder at him, concern pooled in her blue eyes. "My family is depending on the coin I make."

There was nothing he could do about that, but perhaps he could make her forget about everything she struggled with for a short while. "Hush, Amelia. No good will come of worrying." He scooted further onto the bench with his back against the side, and as he extended his legs along the squabs, he pulled her backward until she settled onto his lap, her body stiff. "Relax." He whispered the word into her ear, then followed the request by gliding his lips along the side of her neck until she reclined against his chest. "Relax."

"I can't. Not until she's found safe."

"I rather doubt Millie is in any danger." He tried to bite back a snicker but wasn't successful. "Well, her innocence might be if she *is* with young Percy." As he drew his hands up and down her arms, a sigh escaped. "What are you doing?"

"Helping to get your mind off things the best way I know how." Up and down, he danced his fingers over her arms. Gooseflesh popped over the skin, whether from the chill or his attentions, he couldn't say.

"I told you flirtations won't work on me."

"You did, but after that kiss in Hyde Park, I don't believe you're as immune to me and my teasing as you hope I'll think." In fact, he would wager everything he owned on that fact and meant to prove it. He nibbled the skin just below her earlobe then went on to explore her nape with his lips. "Curious?"

"No." But the word was a breathy affair even as she brushed at his hands.

"The tension that has brewed between us since we met now needs an outlet, don't you think?" As he spoke, he worked the laces at the back of her dress.

"I…" She blew out a breath. "Perhaps, but that doesn't mean we need to act on it."

"I never thought you'd be a coward," he whispered, and when the dress sagged about her upper body, he grinned. "Let me explore you, Amelia. Surely you can feel how much I desire you." Already, his hardened shaft pressed insistently against her arse.

Damn, I want this woman.

"I shouldn't. It's not proper for a companion to indulge in such things." Yet there was a note of doubt in her voice he couldn't wait to exploit.

"No one will know; it's quite private here." Gently, he tugged on the dress, eased it off her shoulders and down her arms until the bodice clung precariously to the upper slopes of her breasts.

"With the rain and the wheels against various things on the road, it's doubtful even the driver will hear the sounds of your pleasure." Every word caused his lips to brush the column of her neck, the underside of her jaw, and the faint floral scent of her drove him slowly mad.

"But I…"

"Do you wish to arrive at the end of your life and know you had a chance to feel what it was like to be wanted by a man, but you turned it down for some silly notion of propriety?" That wasn't well done of him, but he couldn't help it. She only needed to thaw a bit more to let that flame she'd long denied herself flare.

"Oh, I think I hate you, Nicholas," she said in a whisper as she shivered again while he nibbled the skin beneath her ear. "This is as much your devil's game as I likened your seduction to the other day, and I no longer understand the rules. Either path I choose, I'll come up the loser."

At least she hadn't flat-out refused him. "Or you'll find there are no rules when it comes to carnal delights. Easily that hate will become something more." He licked and kissed a path along the side of her neck, couldn't have enough of her satiny skin. All the while, he continued to stroke a hand up and down her arm. When she fidgeted, apparently restless, he brushed the fingers of his other hand along the top of her loose bodice.

"I am not an innocent, you know." When he dipped a finger beneath her dress to oh so briefly graze a hardened nipple, she sucked in a breath.

"In one way, perhaps you are not, but in all the ways that matter, you are so completely naïve that I cannot wait to show you everything you should have had from your fiancé."

"Why are you so impossible?" Amelia reached up a hand and hooked her fingers about his nape, gently pulling his head closer. Ah, that sweet agreement was heady indeed.

There was no doubt in his mind she wanted him as much as he did her, but he didn't wish to rush his fences. "Why are you?" he asked instead. When she turned her head, Nicholas captured her lips with his, and for several minutes, they spoke with kisses and fleeting caresses. It was all too easy to tug the dress ever downward until her breasts were bared, nestled beneath a thin lawn chemise that was no longer new, as well as low stays.

A gasp was her only answer, but she didn't bid him nay when he freed her breasts from the remaining barriers, glanced his fingertips fleetingly over her pebbled nipples.

"As I said in Hyde Park, you were meant for pleasure, not for being a companion to a spoiled chit with more coin than brains," he whispered against her neck, and ever so gently he drew his fingers along her sides, played her ribs in an effort to draw out the teasing, the anticipation.

"*Your* brain must be addlepated. I am nothing like that."

"Then you haven't truly looked into the mirror I gifted to you." When Nicholas cupped her breasts, she sucked in a breath of apparent surprise. "You are lovely when you are hovering on the edge, in the moments before I send you over."

"Over where?"

"Oh, my dear dragon, you have so much to learn." Pure, unadulterated lust pushed through his blood as he squeezed her breasts, rolled the nipples at the roots. This would be such fun.

"Oh, do that." She squirmed on his lap, which only sent spikes of need through his shaft. "I never knew I could feel so... feel like floating." Wonder wove through her voice and made him grin.

"I'll wager you'll feel so much more before we're through." With new confidence surging through his form, Nicholas applied himself to the task of seducing the woman in his lap. When he glanced his palms over her erect nipples, a shuddering moan escaped her. It was as if angels sang from the heavens, and he selfishly wanted to hear it again. Amelia arched her back, curled the fingers of one hand into the side of his thigh, her fingers clenching and unclenching the more he manipulated her breasts. "Concentrate on what I'm doing to you and let your worries fall away."

It would be a task to remind himself to go slow, to not rush things, to not frighten her, but he would do it because she deserved to know what it felt like to be wanted, desired, understood.

"Please don't stop." The insistence in her whispered plea continued to tighten his shaft, bringing him quickly to a place he desperately wished to explore with her.

Damn but she felt amazing in his arms, the sounds she made in enjoyment or encouragement set fire to his veins. After a week of teasing, of stolen kisses, of verbal sparring, of looks full of longing and hunger, he had this fascinating woman front and center, and beyond that, she was willing.

Oddly enough, it humbled him as he caressed the perfect globes of her breasts. With each pass of his hands, each stroke and twist of his fingers on those bright pink, pert nipples, she moaned and arched her back. Clearly it had been years since she'd been pleasured by a man, longer than that if her fiancé's ineptness was anything to go by, and if she was this wanting, it wouldn't take long for her to fall into bliss.

And he would be the one who taught her to fly. No one else. He would be the man she would always remember. Heady stuff indeed.

His hand shook as he slipped a hand down her torso, past the yards of fabric that made up her skirting. Once he'd pulled up the garment, he delved his hand between her thighs, gently urged them apart, and let his fingers drift into the curls shrouding her sex. When she tried to pull at his hand, he made soothing sounds into her ear and batted her hand away. "I won't hurt you, love, but you need to let me in for me to show you how you can fly." Her innocent want to dissuade him went straight to his shaft. It was only a matter of time before he embarrassed himself by spending too soon, for it had been a while since he, too, had indulged, but he gritted his teeth and ignored the throbbing discomfort.

"This is exactly the scandal I've cautioned Millie about. I'm hardly setting a good example," she managed to say between panting breaths.

"Yes, well, she is young and vying for a titled man, while you are nearly a widow. You are older and know your own mind."

She snorted. "Meaning I'm well past an age where a man would care about my reputation?"

"Of course not, and age is meaningless, for a woman can be valued no matter how old." It was another truth, which just went along with everything else he'd said this week, but it was doubly so now.

"Must you always try to charm me?" The dear woman parted her legs to allow him greater access, and as he spread her folds to uncover the swelling pearl at her center, she whimpered.

"Is it working?" He could barely believe his luck in that she was allowing any of this.

"May God strike me dead or mark me as a fool, but yes." Amelia's back arched again. She held his other hand to her breast, pressing it to the nipple. Oh, yes, she would break, soon, and he couldn't wait.

Truly, being with her was so completely different from the other women he'd bedded, it was almost as if he were discovering all of this with her for the first time.

At the first pass of his fingers, she moaned. The shiver that went through her delicious body transferred to him. By the second, she was shaking with need. Nicholas circled that tiny bundle of nerves, experimented with varying levels of friction as he worked it over, and all the while, he kissed the side of her neck, plucked and rolled her nipple, did everything he could to bring her to a shuddering climax. When her breath grew labored, he grinned and whispered words of encouragement into her ear.

"What... what should I do?"

"Nothing. Go through the experience, discover what you enjoy, and perhaps next time we can incorporate that." Would she allow him to violate her in this way a second time? Only fate knew but he hoped so, and still he worried that swollen bud, rubbed it, flicked it, circled it as if that were his only purpose in life.

A moan mixed with a gasp. "Oh, heavens." The lady writhed against his body, and his hardened length pulsed with a need of its own. "I'm being swallowed by such big sensations. Drowning, and I might not survive." There was both marvel and fright in her tones.

"You will, and I'll wager you'll adore hitting release." As she fought through all that she experienced, he sought to push her toward the brink, and for one second, he left off working her nubbin in favor of slipping two fingers into the honeyed heat of her passage. "Dear God, you feel amazing." A ragged moan left his throat. Damn but he couldn't wait to claim her; she was warm and tight, and as he stroked, her body greedily pulled at his digits.

"What are you doing to me? I'm going to fall apart."

"That is the general idea." In and out, he thrust into her, enjoying the heat of her. "Let yourself go. Do this one thing for yourself. Be selfish and take exactly what you want."

"How, though?" A slight wail entered her voice as her head thrashed on his chest. "Something is just there…"

"It's all right. Don't fret." Renewing his attentions at her breast, Nicholas withdrew from her passage only to bedevil her nubbin with greater intensity. "Don't think about anything except what you feel, at the sensations crashing through you."

"I—Oh!" A shiver racked her whole body, but he didn't ease with the friction, the play he did to her button or her nipple. "Ah!" When she fell into that release, she did it in spectacular fashion. Put simply, Amelia Hasting shattered in his arms. A low, keening cry left her throat as her body stiffened, then relaxed.

Would the driver hear those cries? Only God knew, but Nicholas couldn't help his grin of satisfaction.

The play of expressions on her face tugged at his chest, as did the way she clutched at his thigh while the climax crashed over her. As her eyes shuttered closed, she reached backward and curled her free hand behind his nape, lost while contractions and waves of pleasure no doubt stole through her person.

It was one of the most glorious sights he'd ever seen, even though he'd long ago become jaded regarding couplings.

"I… I seem to have no words," she whispered as he held her. In that moment, it didn't matter that he was close to exploding with his own need, that he hadn't bedded a woman since meeting Miss Hasting, that he'd thought of nothing more than joining with her for days. Seeing her flushed cheeks and chest, listening to the frantic beat of her heart as she twisted on his lap and put frantic pressure on his engorged shaft, the thought that he'd been given a rare and special gift slammed through him.

Clinging to the last vestiges he had of being a gentleman from deep down inside him, Nicholas drew her to him and kissed her, slowly at first because he was in awe of her and suddenly uncertain of himself. Then, once urgent heat roared through him, he deepened the embrace, sought out her tongue in the hopes of finding redemption in her.

A sharp rap on the roof broke into the passion that fogged his brain. "No sign of the young couple, my lord, but we're now approaching Captain Featheringham's townhouse."

Those words completely destroyed the spell the afternoon had woven around them, for as soon as the carriage slowed and then rocked to a halt, Amelia scrambled off his lap. She set herself to rights faster than any woman should need to after finding release. In the gloom from the interior of the vehicle and the rain, emotions flitted over her face, but shock and perhaps guilt were all too obvious.

"What you did… What *we* did…" She shook her head, and a few locks of hair fell from the pins of the tight bun at the back of her head. Her breath came in fast pants. "How could you? How dare you!" As tears sprang to her eyes, she lifted a hand, and even though he knew what would happen, he was wildly unprepared when she slapped him.

"You *did* agree to the events of this afternoon," he said into the tense silence.

"You could have been a gentleman instead of…"

"Giving you the best experience you've ever known?" Nicholas provided helpfully, grinning in the face of her ire.

"Oh, you aggravating, annoying bounder of a man!" Amelia wrenched open the door to the carriage. Her gaze bore into his. "This will *never* happen again." Without another word, she hopped from the vehicle, then turned back to him. "And you'd better hope Millie is inside, else there will be hell to pay, and if she *has* been with Mr. Marsden this whole afternoon, I shall be *furious* at you."

He held a hand to his burning cheek but couldn't help but grin. "Even more than you are now?" Why did he always feel the need to needle her, especially when she was in a temper?

And dear God, she was magnificent in her rage.

"Argh!" When she slammed the door, the sound of it resounded through the cabin and his mind.

Switching benches, Nicholas rapped on the roof. "Home, if you please."

"Aye, my lord."

He leaned back against the squabs, watching the dragon as she stormed up the short walkway *sans* her cloak looking for all the world like an offended fury of old. Oh, he'd made an impression on her, and what was more, she hadn't left his blood after that heated session. If anything, the obsession had grown, and he wanted her more than ever.

Damn if he didn't look forward to furthering the pursuit, and it wouldn't end until he'd properly bedded her.

Twice.

Chapter Ten

February 8, 1817
Masterson House
Mayfair

THE LAST THING Mia wished to do tonight was attend a rout, but that was what the captain wished for his daughter to do, so she would escort Millie to the event.

She frowned out the carriage window as the vehicle waited in the long line of similar conveyances that approached the townhouse. In fact, the only thing she wanted to do was remain locked in her room and try *not* to think about the Viscount Wycliffe. What sort of weak-spined ninny had she been yesterday to let him have intimate access to her body, to become so lost in him and his ministrations that she'd completely separated herself from reality for a time?

Especially when, as soon as she'd entered the Featheringham townhouse and located Millie, she'd given the girl an overly strict dressing down against doing the same? Heat filled her cheeks, and she hoped to any deity that was listening she hadn't been observed exiting Wycliffe's carriage looking as undone as she'd felt. What was more, she'd accidentally left her cloak in the vehicle, which gave him an excuse to call.

But he hadn't today, and that had made her a tad out of sorts as well, for she'd become accustomed to him bedeviling her on a daily basis in the guise of calling upon Millie. *What is wrong with me that I'm actually missing him?*

"If you are going to be so dour and rainclouds tonight, please do not stand anywhere near me, Miss Hasting. You'll scare away all the men." The annoyance in Millie's voice was quite clear.

With a huff, Mia focused her wandering attention on her charge. "I'm sorry to put a damper on your fun for the evening, but that is literally what my position is." And she'd been doing a poor job of it to this point, but at least Nicholas hadn't truly been pursuing the girl. "I'm to steer you into the directions of appropriate, eligible men with titles as well as keep you out of their beds until you've accepted a proposal."

The girl shook her head, and in the dim illumination coming from a nearby gas lamp on the street, a trace of vulnerability and doubt went through her eyes. "What if I personally don't want a titled gentleman any longer?"

"Oh?" This was a new path for her. "What has made you change your mind?"

She waved a hand. "It seems to me the pool of men who hold titles are small, and the men inside that pool who aren't old or unattractive is even smaller."

"True." Had the girl suddenly matured or was there a reason for the statement? "What will you tell your father if you should find this paragon of a man who isn't titled or part of the English aristocracy?"

"Uh, I'd hoped *you* would break the news to him if such a thing occurs."

Their carriage moved forward and would be the next to offload. Mia shook her head. "If you wish to guide your life for yourself, then you need to have the bravery to tell others in that life of your intentions. You will not always have someone there to deflect criticism or ire."

Perhaps she needed to follow her own advice.

"I don't want him angry at me for something I feel strongly about."

Mia snorted, for that was much of what life was about. "It is how you know you are maturing, I'm afraid." She narrowed her eyes on the girl. "Did you have a specific gentleman in mind?" *Please don't say Mr. Marsden.*

"That remains to be seen." Millie brushed at a section of her skirting. "Spending your time watching what I'm doing must be dull for you as well, Miss Hasting. Why don't you try to flirt and attract a man? Then once I'm married, you won't be thrown to the wolves or need to take another position."

"Thank you for the concern. I shall keep that advice in mind." She couldn't quite remove the sarcasm from her voice. Why did everyone assume she needed a man in her life?

"You're welcome. I'm certain there are men around your age, and I know there are older men in need of a wife," Millie continued, completely oblivious to Mia's mood. "Of course, you might be subjected to his already formed family, but then, I don't suspect you could bear children at your advanced age."

If that didn't make her feel every bit her one and thirty years. "It's so good that I have you here to remind me of things I might have forgotten." Though it was a fear and worry of hers that she strove to ignore most days, Mia liked to hope she wasn't too old for motherhood if fate might grant her a husband.

Then the carriage stopped again, and this time a footman opened the door and put down the steps. "Welcome to Masterson House."

"Thank you." Millie assumed command of the situation. She swept out of the carriage with the footman's assistance, then shook the wrinkles from her pale blue satin skirting. "Don't dawdle, Miss Hasting. I can't wait to see who is in attendance tonight."

Tamping down hard on the urge to form a less-thanladylike reply, Mia accepted the footman's hand as she descended the steps. Why had she ever thought taking the paid position as a companion would be a way to see London and pretend, if only for a few moments, she was a member of good standing within the *ton*?

By the time they cleared the reception line, she could no longer curb Millie's enthusiasm for mingling, so she didn't even try, but when they came upon young Mr. Marsden quite by "accident" wherein Millie gushed on and on about how it was *such* a coincidence to meet at the rout, Mia's eyes narrowed. Had the two of them concocted the scheme to meet socially yesterday when she'd snuck out to presumably meet him?

"Good evening, Mr. Marsden." Despite herself, she glanced around the immediate area but didn't spy Lord Wycliffe. "Are you attending by yourself?" Both of the young people were in need of a lecture on proper deportment and the possible consequences of physical intimacy, for society didn't look kindly on fallen women, while the men were able to go through their lives with rarely a word spoken.

"For the moment. I, uh, haven't seen Lord Wycliffe for a couple of days." He tugged on the knot of his cravat. "The viscount is cross with me more often than not."

Millie sniffed. "He's as big a curmudgeon as Miss Hasting."

Mr. Marsden shrugged. "My uncle is supposed to be in attendance, though, so you shall meet him soon."

"Oh!" Surprise and a hint of nervousness flitted across Millie's face. Why? Was that meeting also pre-planned as an underhanded way for her to begin being introduced to Percy's family? Before Mia could ask, the girl glanced toward the staircase. "Shall we go up? It doesn't seem as if there is much of a crowd going into the drawing room."

"I'm told the hosts are planning to have dancing straightaway. It's one of the things they enjoy most." Mr. Marsden offered Millie his arm crooked at the elbow, which she took, and then they both headed toward the stairs.

With nothing else to do, Mia trailed after them. This had all the makings of trouble, and she suspected Millie intended to choose Mr. Marsden as her husband regardless that he had no ambition, a title, or a place of his own to live. *The captain is going to be furious!*

Barely had she chosen a spot at one wall near the other wallflowers and companions who sat in delicate chairs, prepared to keep a hawk's eye on her charge, when a pianoforte was wheeled into the room now that the rugs had been rolled back. There wasn't exactly a crush of people in the drawing room, but there were a decent number of guests for her to temporarily lose sight of Millie a few times as she and Percy made a circuit about the room.

"Imagine finding a dragon here among so many rabbits."

The sound of *his* voice, couched in a whisper that sent tingles shivering down her spine, accelerated Mia's heartbeat and had her turning about to face the viscount. "Ah, Lord Wycliffe. I wondered when you would slither in."

A chuckle quickly covered with a fake cough drew her attention to the man coming abreast of Nicholas, who she recognized from the first night she'd met the viscount. "This must be the much-lauded Miss Hasting." He slowly grinned as he looked her up and down. With his lean form, his blue eyes, and blond looks, he could easily have been mistaken for a Grecian god come to life. "Forgive Wycliffe. He's naught but a nodcock if he considers you a dragon. Frankly, I would choose you as a dance partner over the chits making Come Outs, for I'll wager you're a lovely conversational partner."

"Thank you." Temporarily ignoring the viscount, who fumed to have his entrance voided, Mia offered her hand to the newcomer. "I *am* Miss Hasting, and unless I miss my guess, you are Mr. Chapman, uncle to the young Mr. Marsden."

"Charming, intelligent, and a looker." Mr. Chapman took her gloved hand and brought it to his lips where he kissed the back. "I definitely wish to speak with you more at length, but I need to tell my nephew I'm here, to make certain he remains a gentleman." When he released her hand, he glanced at Nicholas. "Let us hope you can do the same while I'm gone."

Left alone with the viscount, Mia faced him with narrowed eyes. "Why are you here?"

"Why shouldn't I be here? I was invited." A trace of confusion clouded his dark eyes before being hidden behind his typical mask of boredom. "Also, Miss Featheringham is here."

"Ah, and you are still trying to win her hand." Behind her, someone began playing the piano. Rustling fabric indicated couples were taking positions for a dance. Though she knew that was the only reason for her own attendance at the rout, it still rankled. Careful to keep her voice at a barely audible whisper, she asked, "Why don't you go dance with the heiress, then, instead of lingering here with me? I'm the companion, remember."

With a quick glance at the wallflowers who stared at them, clearly curious, Nicholas urged her a bit away from that gaggle and the potential gossip therein. Then he peered into her face. "Why are you in a temper with me?" His hiss of a whisper, the way the warmth of his breath skated over her cheek as he leaned closer to be heard over the music and the sound of shoes over the hardwood.

"Why do you think, Lord Wycliffe?" If he wasn't clever enough to puzzle it out, she certainly wouldn't tell him.

His eyes darkened. "Are you still out of sorts over what happened in the carriage yesterday?" When she didn't answer, he chuckled, and she ignored how that sound resonated in her chest. "You *were* willing. It has never been my habit to take women by force."

Heat poured into her cheeks. "That isn't the part I've taken issue with." Under cover of the country reel, Mia continued. What would it hurt to tell him why? "After what you did to me, I was... curious about other things, which you did *not* do."

"What I didn't... Bloody hell. I was being a gentleman!" His eyes rounded. Shock etched through his expression even as his eyes glinted with wicked promise. "I can certainly rectify my oversight, though, Miss Hasting." As he roved his dark gaze over her décolletage, she shivered. "If you'd like, I can have my driver summoned—"

"Stop." As tempting as that was, she held up a hand to ward him off. "That might have been what I wanted yesterday afternoon, but that urge has faded."

Oh, it was quite a lie, and that further drove annoyance through her chest. Being claimed by him, feeling him moving inside her body in an effort to dispel that restless longing circling through her that had begun from the moment they'd first met had been uppermost in her thoughts. It had dogged her every step, chased her every heartbeat since the second she'd left the carriage yesterday and had haunted her all of last night.

A few seconds passed in silence as he stared at her while she glared. Then a knowing grin spread over his face. "You are not a gifted liar, Amelia." The way he said her name, as if he caressed the word with his tongue and lips before releasing it into the air, awoke the butterflies in her belly. "You want me still."

Even now, a tremor of desire throbbed through her core. *Do not show him he's gotten beneath your skin!* Thankful for the dance that would conclude at any second, Mia huffed out a breath. "That's not it at all, my lord. In fact, I rather think your alleged skill in that arena has been over-inflated since that reputation depends on word of mouth from unreliable sources." She refused to feed his ego, but she would give him something that would make him twist in the wind. "However, I *am* cross with you."

"Why? Please tell me so I can correct it." Was that truly a note of desperation in his voice or was she imagining it? Surely none of this mattered to him.

"The only reason I haven't slapped you again is the fact that Millie *was* at home when I arrived there." She let her hands fall to her sides, hid the fingers in the folds of her plum-colored silk skirting, the gown over three years old. "I lectured her about her behavior, of course, but I believe it fell on deaf ears, thanks to the young man you've trained into your likeness."

He snorted. "I've hardly done that. In fact, I only met the

young man nearly a week ago."

"Be that as it may, I don' t wish to discuss Mr. Marsden." Daring much, she moved a step closer to him. "I'm annoyed at you because you never noticed that I wore the stockings yesterday."

An expression of delight crossed his face, but she didn't quite trust the look in his eyes. Nicholas scooped up her hand and brought it to his lips. "Why, my dear Miss Hasting, I did in fact notice, but time got away from me before I had the chance to properly explore those fantastic legs of yours." Even though his words were a whisper, they glided over her skin like satin. "Are you wearing them tonight? I would adore slowly removing them, kissing your glorious skin as I do so."

Mercy. If she lingered too long in his company, she would melt into a puddle. "If I am, you will never know." She stepped away from him as the music ended and the reel came to a close, but she winked, to let him know that she was, indeed, wearing the hosiery.

He put a hand to his chest. "You don't play fair, dear dragon."

"Perhaps now you will understand I am *not* your quarry." That was the fact of the matter. "I'm a companion only. Employ that energy on the woman you will eventually marry." Her voice wavered slightly on that last word, but she hoped he didn't notice.

"I don't want to spend my time tonight pursuing the girl when I could have you instead." There was nothing except earnestness in his expression, as well as scandal in his eyes.

She almost crumbled, but then Mia steeled her spine and shook her head. "You know that can't happen. I need to set an example. As I've said numerous times."

"For Millie who's probably already given young Percy everything he's wanted?" The viscount snorted. "She is entirely too impulsive and reckless."

"Perhaps the right man will tame her." She ignored the heat in her cheeks. "I also need to keep my position and you need to find an heiress. Those are the facts, and nothing has changed. You know this."

"Sadly, I do." The viscount stared over her shoulder at the makeshift dance floor. "How is it one lives one's life as if there is no tomorrow, and suddenly when that tomorrow comes, it doesn't hold nearly the same fascination or excitement as one dreamed that it might years ago?" Far too much maudlin emotion riddled the inquiry that it touched her own, drew it out.

"Perhaps that is what it feels like when one matures, Lord Wycliffe. One has responsibilities one needs to attend even though they demand one sacrifice themselves." To her horror, tears welled in her eyes. The conversation had veered into highly personal territory, but now wasn't the time for such confidences or truths.

They were both spared from responding, for Mr. Chapman joined them again.

"I apologize, but I was asked by my nephew to partner Miss Featheringham in that set, and since my dimwitted best friend is supposed to be plying his charm to her, I thought I would try to vet her for him." But he studiously ignored Nicholas in order to speak directly to Mia. "The next set is a waltz. Would you care to partner me?"

"Oh, thank you for the invitation, but I'm here as a companion. It wouldn't do for me to dance with one of the eligible men." Though it would serve Nicholas right if she were to favor someone else over him.

"Nonsense. You are also the daughter of a baron and therefore a member of the *beau monde*," Mr. Chapman answered with a smug grin at his friend as he held out a gloved hand.

"Ha! A family plagued by gossip and now with pockets to let," she replied but with a smile, for this was far too much fun.

Amusement twinkled in Mr. Chapman's eyes as Nicholas stood tense and looking on with a fierce frown. "Very well, then indulge me at the refreshments table in the corridor. We'll let Wycliffe do the pretty here while we talk."

"I was engaging her in conversation first, Chapman," the viscount said in a tension-filled whisper as the impromptu dance floor filled with couples.

"Not well, I should say, since a woman should be simpering and smiling when she converses with a man," Mr. Chapman was quick to note. "Let me show you how it can be, Wycliffe."

"I'd find that quite acceptable." When she slipped her fingers into Mr. Chapman's palm, he drew her hand to his sleeve. Flashing what she hoped was a demure smile at the viscount, she fell into step with her escort. If Nicholas thought to play a game with her, she could do the same with him. To Nicholas, she said, "Go charm Millie. After all, that *is* why you are here, correct?"

Once they exited the drawing room, Mr. Chapman put his blond head close to hers. "Why do I have a feeling you only went with me to spite Wycliffe?"

Mia allowed herself the freedom to laugh, and it felt good to do so. "Why do I have the feeling *you* only asked *me* to do so for the same?"

Though his chuckle was pleasant and deep, the sound of it didn't ignite something in her soul like the viscount's. "Touché, Miss Hasting. I did, indeed, wish to annoy him, but I never thought he'd show jealousy before. It's something I've not encountered from him in all the years I've known him."

"Why would he have need for jealousy?" They were nothing to each other. Not even after what happened yesterday afternoon.

"That is what I intend to discover." He escorted her to the table that bore glasses of lemonade as well as flutes of champagne. "What do you prefer?"

"If I'm honest, I'd say champagne, but if I'm responsible, I would answer lemonade."

He glanced quickly at her, but his expression was difficult to read. "One should never be too responsible, especially all at one time in the same evening." After snagging two flutes from the table, he led her over to an empty spot near the stairs but diagonal to the drawing room. "You can see into the room and thereby keep an eye on your charge."

"Thank you." She accepted the bubbly wine from him and took a sip. "Heavens, I'd forgotten how that tickles," she said and pressed the fingertips of her free hand to her upper lip. "It's been ages since I've imbibed."

"You should do so more often."

"Not on a companion's salary and certainly not while I'm on duty." With a frown, she peered into her champagne as if the bubbles would give her the answers she sought. "How well do you know Lord Wycliffe?"

"Well enough, since our university days." He steadily watched her as he sipped his champagne. "Why?"

"I have the feeling Nicholas isn't the rake he wishes the world to see." Slowly, Mia took another sip of her bubbly wine. "However, I don't understand why that is the type of man he wants everyone to know him by when the truth of him is by far more fascinating."

"You are quite clever, Miss Hasting." One of Mr. Chapman's eyebrows rose. "I agree. I have never understood that about him, but he keeps secrets for his own reasons." Speculation clouded his eyes. "However, there has been a slight shift in him over this past week that is most peculiar, and I'm at a loss as to why."

"Perhaps he has grown tired of the charade. Who can tell with Wycliffe." She took one last sip then handed her flute to Mr. Chapman. "Thank you for the interlude. I need to check on Millie, and if I were you, I'd talk to some sense into your nephew and your friend. They both seem to need the same sort of advice."

Then she reentered the drawing room with a curious pain twining about her heart.

CHAPTER ELEVEN

February 9, 1817
Royal Opera House
Covent Garden

MIA COVERED A yawn with her hand. The second show of the evening had only just begun, which meant it was around eight o'clock in the evening, and already she wished she'd feigned a megrim to stay home curled up in her bed, reading a novel.

Slumber had been elusive last night after the rout. Perhaps it was because she'd seen Nicholas or perhaps it had been the excess of excitement brought on from the society event, but she tossed and turned all night, and her thoughts revolved around the viscount. Though she'd been in a temper with him, she couldn't shake her maudlin mood, for she had her life, and he had his, and never should those paths cross.

Yet he was like a fever. He'd gotten into her blood and now it was difficult to heal from it. No matter what she did to occupy her mind or how much she kept Millie occupied when they were home, her thoughts always circled back to Wycliffe and how his hands had felt on her body, how his whispered voice sounded like in her ear, how the heat of him and the strength of his arms around her had made her feel safe and wanted.

And how, in a tiny abstract part of her heart, she wished life was different for them both.

That was easily enough forgotten, or at least shoved into a box and ignored, for Millie did keep her quite busy, especially because there was an upcoming ball at the end of the month hosted by Lady Evelyn, who just so happened to be Mr. Marsden's mother. It had come as a shock to her that the young man was the grandson of an earl, but she supposed stranger things had happened. No longer was he a man adrift, and if Millie *did* bring him up to scratch, it wouldn't be so bad. There was no hope the boy would ever take the title, for apparently the earl had four sons—Mr. Chapman being the fourth—as well as a daughter, and all of those siblings, with the exception of Mr. Chapman, had many sons among them.

Why am I trying so hard to keep Millie and Percy apart?

If she gave in, then she wouldn't need to worry that Nicholas would manage to charm his way into Millie's heart or rather her father's coffers, but what good would that do? He was in need of a fortune, and her charge wasn't the only heiress in the *ton*. If it wasn't Millie he chased, he'd need to move on to someone else, and that would take him away from *her*.

Yet she had no claim to him.

Mia sighed. The actors upon the stage didn't hold her attention. Granted, the opera was more serious than the comedy the evening started with, but as Millie nodded in her chair and the captain not far off, there was no one for her to talk with. The other people within the box—Mr. Chapman was the one who'd given the captain the loan of it tonight—were strangers to her and merely a collection of individuals whom the captain assumed would make him and his daughter seem more attractive to the powers-that-be in society.

Needing to do something to help jog her mind away from the viscount as well as keep her awake through the final performance of the night, Mia stood and quietly made her way from the box.

Since she'd been seated behind Millie and the captain, there was no need to excuse herself. The red velvet curtain was easy enough to slip through, which deposited her into a small room behind the box where dinner had been served between shows. It was empty of staff and foodstuffs now, and everything had been put back to rights, but before she could reach the door on the other side, that panel opened, and Viscount Wycliffe came in.

Well, drat. Her blood both heated and chilled upon seeing him, for he was devastatingly handsome in his dark evening attire. The silver thread on his black satin waistcoat glimmered in the dim light from one of the gas sconces that had been left burning. Was there ever a more captivating sight than him dressed like that? "Nicholas," she breathed in a barely audible whisper, pausing midway through the room.

"Amelia." When his gaze alighted on her, a play of emotions went over his face, but it was too shadowy in the room to read them. "Why are you not in the box watching the opera?" He kept his voice low, which was all to the good, for the last thing they needed was an audience.

"I am far too restless to sit and watch a play." She could scarcely breathe; his presence was far too large for the small space, and it seemed as if he filled every portion of it. "Why are *you* here?"

"Marcus mentioned in passing you were attending the opera tonight with the Featheringhams. I had business that kept me away until now, and I wasn't allowed in until later anyway." As he spoke, he prowled toward her with slow, measured steps. "But I am quite delighted to find you alone."

She retreated, led him toward the far side of the room toward the door and away from the heavy velvet curtain so they wouldn't be overheard, and he continued to follow until her back connected with the wall near one of the sconces that hadn't been lit. "What are you about? You should go inside and sit next to Millie, try to charm her since that has always been your goal." The sooner he focused his attentions on the chit, the sooner she could put him from her own mind, yet… If she were honest with herself, she should have attempted to get away from him, leave the room, put space between them, but perhaps she was in denial and the craving to be in his vicinity, to perhaps feel his lips on hers was too great to ignore.

"Don't pretend you don't feel the attraction between us." As if he had all the time in the world, he divested himself of his gloves and then tossed them to an ornate and empty sideboard at her right. When he rested a palm on the wall at her head, he leaned his body into hers, effectively trapping her. "That short session in the carriage the other day wasn't nearly enough to clear you from my blood." Every whispered word sent heated breath sailing along her cheek. Though the desire in his dark eyes was all too clear, confusion lined his face. "I don't understand why you've enchanted me, bedeviled me, but I cannot move forward until it's been exhausted. What is aligning myself with the girl compared to that?"

The words were flattering enough, and ninny that she was, a few stupid flutters went through her heart. "But, I…" It didn't matter that she craved his touch, his kiss, his notice. He wasn't for her, couldn't be, because letting a man of the viscount's caliber trifle with her emotions wouldn't end well. She would be hurt, to say nothing of the consequences should other things occur. As she tipped back her head, he dipped his down, and with her every word, their lips nearly touched. "How many times must I tell you nothing else can happen between us?"

"I have never been one to follow instructions, my dear Miss Hasting, and from the looks of it, neither have you, for your gloriously expressive eyes are telling me you feel the same." The viscount put his free hand to the small of her back, pulled her closer still, then eased his hand downward to rest at the curve of her arse in a move that was quite possessive and sent thrilling frissons twisting up her spine. "Right now, I want you over everything else. It's a madness, really."

"In this moment, I quite agree." Before Mia could say anything further, he claimed her lips in a searing kiss that made every portion of her body feel more alive than she'd ever been. Those fires in her blood he'd ignited became molten rivers of need, and she gasped at the intensity of desire sparking between them. So much so that she looped her arms about his shoulders and fairly clung to him without a shred of decency or decorum as she returned that embrace with the hope of more to come.

There was no going back. For better or for worse.

"What the devil have you done to me, for my mind is not my own; you are a siren," he whispered while taking her more comfortably in his arms and teasing her—torturing her—with intense kisses that hinted at exactly what he wished to do next.

"Only because I don't allow you to manipulate me." Except here she was, fairly offering herself to him in this moment.

"You are like no one I've ever met, and I'm half crazed to possess you."

Because no other man wanted her or because he knew he couldn't have her? "We cannot both be driven insane, so either continue this interlude or let us deny ourselves the pleasure, for this isn't proper." Her commonsense fled along with propriety, for she dragged her lips beneath the sharp line of his jaw, licked a path down the strong column of his throat merely to imprint his taste and scent upon herself as a consolation for when he came to his senses and set his sights elsewhere for entertainment. "None of that negates this inexplicable hold you have on me, this terrible want I have for you."

Sadly, that was all there was between them, for nothing could come from this, neither should it. She was no one but *he* had the potential to be someone. Why couldn't he see that?

A groan issued from him as he drew his palms up her sides to cup her breasts. "Then by all means, let me indulge you." Nicholas held her breasts, squeezed them, teased her nipples through the fabric of her gown until she whimpered with anticipation. "Rather desperate, aren't you?" he whispered when she arched her back.

"Yes. God help me, yes," she said on the heels of a gasp while he yanked the bodice of her gown down to bare her breasts. "I fear you will be my destruction, as a devil would be." In this moment, she didn't care, for at least then she would have made a decision that benefited her over her family. When the viscount stimulated her nipples, intense sensations streaked from her breasts to her core. "Touch me. Please." If that made her a wanton, then so be it.

"I adore that begging," he murmured and gave her nipples a quick pinch. When a sound that was a mix of a gasp and a moan escaped her, he chuckled. "I would love to hear you do much more of that for many other things we have no time for tonight."

Already, they were tempting fate being scandalous here where anyone could come upon them, and if they were found out, disaster would follow, for she rather doubted Nicholas was one for being forced into marriage to a nobody like her who hadn't the coin to make a difference. Yet in an odd sort of way, there was a certain freedom she found in him, and it made her drunk with the choice.

"This is the last time, but I cannot forget about you until I know what it feels like to be thoroughly claimed by a man who is so carried away by desire for me he throws caution to the wind in that one moment."

"Surely this is insanity, but then, I have lived my life for much less."

Mia's head lolled onto his shoulder. "I refuse to stroke your ego any more than I already have." A shiver racked her being while he continued to manipulate those aching buds.

"Which is but one reason you're so maddening to me. However, you have my permission to stroke something else instead," he whispered into her ear and followed the quip with a light nip to her lobe. Once he'd urged her arms above her head, he caught her wrists in one hand and cupped a breast with the other. "Would there was time to see you naked." He nibbled a path along the column of her throat, licked and nipped her breasts, teased her with his hot breath on her skin. "There is so much I wish to do to do merely to see your reaction, hear the sounds you'll make as I send you to the brink."

"Oh…" She expelled a soft moan when he teased her nipple with his tongue and teeth. This was so much different than how he'd pleasured her in the carriage, so much more intense. "I need you inside me."

"Not just yet, I think, unless you can convince me." With a wink, he released her wrists and then spread his arms wide. "Explore at your will. I know you want to."

Damn his eyes, but he was too smug. "Don't be an arse any more than you can help." Now was her chance to tease him. Perhaps she'd leave him wanting as he'd done her, except she craved him far too much. This would be the last time they were given an opportunity to be alone like this. "Forgive my ineptitude, but I have always dreamed of doing this, thought I might have a knack if given a chance…" Mia dropped to her knees before him. Quickly, she divested herself of her gloves, let them fall to the floor. Only then did she reach for the buttons of his trousers. Before he could protest, she'd opened his frontfalls and then eased his rampant shaft from the fabric. "Oh…" He was magnificent. "Much bigger than my fiancé." The pale length of him that bobbed so near to her head stole away her breath, and as she tentatively wrapped her fingers around that appendage, the hard heat of him had a wave of intense awareness washing over her. "Simply wonderful."

"Amelia." A warning growl propelled her name from his throat. The breath hissed from him the first moment she touched her tongue to his cockhead. "You needn't do this if…" The remainder of his statement was lost in a groan.

"Hush, my lord. Let me explore, bring you pleasure, but we must be quick." Perhaps this would be another opportunity that would never come her way again, so she smiled up at him and then applied herself to her task even though her stomach clenched with nerves. For the situation as well as the act. Since meeting this man, everything she did was new and fresh and thrilling. Shoving away the doubts crowding into her head, she teased the skin just beneath the tip of his gloriously hard shaft, and when she was done, she licked the silky skin. How interesting and scandalous. Emboldened by his half-stifled sounds of encouragement, she took as much of his length into her mouth as she could.

"Oh, God." Nicholas held her head in his hands, and the longer she bobbed on his rigid member, the more he matched her movements. He thrust into her mouth, his eyes closed, and his head thrown back, his breathing ragged.

It was a crime for any man to look so beautiful during such a wicked act, but Mia hummed her approval. Once she found a rhythm and understood how to both suck at his length while moving upon it, it was oddly entertaining. She fondled his stones as she worked and wished she had more time to explore. Again and again, she continued to push herself, discover what he enjoyed, simply by employing her tongue or fingers in different ways, and all the while she imagined that hardened member moving inside her body.

It was far too heady and nearly saw her undone right there in the shadows.

"Enough." Desperation propelled the word from his throat. Nicholas pulled away only to wrench her upward to her feet. "Damn it, Amelia, your teasing has brought me too close to the edge. I have entered insanity."

"Then I did it correctly." And she rejoiced in that knowledge, for she hadn't been certain. "Show me you're primed, that in this moment, I am all you want," she demanded, her whispered voice low and smoky with desire. Then she would return to her dull life as a companion, ignored by the aristocracy, overlooked by respectable men, and resented by wallflowers and companions.

He didn't answer with words. With an intensity that stole her ability to speak, the viscount pinned her between the hard wall of his chest and the wall at her back. The kisses he treated her to were deep and drugging; he dueled with her tongue as they both fought to not be forgotten, but eventually he won, and she gave herself over to his mastery.

When he encouraged one of her legs up, shoving skirting out of his way as he went, she hooked it over his hip and wrapped her arms about his strong, broad shoulders. In this moment, in his arms, she had everything she'd ever wanted: security, contentment, desire. His eyes were dark with need, nearly as black as the devil's, and his hands were at her buttocks holding her against the wall as he set out to apparently devour her whole. Mia forgot everything as she wriggled into a better position, clung to him while she kissed him back. She shuddered as he fit his tip to her opening. Her moan of satisfaction sounded overly loud to her ears, but he swallowed the remainder of the noise and at the same time, he flexed his hips, penetrated her swift and deep, without stopping until he'd penetrated her to the hilt.

"Merciful heavens." Awe threaded through her utterance, for this was so much more than she'd had from her one and only time of coupling with her fiancé. The viscount was so large, so thick, and he filled her so completely she wanted to cry from the perfection of that joining, but instead, she dug her nails into his shoulders as her eyes shuttered closed. The most delicious sensations bounced through her insides, and she shivered with anticipation.

Then he moved, thrusting with short strokes, forcefully spearing into her which set her blood on fire and each nerve ending tingling.

As best as she could, Mia attempted to match his rhythm, but the position was awkward, and her inexperience hindered her efforts. It didn't seem to affect him, for Nicholas continued to move, so she clung to his shoulders and pulled him closer with her leg around his waist.

Over and over, he drove like a man possessed. She held him to her, kissed whatever portion of his body she encountered. The scrape of her nipples against his evening attire added another layer of acute cognizance to their actions, as did the friction put on the button at the center of her pleasure, for her body was opened to him and nothing was uncovered. His ragged breathing echoed in her ears. His fingers dug into her hips with a savageness that would no doubt leave bruises. Sweat dampened his forehead, his upper lip, and as she kissed him, the taste of salt came away on her tongue.

She couldn't have enough of him, and in that moment, she gave herself over to the devil himself without a second thought.

When he delved a hand between their bodies through layers of skirting and he strummed his fingers over that swollen bud, she sucked in a breath. Before the scream could leave her throat, he kissed her again, took the sound into himself to prevent premature discovery. Quite simply, they shared a few breaths as their bodies worked to become one. All too soon, the pressure building and circling in her lower belly broke, for the sensory overload had finally overwhelmed her. Dear lord, it was all too easy to fly when she was with Nicholas, and equally easy to lose all sense of who she was in him as well.

"Mmm... ah!" Contractions fluttered through her core as pleasure swamped her in ever-increasing waves. Mia dug her fingers into his shoulders. She whispered his name as if in prayer, buried her face in the crook of his shoulder, and still the bands of release kept coming. There was no relenting, no cessation, and she feared her body would break apart.

Another two thrusts sent him into the vortex with her. The viscount claimed her mouth in a hard kiss that completely swept her off her feet and separated her from reality. As he ground his pelvis into hers, he lifted her up, and she locked her legs around his waist as the warmth, the aftermath of his own release filled her core. Completely spent, she collapsed against him, and he did the same to her until they were more or less draped against the wall, panting in the shadows with the muffled sound of the orchestra playing behind them.

Eventually, her heartbeat returned to normal, and her breathing evened out. When Mia came back to her senses, the horror of what she'd just done—allowed to happen—seeped into her. This was highly improper and could result in a pregnancy that would completely shred the remainder of her family's reputation. With a gasp, she pushed at his chest until he released her. When her feet hit the floor, she continued to shove at him until there was a fair amount of space between them.

"You must go," Mia implored in a barely audible voice as she smoothed her skirting back into place. "We cannot be seen together." She tugged up her bodice next and hoped to goodness no one would notice if she appeared slightly disheveled.

"Calm yourself, Amelia." His voice was just as low as he dropped his hands on her shoulders and peered into her eyes. "We are safe. Neither were we heard. No one suspects."

"That is the least of my worries." With the shake of her head, Mia slipped from his hold, put a hand up as if to ward him off. "I went against my own rules tonight, Nicholas, because *I* wanted that coupling, but I won't dissolve beneath your teasing again." To her horror, tears sprang to her eyes. "I will not be your next conquest, your next mistress for you to lose interest in when someone else better comes along, and I certainly refuse to be your solace once you take a wife with more money than brains, for even that woman deserves all of you."

"Now is not the time to discuss any of that." When he held out a hand, she shook her head so violently that a lock of hair escaped its pin.

"No." She took a step toward the curtain. "You only pursued me because I was different, I fought against falling into your web like all the rest, but in the end, I fell anyway, and in some ways that is good thing because now that you have what you wanted all along, you can continue with your life as can I." Even then, there wouldn't be peace, for if he courted Millie, then she would always have him underfoot, yet if he decided to chase after a different heiress, then she wouldn't see him again.

Both were terrible choices, and already she feared her heart had been singed.

"Amelia…" Confusion lined his face, but in the shadows, it was too difficult to read the emotions in his eyes. "This conversation isn't finished." His whisper was graveled and strained with the things he refused to utter.

"It is, and I think you already know that." Only half stifling a sob, Mia slipped behind the heavy curtain and back into the opera box. She hoped he would choose an heiress quickly, for she truly needed to look at securing her next position…

…or run back home where she could suffer a breakdown in the privacy of the same room she'd first dreamed of finding a man to fall in love with.

Oddly enough, the reality wasn't at all what the fantasy suggested.

CHAPTER TWELVE

February 10, 1817

"WHERE THE DEVIL are they?"

To say Nick wasn't best pleased was an understatement. He'd sent a note 'round to the Featheringham residence earlier this morning asking that the chit and her companion meet him at Hyde Park this afternoon for a stroll through the acreage since the day was overcast but without rain.

Since there hadn't been a decline of his invitation sent to his townhouse—and he'd half thought there might be one out of spite from Miss Hasting—he'd gone ahead to the meeting point at the main arch, but here he was, milling about on foot by himself while his breath clouded about his head, and he hunched further into his greatcoat.

Why had he gone to the opera last night? Beyond that, why had he lost his mind the second he'd seen Amelia? There was no explanation that would make sense, but ever since she'd snubbed him at the rout in favor of talking with Marcus, he'd let jealousy roil within his chest. Which was stupid because he had no connection to the companion except for the teasing and innuendo and verbal sparring they'd shared over the course of a week.

When she'd told him he had to make a decision about courting the chit or a different heiress, he'd wanted to retch. For the first time in his adult life, he'd found himself fascinated by a woman in a way that went beyond the bedroom. And also for the first time, that same woman left his gut in knots, his mind in confusion, and his prick in a near constant state of arousal.

He'd assumed all of that would have faded after the events in the carriage, definitely after the quick, intense coupling at the opera last night, but what he'd expected never materialized. If anything, he was even more invested in Miss Hasting, wished to know more about her than what she'd told him, and that worried the hell out of him because that just wasn't what he did with women while they were in his company.

To say nothing of the fact she was as skittish in his company as a newborn colt.

Why?

"Lord Wycliffe."

The sound of *her* voice had him spinning around so quickly the tails of his greatcoat flared slightly. "Miss Hasting." A subtle glance of the surrounding area didn't show her young charge. "Where is, uh, Miss Featheringham?"

Doubt reflected in her eyes, and the overcast skies made them all the bluer. "She said she's suffering from a megrim, and since the hour grew too late to send a courier to your townhouse, I decided to come out here and tell you in person." From the scowl that marred her expression, she didn't appear too thrilled with that prospect.

"I see. Has she often suffered these headaches?"

"Only a couple of times since I've known her."

"Ah." Knots of worry pulled in his gut. He had his suspicions regarding Miss Featheringham, for they were the same he harbored about Percy, but he didn't know if he should bring up those concerns with Amelia. She might blame her distracted state on him—Nick—and think she'd been lax on guiding her charge toward men she should be meeting. Knowing the companion, she would absolutely refuse to let him come 'round any longer.

Worse yet, she might quit her position, find another, or leave London altogether. Then he would have no more excuses to see her. "So she locked herself in her bedchamber, then?"

"Millie's maid assured me she was resting in her bed with a cool cloth on her brow." When she briefly held her full bottom lip between her teeth, he swallowed a groan. "I didn't check on her myself before I left but I did talk with the girl through the door."

"Mmm." Knowing how the girl had already sneaked out of the house to meet Percy, he had grave doubts she had told the truth. "I'm not certain I believe she is ill." It was too damned bad he didn't have the young Mr. Marsden with him. Would that have affected Millie's mood?

"Neither do I, but I'm reserving judgment. I'm sorry you have been thwarted in trying to woo the girl and that she's proving stubborn."

"Miss Featheringham isn't the only who possesses that trait." He lifted an eyebrow in challenge.

A slight blush stained her cheeks. "Yes, well, we can only be who we were destined to be."

"Except I think most of us deny that destiny." Why was she fighting the attraction between them? Though he understood her reticence at being a mistress or a conquest—not that he could afford to keep any woman under his protection in the coming months—wasn't she at all curious to see what could happen?

For that matter, was he? Everyone in London knew he must marry an heiress or at the very least, a woman who was connected to deep pockets, yet here he was befuddled and confounded by a companion well past the first and second blushes of youth.

Why?

She glanced between him and her carriage that waited at the curb. "Well, now that I've told you, I should go."

"Amelia, wait." He despised the forced propriety that had sprung up, hated that they'd lost the easy verbal sparring they'd always had. "Please stay. Walk with me through the park. Who knows when we might have long stretches of rain or even snow that confine us indoors." For the space of a few heartbeats, he remained silent while resting his gaze on her. "You and I should talk in any event."

"I said everything I needed to last night." That hint of frost in her voice had the power to stab through his chest like tiny knives. "There is nothing else to discuss."

"Can we not be friends, then, after everything?" If he couldn't have her for a lover, he hoped he could enjoy at least that with her, for it would tear him apart to watch her walk out of his life forever.

Her chin wavered, and that slight tell of vulnerability nearly had him on his knees, begging for forgiveness, promising her anything if it would keep her close. "I don't know if we could be just that to each other, Nicholas," she said in a low voice with pain reflected in her eyes.

Did that mean she wanted him still? "I promise to keep my hands to myself." So saying, he tucked those appendages behind him, clasping them at the small of his back. "Will you stroll with me? I can be a gentleman if the occasion warrants."

Remarkably, Amelia snorted. "I haven't seen evidence of that yet." Then she gasped and her eyes widened. "Except that afternoon in the carriage when you…" She pressed the gloved fingertips of one hand to her lips. "You *were* being a gentleman as you'd claimed. Your conscience got the better of you that day." Her expression softened. "Yet you never said anything until the other night when I was aggravated, and I missed it."

Heat raced up the back of his neck. "Guilty."

"I knew you weren't the rake you want everyone to see." Without a word, she spoke to her driver. "You may take the carriage back to the Featheringham house. I'm going to walk with Lord Wycliffe for a bit and he will convey me home."

"Of course, Miss Hasting."

Nicholas held his breath during that exchange, but when she turned back to him, and with the concern and annoyance vanished from her expression, she was easily the most beautiful woman he'd seen in an age. "Thank you."

"Don't make me regret this decision."

"I won't." *Please God let her see someone in me who is a much better man than I truly am.* He offered her his crooked arm. "Taking in the air is good for us regardless." Never had he been as pleased and redeemed as he was when she slipped her hand into his elbow.

For a time, they walked in silence, and for the first time in his life, Nicholas felt… content, almost at peace, and he reveled in it. For reasons he refused to analyze just now, Amelia brought out a calm in him, and he drank it up as much as he did the way his desire for her carried him away from all reason.

"You seem quite relaxed." The dulcet sound of her voice broke the pleasant quiet as they strolled. "It is rather disconcerting after what I've come to know about you."

"I'll admit, it has been some time since I considered my world balanced. Probably not since a young man while visiting Moss Cottage in Ireland to see my grandmother when she'd been alive." Just for her, he brought out a bit of his brogue. "God, but I miss that land. Acres of lush fields and rolling hills dotted with sheep. Lakes so glassy they reflect the bluest of all blue skies. Fresh crisp air a man can fill his lungs with and find himself at the feet of God, with nights so velvety dark every star is visible it's as if the heavens crept close merely to show off their glory."

"That sounds lovely, and there is genuine fondness in your voice for that place." She turned her head and peered at him past the shallow brim of her bonnet. "If you cannot find such ease and contentment here in London, perhaps you should visit that cottage and discover a new perspective your life is lacking."

"Why?" When his muscles tensed, she squeezed his arm in a subtle reminder to relax.

"Are your coffers as empty as you let on?"

"Not quite but they will be soon if I don't turn the country estate around. Otherwise, I might need to seek out a paying position."

"There is no shame in it."

"There is for a titled gentleman to sully his hands." God, but his father would be so disappointed in him.

"Times are changing, Nicholas. As the thought of reform sweeps across more portions of the country, the huge divide between rich and poor will shrink. Whether a man is titled or not will hold less importance than if he is proud of himself at the end of the day."

He stared at her in awe. "You follow politics?"

"I am interested in everything and anything that exercises the mind or affects change." Amelia shrugged. "If something interests you, go out and chase it, regardless of how others will see you." She blew out a breath in an effort to remove a few escaped hairs from her face. "You already adore farming and advanced practices therein, and I'll wager you've been ridiculed for the same."

"I have."

"Then taking a paying position for a time until your estate begins working for you again is a sound business investment, only you'd be putting that time into yourself." Gently but firmly, she steered him around a large boulder and then back on the path that would lead to his waiting carriage. "Give it some thought."

"I will." As they strolled along the Serpentine, he couldn't help a grin. "Regarding what happened last night—"

"There is no need for an apology or rakish words that will ruin what we shared." Her hand trembled on his arm. "It was an indiscretion I will remember until the day I die, and there will be fondness as well as excitement in that memory, but I will also use it as a cautionary tale when I look after my future charges."

Did that mean she regretted joining with him? He stole a glance at her, and when he caught amusement dancing in her eyes, he allowed a small grin. "As how to bring a rake to heel?"

"No." The corners of her mouth twitched. "In how to remain firm in their resolve and not let themselves be swept away by charm, good looks, and a man who smells delicious but is quite wickedly determined to ruin a lady's reputation."

He gawked, for there was much to digest in that statement. "It wasn't my intention to see you ruined." But he supposed that was exactly what had happened, for she'd probably told no one of her coupling with that long-ago fiancé.

"No, I don't suppose it was. You were as carried away in the moment—or rather moments—as I was, but for different reasons." For long moments, she was silent, apparently content enough to walk beside him. "If I were a scheming woman or a social climber, I would demand you marry me, but I am neither of those things. I believe when a couple weds, both parties should be happy and in love, or at least have the hope they will find those things together at some point in the future."

The words were like a blow to his gut. "You assume you and I wouldn't suit?" Not that he wanted to marry her or anyone.

"It doesn't matter, for you still need a fortune and I must get a living for my family. After you decide whether or not you wish to woo Millie, I rather doubt our paths will cross unless I'm chaperoning another young society miss."

"A clandestine relationship while you're in Town isn't something you would indulge in?" Perhaps then he could still see her regardless of his marital status.

Amelia snorted. "You know it is not. After all, I do have some respect for myself." Then she sighed. "As silly as it is for a woman of my advanced years, I do persist in having a few dreams for myself. Perhaps they will come true one day. Perhaps they won't, but at least they are mine."

"It is good to hold tight to dreams." Yet his chest tightened. He would go on to follow the path fate had handed him and she would do the same, for they had met by chance but were never meant to be together. "At some point, you will need to tell me about your family. I would enjoy knowing how you came to be the woman you are. Since we have formed a tentative friendship."

What if that is all I want from her? Yet in order to advance that relationship, he would need to be brutally honest with himself and what he wanted from life, and being alone with his thoughts terrified the hell out of him because he might find a few truths.

"My sisters are quite the handful." A genuine smile curved her kissable lips. "You might even like them, and I suspect you'd charm them all, including my mother."

"Ha!" Longing set up behind his breastbone, made it difficult to draw a deep breath. "There are times when I miss having family about. Perhaps I should write to my sister."

"You should. Family is vital to one's well-being… *if* they are good people, so when you are reordering your life to fill your coffers, don't discount that."

By then, they'd reached his carriage, but he wasn't in a mood to further the conversation. She had given him much to think about, which was a horrible endeavor, for thinking was a singularly bad idea.

And he'd forgotten all about discussing his concerns regarding Millie and Percy.

⟫⟫⟫✕⟪⟪⟪

ONCE THEY'D REACHED the Featheringham residence, his stomach was rumbling, so Amelia took pity upon him and invited him in for tea.

General conversation kept them occupied until the tea things were brought in, and as the footman set everything out on a low table in front of them, he mentioned in passing that Miss Featheringham still suffered from a megrim but that she'd taken a hearty tea on a tray in her room not half an hour past.

"Thank you for telling me. I'll check on her in a while." Clearly, Amelia didn't suspect any wrongdoing, but the whole arrangement stunk of a farce.

"I don't like this by half," Nick whispered as he accepted a cup of tea from her. A hearty tea for a girl who was sick with a headache? Hot annoyance filled his chest, for he was certain that somehow Percy had come over. "What side of the house is Millie's bedchamber?"

"Why, so you can sneak upstairs?" There was no malevolence in Amelia's tone, merely humor, and he was beginning to know she enjoyed needling him.

"No. I only wondered."

She shrugged. "At the rear. Her rooms overlook the back garden and the square beyond."

And quite easy for an enterprising—and randy—young man who wished desperately to see an equally lust-driven young lady who had no business trysting with said man. If Millie lost her innocence, it would completely destroy everything *he* was building with Amelia, and suddenly, he didn't want that damaged, for it was more precious than wishing to tumble her into bed again. Well, he wouldn't be routed by a stupid chit who had her head turned by a young man with nothing to his name.

This ends now. And he'd wager the rest of his coin that Percy was even now enjoying himself in Millie's room.

After taking a gulp of tea and then coughing from the heat of it in his throat, he set the cup into its saucer on the table with rather more force than necessary. "If you will excuse me for a moment? I need to attend to a personal… matter."

With a bemused expression, Amelia nodded.

Seconds later, he dashed upstairs, taking the treads two at a time. It wasn't a difficult endeavor to discern which bedchamber belonged to the girl, for she and her would-be lover weren't exactly quiet, which meant they would learn from their mistakes. After a preemptory knock, he swung the door inward with such force it crashed against the wall. Both Millie and Percy were twined together upon her bed, kissing as if they had nothing better to do while hands roved everywhere and Millie's bodice was half askew. They sprang away from each other when the door crashed, and she gasped in outrage.

"This is my private room!"

"Ah, it's good to know you aren't suffering from a megrim. Just a lack of common sense." His gaze fell on Percy, then he strode forward, grabbed the boy by the back of his cravat, and then dragged him off the bed. "Come with me. The both of you should be ashamed of yourselves, and you're damned fortunate the young lady's father isn't in residence right now!"

"How dare you, Lord Wycliffe!" Millie sprang from the bed, her dark hair tumbling down her back as she quickly stuffed her overflowing bosom back into her loosened bodice. "You have no right to tell me what I can or cannot do, especially when you have the same designs on Miss Hasting."

He refused to acknowledge the barb. "I can when your virtue is endangered." Never did he think those words would come out of his mouth. Was this what maturity felt like, this constant state of outrage and caring about others, worrying over their fate? "I'll tell you something else, Miss Featheringham. You should save yourself for the man you'll marry. Intercourse, while lovely in the moment, will mean more when there are emotions involved." What the hell was happening to him? And why the devil did he suddenly sound like an outraged parent? "There might be consequences of doing... this." He wildly gestured between the two young people.

"We can do what we want. Nothing will happen, and besides, we are in love, and you are trespassing here."

Was the young lady that stupid? Love was fine in its place, but it wouldn't pay the bills, and it didn't guarantee Percy would marry her. "Do not let your companion know you're courting scandal and disaster, for that isn't fair to her. If you allow this," he shook Percy as if he were naught but a sack of laundry, "boy to tup you next time and your father comes in instead of me? He'll demand you marry, and this boy has nothing to recommend him. Or worse, he'll toss you out because he wants a title for you."

"That doesn't matter!" Millie stomped her bare foot.

"We're in love, Lord Wycliffe. The future will work itself out." Percy's aside went largely unheeded.

Nicholas groaned. *Spare me the theatrics of the young.* "I refuse to hear your excuses, Miss Featheringham. They only make you seem petty and immature. Certainly not ready for the life you're courting." He glared at both of them in turn. "Put yourself to rights and go apologize to Miss Hasting. She's sacrificed much for you, yet you thank her by betraying her trust."

She pouted and crossed her arms beneath her breasts. "As if you aren't betraying her in your own way."

"Meaning?" Oh, he couldn't wait to hear her reasoning.

"Flirting with her, getting in her good graces, making her care for you, when you have no intentions of being with her in a forever sort of way, have no intentions of marrying her after you coerce her into *your* bed." The girl paused for effect while he gawked and ignored the second round of shock exploding through his chest. "If you still think to marry me for my father's money?" She laughed at him as if he were naught but a bounder, looked him up and down and found him lacking as only a young woman could. "I would rather *die* than let you touch me in *that* way. You're so old!"

Heaven spare me from all women!

"Enough!" Not wishing to discuss the matter further with her, Nicholas marched Percy out of the room. He didn't much care what Miss Featheringham did as long as she didn't put Amelia's position or reputation into jeopardy.

He didn't pause until he pulled Percy into the captain's study, which sadly was only a couple of rooms down from the drawing room where Amelia waited. There was nothing for it, though. After slamming the door, he released the young man and gave him a bit of a shove.

"How dare you betray everyone's trust by trying to bed Miss Featheringham! Do you wish to destroy her life and yours?" When had he become the responsible one?

Percy's face turned red. "You have no say in this, Lord Wycliffe. It is our decision."

"I'm quite certain your parents don't wish you to involve

yourself with a woman not of the *ton*." There were other choice words he said to the young man in an attempt to frighten him, but Percy remained firm in his decisions.

"I love her, my lord. Have never felt this way before, and if I wish to marry her, I don't need anyone's permission." For the first time, Percy met his gaze without flinching. "If the match is opposed, we'll go to Gretna."

Bloody hell. The boy was a lost cause if he was that determined to attach himself permanently to such a spoiled young lady. "At least talk it over with your parents, but if you bed the girl before that happens, be aware there *will* be consequences, and you'd better be able to square with them. Ask yourself if you can support a wife and a child with no income and no plans, for I rather doubt your uncle or your grandfather will help you out of that coil."

"You only say that because you are afraid of marriage for yourself, afraid to dare to love."

That statement hit far too close to the truth to be comfortable. With a sound akin to a growl, Nicholas grabbed the young man's upper arm. He slammed out of the room with Percy in tow, ushered him through the corridors, rather roughly tossed him from the house and told him to go home. By the time he returned to the drawing room, he was out of breath, out of patience, and quite ruffled, but seeing Amelia sitting calmly on the gold brocade sofa sipping tea and reading a book made his heartbeat accelerate.

Life wouldn't perhaps be so bad if he could come home to that image after a trying day.

She glanced up when he came in. "Is all well? I heard arguing but couldn't discern the source."

"It was nothing." He tugged on the knot of his cravat. "I hope your charge is better soon."

"I'll check on her soon." Setting down her book, Amelia smiled at him. "Thank you for a lovely afternoon. It's not often I can take an afternoon off and actually enjoy myself as I did today.

I rather like you more when you're not relentlessly chasing me."

Well, damn.

The earnestness in her words and expression had the power to bring him to his knees. Before he could reply, Millie entered the drawing room looking far too tousled, but more or less respectable.

"Millie? Are you feeling better?" Surprise wove through Amelia's tones as she frowned at the girl. "You should be abed."

At least the girl had the grace to blush. "Oh, I..." A quick glance at him made her clear her throat. "I didn't really have a headache; I just wanted time alone. However, I should like to share tea with you." Maneuvering around him with a sniff, Millie then settled herself on the sofa next to Amelia and completely ignored him. "I'm also grateful for all you've done for me and appreciate your efforts on my behalf as we try to find an appropriate husband for me."

"Oh!" The shock and happiness on Amelia's face tugged at his heart, and he didn't know what to do about that. This day was full of new experiences. "Uh, you ladies should spend this time together. I'll show myself out, but thank you for spending the afternoon with me. Perhaps we can go on an outing tomorrow."

⊱⊱⊱⊰⊰⊰

LATER THAT EVENING, when Marcus joined him at the club, he wasn't best pleased with his friend, and proceeded to give him a dressing down regarding his nephew's behavior.

"He means to take her to Gretna Green if the parents oppose the match, and I fear if something isn't done soon, disaster will befall all of us." He followed the speech with a large gulp of brandy that burned painfully as it went slowly down his throat.

An expression of unmitigated glee went over Marcus' face as he stared. "You were the one who wanted to give the chit a distraction so you could focus on bedding the companion."

He huffed. "Oh, she's distracted, all right, and if we're not careful, those two will be copulating like rabbits!"

"Why do you care?" His friend hooted with laughter. "Isn't this how you live *your* life? Didn't you teach Percy all too well that is how to behave like a rake?"

Heat poured up his neck into his cheeks. "I suspect I have been... wrong."

"What?" Incredulity propelled the word from Marcus' throat. "Do you regret how you've lived your life to date?"

"I don't know, but I am confused. Everything is changing." Nicholas rubbed his free hand over his face. "I suddenly feel responsible. For everyone. Miss Hasting will lose her position if Millie is ruined or left with a babe in her belly."

"Ah, before you can do the same to her?"

"Bah." The back of his neck heated. "I'd still marry the chit for her money. After I have an heir, she can do whatever the hell she wants."

Except, did he even want *that* any longer? Spending so much time in Amelia's company had caused his brain to rot. Especially after their two scandalous sessions together and being with her this afternoon without trying to charm her.

He pulled a face. "Yet the thought of getting the girl with child nearly turns my stomach. She's beyond spoiled and wastes no time in reminding me how old I am."

"Oh, this is too rich!" Marcus uttered a string of laughter that made more than a few men turn their heads and glare in their direction. "Wait until the men at White's hear this story. Wagers will fly and reverse. Much coin will exchange hands. People will be rich while others turn pauper." He followed the statement by draining his brandy glass.

"Why the devil for?" Suddenly, Nicholas was out of patience with the whole of the human race. He had no use for any of them.

"You don't know?"

"It's been a rather confusing and trying day. Enlighten me." There was no point in keeping the sarcasm from his voice.

The grin on his friend's face was wide. "Well, my friend, you're about to toss your hat over the windmill and go tip over tail for the companion!" Again, he hooted with laughter and this time had to pause to wipe away the tears. "The woman with no dowry and no fortune, and a family about to be evicted for not paying taxes on their country property. Who would have thought *that* would happen? You're caught up in your own game?"

Who indeed? Certainly not I. Damn it all to hell.

"Do shut up, Marcus." What was happening to his life? He didn't like it by half.

CHAPTER THIRTEEN

February 11, 1817
Featheringham House
Mayfair
London, England

Mia couldn't concentrate on the book in her hand. It was a rainy afternoon, which meant no outing was in store, or at least not one which required the out of doors.

Though Nicholas had told her yesterday that he would call today on Millie, she had yet to see him or Mr. Marsden. Not that she minded, of course, because both of the men weren't good for her charge, but she detested the silly little flutters that had gone through her belly when she'd anticipated the viscount's arrival.

Since tea would be served soon, she'd settled in the drawing room thinking Millie would come down and Lord Wycliffe would eventually arrive. Neither of which had occurred, so she attempted to busy herself with reading, except her mind refused to concentrate on the print.

Why? Why the devil couldn't she read past one or two paragraphs before the words blurred and her mind was once more hung up on Nicholas?

Mia blew out a breath. Oh, she knew, and the reason terrified her, for she was falling in love with the absolute worst man for her. The dratted man had spent copious amounts of time worming his way beneath her skin, infecting her blood, and now she craved his touch entirely too much.

Nothing about him had indicated he was doing anything except flirting and teasing her. He would never marry her, and she had no dowry besides. She wasn't an heiress and neither did she enjoy a high position in society. And if the taxes on the family ancestral home weren't paid soon, she would be properly homeless. So why was he still bedeviling her? More to the point, why was she letting him?

With a soft cry of annoyance, Mia tossed her book aside. It bounced on the cushion next to her then flipped to the floor with a dull thud. As if she had no brains, she'd let his attention turn her head. She'd enjoyed his notice far too much, and been over-whelmed to the point of drowning at his physical teasing and coupling. None of that equated to love or even respect, yet here she was, practically pining over the man's absence like a lovesick puppy.

What is wrong with me?

Anyone could see he was naught but a rogue, a rake, a scoundrel who played with women's affections until he had what he wanted from them, until he bedded them, and then he unapologetically moved on to the next as if he were a bee in a flower field.

And she had believed that of him until he'd accidentally admitted to her that he'd been acting as a gentleman the night in the carriage when he hadn't fully bedded her, when he hadn't taken his pleasuring to that final step. To say nothing of the books he'd admitted to reading, to the new ideals he had about farming, to the care he'd shown, the intense way he'd claimed her body while at the opera, and the small hints of vulnerability he'd shown when they'd walked through Hyde Park just yesterday. Oddly enough, if fate had handed her different cards, they could have been well matched in a puzzling sort of way, but as it was, they were on opposite sides of the same coin.

A bit of hysterical laughter climbed her throat. Wasn't that ironic, though? He needed coin and she had none. Did she believe he was the rake that all of London did? No, she did not. In fact, she believed he was hiding his true self for some reason unknown to her, but perhaps he might divulge that reason if she perhaps had more time.

Get hold of yourself, Mia. The viscount is not for you, no matter how much of an affinity you have for him.

It was ridiculous sitting here all by herself when she should be figuring out a gown to wear for the ball to which she and Millie had been invited. For that matter, how *had* Millie fared lately? Hot guilt cut through Mia's chest, for she hadn't done a great job of being a companion ever since Nicholas had slipped beneath her skin and stole away her ability to reason or think with any sort of common sense.

Might as well go upstairs and invite the girl down for tea. Ever since the miracle yesterday when Millie had apologized to her, her charge had been oddly clingy. Almost as if she wished to ask for advice or seek council but couldn't quite summon the courage.

As she rose from the sofa, she frowned. What did that mean? And why had Millie suddenly seen fit to try and be a friend to her? No one made such a change so suddenly unless... *Oh, dear lord.* Unless the person willfully wished to change because they'd either met with a life-changing bit of news or wanted to do so for someone else.

She hastened from the room. Knowing that Millie had quite the talent for dissembling as well as sneaking out of the house, she took her skirting in hand and ascended the staircase rather more quickly than she should have. *You had better be in your bedchamber, my girl, for I will not tolerate more of your deceptions.* As she neared Millie's door, the sounds of a scuffle met her ears, accompanied by angry voices.

Gooseflesh raced over her skin, for she recognized them both as Millie and the viscount. "Millie? Is all well?" A squeal from her charge was her only answer.

With her pulse pounding in her ears, Mia thrust open the door and then gasped, for she couldn't believe what she saw. Millie was layered against Nicholas. There was no space between their bodies, and they were locked in what appeared to be a heady embrace, the likes of which made her cheeks heat, for Millie seemed to be enjoying herself immensely. Or rather, Millie clung to him as if he would suddenly evaporate into the air while one of his hands clawed at her arm and the other pushed at her opposite shoulder.

Had the kiss not been consensual?

Though that was the reason for the viscount to come calling to begin with, how had he gained entrance to her bedroom if he hadn't come through the front door? Wouldn't the butler have informed her if he had? And why would Nicholas go directly upstairs?

"Nicholas! Millie!" Heated shock chased cold disappointment through her chest as they sprang apart. In a remote part of her mind, she'd entertained a tiny hope that it was her he'd truly come to see during those outings, her he preferred kissing, but apparently, she was wrong about that as well, for the bedclothes were rumpled as if someone had enjoyed energic activity upon them.

"It is not what it looks like," the viscount blurted out as he wiped his lips with the back of his hand while ruddy color filled his face.

Millie, oddly enough, appeared supremely satisfied as if she were the proverbial cat who stole the cream. "He is quite a good kisser, Miss Hasting." As she spoke, she scooted over to the window, which was open. Perhaps the two of them had been all too heated.

God strike me dead, but I know that too well.

"Once a rake, always a rake," Mia said in a dull voice. An ache had set up about her heart. It was so unexpected and acute that she gasped from it, then promptly berated herself, for she had no claim on the viscount. It was common knowledge he needed an heiress. Swallowing down her emotions, she lifted her chin. "This is highly improper, and you both should be thankful the captain isn't in residence just now. He'd have the two of you engaged and Lord Wycliffe signing marriage contracts in a thrice."

"As if I would ever marry this scheming, lying girl." For one second, it appeared as if Nicholas would spit the taste of her from his mouth, but then he remembered his manners, took his handkerchief out of an interior pocket, and proceeded to wipe his tongue with the fine lawn square.

Why? Hadn't he been intent on wooing, seducing, and then marrying the girl not a few days before?

"You know how it goes when a man sneaks into a young lady's room," Millie said with a grin that smacked of mischief. "He only has one thing on his mind." Quickly, she leaned over and drew the window panel closed. "I'm an innocent in this whole mess."

Nicholas, to his credit, snorted and scoffed. "Surely you don't believe her. She's lying in the hopes of covering her own scandalous tracks. In truth she—"

"Oh, Miss Hasting, please don't believe him!" A trace of fear sprang to Millie's eyes. She hurried across the room, narrowing her eyes on the viscount in the process, and then stood at Mia's side, clutching at her arm. "I didn't have time to protest before he'd coerced me into an embrace. The next thing I knew, we were carried away!"

"Liar!" He implored Mia with his eyes, and to his credit, there was earnestness there vying for dominance with fury. "It wasn't me who embraced her. In fact, I was actively trying to disengage her, but she clung like a demented squid!"

"Please, Miss Hasting," Millie pleaded with a puppy-dog expression that had no doubt gained her whatever she'd wanted over the course of her life. "He is quite persuasive. I stood no chance of breaking from that spell."

Fair point, and the longer they played at this poor Drury Lane production, the less his spell held power over *her*. "Miss Featheringham, go directly downstairs and wait in the drawing room for me." She pointed to the door. "Now."

With a contrite expression, the girl left the room, but she glanced back over her shoulder at the viscount with such victory in her eyes that Mia almost felt sorry for the man.

Almost.

Alone, she rounded on him, letting the full power of her ire surge through her veins. "How could you? Was it your intent to compromise her and thereby secure an engagement?" she hissed as she advanced upon him.

"Of course not." Nicholas stuffed his handkerchief into his jacket pocket. Fire fairly crackled in his dark eyes, and she *would not* think about how his jacket of sapphire superfine only enhanced the width of his chest and breadth of his shoulders. "If you must know, I came chasing Mr. Marsden."

She frowned. "Where is he, then?"

"Gone, of course."

"Of course." When Mia crossed her arms beneath her breasts, she narrowed her eyes on the viscount. "I hope you enjoyed pulling Millie down into your scandalous dark world. Only a nodcock wouldn't see she'd been thoroughly explored." And it was like a betrayal of sorts, which caused her heart to ache once more.

"Not by me. I'm telling you, Percy *was* here."

"Yet Millie said it was you who initiated the embrace."

"Haven't you suspected by now the chit is a proper liar?" Worry creased his brow while slight panic clouded his eyes. "She will do or say anything to wrap people around her little finger so she can have her way, and what she wants is Percy. Those two are determined to be together. I fear this is a battle you and I will both lose."

So then he would stick to his version of dissembling. "While that is perhaps true, you and I both know you are in need of wedding an heiress. Millie is the logical choice, and since you were trying to compromise her, here we are. No doubt the servants will talk. The captain will catch wind of the story sooner rather than later and we'll all be in trouble." Yet she couldn't discount her own hurt, even if it was pure folly on her part. "I had hoped you and I might have had a connection."

"We did… We do!"

"Beyond attraction."

"Of course we do." When he took a step toward her, Mia scuttled backward toward the door. "Amelia, please, you must believe that I'm telling the truth."

"I know what I saw, and I know what you've told me before." She shook her head as tears welled into her eyes and heat infused her cheeks. "Please go. Before the situation grows into something else entirely," she said in a low, quiet voice as anger built in her chest.

"Don't close me out." He joined her at the door, took her shoulders in a firm grip while peering intently into her eyes. "Millie is using me, using you, playing us off each other to get her way, to deflect what she's truly been doing—"

"Stop." Wrenching out of his hold, she faced him, helpless to the barrage of emotions battering her. "I found you in her private room. Alone with her. In an embrace. With her upset about the circumstances. How do you think it looks?" When he tried to protest, she acted without thinking. Her hand shot out so quickly, she was barely aware she'd slapped him for the third time in their short acquaintance. "How could you, Nicholas? You have managed to disrespect us both, and I don't appreciate it."

For the space of a few heartbeats, he stood staring at her with a hand to his red cheek. Finally, he nodded. "Then by all means, don't let me tarry here any longer. I have found my interest in both of you has waned, and combined, the two of you are more trouble than you're worth." He strode into the corridor beyond. "You needn't worry, for I won't darken your door any longer. I was a nodcock and a fool to think you might have been different, that there might have been *something* there..." Not finishing the statement, he shook his head. A muscle ticced in his cheek. "Good day, Miss Hasting. I hope you find fulfillment in your spinster's life, because I'm not sure I care any longer."

"Shocking to know you would give up so easily, Lord Wycliffe." Sarcasm fairly dripped from her voice. "But I suppose a rake such as yourself wouldn't dare go deeper in his life or try to pursue something or someone not in his usual style."

He paused, turned slightly back to her. "I'm not the one who refuses to listen to reason or an explanation as to what happened here today!"

"I know what I saw, and my position is in jeopardy the longer you linger. Don't you understand your actions have consequences beyond yourself?" She didn't have the luxury of privilege like he did. "You used me to get to her, and you'll do the same to her with someone else, as if we don't matter because you cannot stop being led about by your damned shaft!" Dear heavens, she shouldn't have said that aloud, but she feared it was all too true.

"Bah!" Nicholas threw up an arm as he resumed his path to the stairs. "Why the hell did I ever think I could take on such a stubborn, foolish, maddening woman?"

Then he was gone, and Mia sagged against the door as her tears spilled onto her cheeks.

CHAPTER FOURTEEN

February 12, 1817
Wycliffe House
Mayfair
London, England

*H*OW THE HELL *has one spoiled girl managed to ruin my life?*

It had been over twenty-four hours since that whole debacle from yesterday when Amelia had burst into her charge's room and found the seemingly damning evidence of a passionate embrace between him and Millie. But looks had been deceiving and the companion had jumped to wild conclusions. He hadn't put the young woman into his arms and neither had he kissed her. The stupid chit had done that all on her own to deflect Amelia's attention, for Percy had been in the process of climbing out the window.

The *only* reason Nicholas had been in Millie's room at all was quite simple—he was trying to protect her from making a damned mistake.

When his carriage had drawn up in front of the Featheringham house yesterday afternoon, he'd anticipated spending the rest of the day with Amelia, perhaps by indulging in conversation over tea, wishing to ask her opinion about how he might turn his fortunes around without needing to marry a chit with a sizable dowry. Except the moment the vehicle had come to a stop, he'd spied shadowy movement out of the corner of his eye.

Wondering why the devil anyone would slink about in the rain and fearing there might be a prowler with criminal intent on his mind, Nicholas had done some investigating of his own. As he'd rounded the corner of the house and went into the back garden, he'd been just in time to see Percy climbing up the side of the house, using the ivy that clung to the brickwork. Beyond that, there had been the unmistakable "rope" of two bedsheets tied together he used for assistance.

The damned man thought to sneak into Millie's bedchamber.

Infuriated beyond reason, Nicholas had sprung into action. The two young people would destroy their reputations as well as Amelia's in the process, and he would *not* allow that. As soon as Percy had climbed into the window, he followed the boy's path up the side of the dwelling. Hell, the muscles in his arms and legs still ached after the fact, reminding him he wasn't as young as he once was. Once Percy had scrambled into the chit's room, the lovers had made quick work of the clandestine meeting, for they'd already fallen to the bed and were kissing with an intensity that would end in disaster.

As quickly as he could, Nicholas pried the two of them apart, took Percy to task, but Millie urged him to climb back out the window because the voices raised in argument would surely bring her companion to the scene. No sooner had the dratted boy done exactly that than the door had flown open, and Amelia had come into the room. That was when Millie latched onto him—Nick—and kissed him as if she hadn't any sense in her head.

No doubt she'd wanted to distract Amelia from seeing Percy's exit, but then the girl had decided to throw him into the gutter by perpetuating the act that he'd embraced her, that he'd been the one who'd slipped into her room for the express purpose of bedding her, telling the lies to Amelia with wide eyes and a tearful expression.

And then one by one, his plans, his budding hopes had crashed to the floor and shattered, for Amelia had no choice but to believe her charge. His own reputation had ensured his destruction, and he couldn't blame her for the emotional reaction. The fact that she'd given him yet another dressing down was testament to the fact he'd gotten under her skin, but how far?

And how *did* he feel about her? Perhaps it was past time to be honest with himself as well as her, but fear sat heavily on his chest, preventing him from doing much more than sitting in a winged back chair in his drawing room, tossing back his second brandy of the afternoon.

Yes, deep down to his soul, he was naught but a coward. So instead of making strides to return to Amelia's good graces, he'd chosen to sulk today, put distance between them, give her space, or rather push her away. Perhaps then the feelings he nurtured for her that grew stronger with each passing day would die an early death. He didn't need a woman in his life, and he especially didn't need one with no coin.

Yet his heart was beginning to wage war with his head and his responsibilities. *What is happening to my damned life?*

When the brandy didn't dull his tortured thoughts like he'd hoped, Nicholas rubbed his eyes and glared into the flames dancing in the hearth behind an ornamental metal screen. Perhaps he should go to one of his clubs, indulge in taking a doxy to bed merely to hide his pain in chasing a release. However, as soon as she launched to his feet, the idea quickly fell out of his brain, for an empty liaison didn't have the same appeal that it used to. Truth be known, the only woman he wanted in his arms was Amelia. He needed her lips on his, *her* body arching from his touch, her heat closing around him, seeing that special smile she reserved only for him.

Surely Marcus wasn't correct when he'd said Nick was falling tip over tail for the companion.

I'm not that far gone, am I?

And if he was, did he want to marry her? That possibility

terrified him, for his parents had been wildly unhappy in their union, and since he'd followed in his father's footsteps by becoming a rake and a rogue, what if he was more like his sire than that? What if marriage wouldn't suit him and he'd come to resent or even hate a spouse after he'd wed?

Beyond that, he rather doubted he was worthy enough of a woman such as Amelia, not good enough for marriage, for his circumstances would only add to the hurdles they would need to overcome as a couple. They couldn't both be poor. It would only exacerbate everything he faced, everything he'd already failed at, make the future more difficult.

Wouldn't it? But what about love? Wasn't that worth chasing?

Dear God, all the changes in his life, coupled with his confusing thoughts, would soon tear him apart. He needed to get away from London, put distance between him and everything that was going topsy-turvy.

I can't breathe.

In a panic, Nicholas tore out of the room, fled up the stairs, and when he burst into his suite, his poor valet jumped and clutched a hand to his chest.

"Is all well, my lord? You look a bit wild about the eyes."

"My life is a mess, Barnes, so I need my things packed."

"Whyever for?" Confusion lay stamped over the valet's face as he held a waistcoat in his hand.

"We are removing to Moss Cottage in Ireland for a while. London has lost its luster." He shoved a hand through his hair. "I am no longer comfortable here."

"First of all, take a breath." Barnes guided him over to a chair in the bedchamber and gently pushed him into it. "Secondly, this reaction is out of character for you, even during the times when your mistresses have thrown things at you after you ended relationships." His eyes were kind as he held Nick's gaze. "What is this really about?"

"Why do you assume this is about anything? I merely miss

Ireland." At least that was partially the truth.

"Oh, I don't doubt that, and it's one of the things you have in common with your father. Ireland is in your blood. Your father was much happier and calmer when he could touch that particular earth every few years." The valet's gaze didn't waver. "However, this link to your past will not help soothe you in this particular problem, I'll wager, and unless I miss my guess, you have been turned upside down by a woman."

Emotion lodged in his throat. His eyes were hot and itchy with the need to cry. Not knowing how to release that torrent but fearing once he did, it wouldn't stop, Nicholas rested his forearms on his knees, let his hands dangle between his splayed legs, and bowed his head.

In a choked voice, he explained what had led him to this pass. "I don't know what to do."

"Why do you care what this Miss Hasting thinks of you?"

"Why?" Why was the sun bright or the sky filled with clouds or a fire hot? She was simply a part of the universe that made up his days. "Why do I care what Miss Hasting thinks of me? Because she is an anomaly, an aberration within the sad, shallow *ton*. She's a riddle I cannot solve, a problem I cannot puzzle out, a law unto herself, and she makes me want to be a better man for her, for me, for that is the only way I might win a woman such as Amelia."

Damnation. He hadn't meant to reveal that much about himself, but there was no going back now.

Surprise sprang into the valet's eyes. "You are in love with her." It wasn't a question.

"I... I'm not certain. I am merely at odds with so many changes in my life."

"Fleeing to Ireland won't help in that regard. The changes will continue because *you* wish to change, and all due to meeting Miss Hasting."

"Then I am a coward, Barnes. I wish to run away from everything I've ever known, but in the process, I'll run from everything that might be coming my way, even if those things are wonderful."

One of Barnes' eyebrows rose in challenge. "Change brings opportunity, my lord."

"Yet none of them bring coin with them." Slowly, he lifted his head and looked at the man who'd advised his father and now him. "I fear I'm not anything without funding, so how could I, in good conscience, even ask Miss Hasting to share a life with me knowing I am nothing, have spent the bulk of my life in pursuit of… nothing?" The emotions in his throat grew until it was difficult to swallow them down or ignore them. "If I had but known…"

"None of us can divine the future, my lord. We can only do our best. Hope for the best." He laid a hand on Nick's shoulder. "And if we're fortunate, we will stumble upon happiness in the process. That is worth fighting for, don't you think?"

He snorted. "I suspect I'll cock that up, just as my father did." With a half-feral cry, he launched from the chair as the valet scooted out of the way. "My sister and I are broken because of my parents."

"Only if you decide to follow their same paths. That choice has always been yours, my lord." Barnes trailed after him as Nick went into the adjoining dressing room. "As I have said before, you are not him. Nancy is not your mother. Once both of you decide to live life on your own terms, everything will change. Doors will open and new ways will illuminate."

"What if they don't?" Near crazed, Nicholas went to one of the armoires, wrenched open the doors, and then pulled out a couple of drawers. "What if I become a better person, continue to clean up my life, and then nothing happens? What if I lose her because of who I am or what I am not?" He retrieved an armful of folded cravats and a few shirts. "I have to leave."

"And then what? Drink yourself into oblivion? Throw yourself into the sea in the hopes you'll drown?" With the patience of a saint, Barnes joined him and gently removed the clothing from

Nick's hands. "Selfish actions, all, and you will leave behind people who care for you, people who will miss you."

"Does it matter?"

"Yes." Barnes dumped the clothing plus the waistcoat he'd held originally in one of the open drawers and then turned back to Nick. "It matters. You matter. Is Miss Hasting upset with you because of something you did?"

"Something she *thinks* I did, but I was only trying to do the right thing when it came to her charge and Mr. Marsden." He rubbed a hand along the side of his face, for he'd already told the valet how Percy was headed for scandal. "She thinks the worst of me, and due to my reputation, there is nothing I can do about it."

"Ah." A slow grin spread over Barnes' face. "Then she cares about you. Perhaps is in deep as much as you, but for whatever reason, she is hiding from those feelings just as you are." He guided Nicholas over to the window. "Look. There has been a break in the rain. It's a perfect time to make a call."

"No." He shook his head. "The woman has slapped me three times since we met. I'm not about to tangle with her temper again, especially since she's sided with that lying, spoiled brat of a charge. There is no point."

Barnes blew out a breath. "Her position demanded at least that, my lord, and knowing your habits, you hid behind fear to mask your confusion or your real feelings."

"I…" How the hell did the valet know him so well?"

"In any event, it will take a week of traveling to reach Moss Cottage. And there is no guarantee you would find solace or peace there while your mind, your heart, are so conflicted. If you feel you can go away without telling Miss Hasting goodbye, without trying to explain yourself, to make things right, then by all means, I'll begin packing your trunks. But if you think there is at least a shred of hope there?" He shrugged. "Fight for it, Nicholas. Fight where your father gave up on his relationship and thereby lost everything of value."

The valet's use of Nick's Christian name made him straighten his spine and truly pay attention. While it was true that he might expire if he didn't see Amelia while away in Ireland, he couldn't help but wonder if he wasn't a fool. "Do you believe there's a chance?"

"There is always a chance, my lord. Are you not curious to see where this one might lead? After all, you haven't had a woman in your bed since you met Miss Hasting. That alone speaks volumes."

"I don't wish to leave while there is anger between us." He had no idea what his life was becoming or where he was going, but he couldn't live with himself knowing she thought him a bounder, who used her merely to go after the chit anyway. "I want to make things right."

"Then, let's get you cleaned up and properly outfitted for such a call, hmm?" Again, one of the valet's eyebrows rose in question. "A well-turned-out lord will always have a greater chance over a man who looks as if he hasn't slept in a few days."

Nicholas took a deep breath, then let it ease out. "Thank you, Barnes. It's appreciated."

"Of course, my lord." He grinned as he swiftly crossed the room to the bell pull. "Perhaps if all goes well, you can spend your honeymoon in Ireland."

"Don't rush my fences, man." But Nick couldn't contain a grin of his own. For the first time in a long while, that tiny little kernel of hope began to bloom in his chest.

Featheringham House
Mayfair
London, England

THE PINK TISSUE paper surrounding the floral bouquet he'd picked up on his way to call on Amelia grated across his nerves, but he'd selected a collection of blooms that he thought she might adore the most: pink and white roses, a few lilies in the same color scheme, with ivy and other greenery mixed within to give the flowers a bit of interest.

Would she even see him? Listen to him? Was now the right time to share what was only beginning to be written upon his once isolated heart?

By the time the tall, thin scare of a butler admitted Nicholas into the house, cold foreboding twisted down his spine, for there was something at play within the air that spoke of things gone horribly wrong.

"What has occurred here today?" he asked of the older man while glancing toward the stairs. Voices raised in anger drifted to his ears, possibly stemming from the drawing room.

"The family is in crisis, my lord. That is all I can say."

"Of course. Would you, ah, inquire and find out if Miss Hasting has time to quickly receive me? I have brought her flowers in the hopes of urging her into a better mood." He held up the bouquet for the butler to see, but the other man merely gave the offering a cursory glance and then huffed.

"Miss Hasting is one of the people involved in the crisis, so I rather doubt she is available."

Nicholas frowned. "Why the devil would Miss Hasting be involved?"

Before the butler could answer, another spate of raised voices reached his ears, and one of them was distinctly Amelia's.

"What the devil is going on?" Protective instincts flared. *I need to defend her against whatever the captain is riled about.* He shoved the flowers against the butler's chest. "Put these in water, will you?" Then he loped through the corridor until he reached the stairs, which he took two treads at a time. With every step, every footfall, his heartbeat accelerated, and his gut clenched. If she was in danger, he would remove her from it.

A whining sort of cry came from Millie as he arrived at the closed drawing room doors, followed by pleading from the girl, and a definitive rebuke from Amelia, but it was the roar of anger from the captain that drove Nicholas onward. Grabbing hold of both handles, he pushed the wooden panels open with such force they crashed against the walls, and as he stepped into the room, it was to all hell breaking loose.

Truly, the Featheringham family and its derivatives had lost their composure along with their minds.

CHAPTER FIFTEEN

I T DIDN'T MATTER that Mia strove for calm or attempted to reason with Captain Featheringham, the man was incensed, and for good reason, but when Lord Wycliffe burst into the drawing room in such dramatic fashion, she couldn't help but think this was all too close to what a production on Drury Lane might look like. Still, a queer sort of shiver went through her heart to see him, for she'd assumed after yesterday he was well and truly out of her life.

"Nicholas..." Shock propelled the word from her suddenly tight throat.

Concern and annoyance roiled in his eyes. "Are you well?" he asked as he strode in her direction.

"Not quite. It's too early to tell."

"Enough!" Captain Featheringham's roar made her flinch. "Lord Wycliffe, your presence is not needed here."

"Like hell it's not. I heard you yelling at Miss Hasting. I am not leaving until you calm yourself, Captain."

"It's not your concern."

As the men glared at each other, the captain migrated to the fireplace with the cheerful flames dancing behind the metal screen with the garish peacock fashioned upon it while Millie stood huddled near Percy's position at the window. She was clad in her fine lawn shift and petticoat while the young man wore only his breeches and a lawn shirt untucked from the waist, for when her father had unexpectedly returned to the townhouse on the excuse of needing to speak with Millie about something important, he'd found her in bed with the hapless Mr. Marsden and both young people in various degrees of undress.

There was no pretending or pleading away from that potential scandal, and once he'd dragged Millie downstairs and into the drawing room regardless of her dishabille, Amelia had come running out of her own bedchamber only to encounter Percy following them, spouting excuses and intentions. Once they'd all landed in the other room, the captain had then turned his ire upon her, because she should have kept an eye on the girl.

"I don't know what game is being played here, but I don't appreciate it." The captain glowered at Nicholas. "You need to leave."

"Not until this kerfuffle is resolved." He took a step toward the captain, and never once did he glance at Millie. "What is the issue? And why the devil are these young people in mixed company dressed like that?" Only then did he bounce his gaze between Millie and Percy as they clung to each other's hands.

"Are you so daft that you can't ascertain what they were doing?" With every word, the captain's voice rose. "Obviously, the two of them thought to sneak around and get into scandal while Miss Hasting stood by and let them." He shook his head while his hands curled into fists. Then the whole of his ire came forth to land on her. "I trusted you with my precious daughter, Miss Hasting! I counted on you to shuttle her through society and find her a titled man."

"I did that to the best of my ability, but you should know your daughter isn't exactly the most demure young lady in the *ton*. In fact, she's a bit fast. She has regularly sneaked away from me, lied to me and all so she could be with the young man of her apparent choice." There was a good possibility she would be sacked, and all because of the brainless Millie.

"I can testify to that," the viscount inserted with a nod to Mia.

"I don't care!" The captain's exclamation thundered through the room. "Obviously I have entrusted my daughter to the wrong person, for I came home today in time to prevent her from being deflowered by—"

"Honestly, Captain Featheringham, I rather think that horse has left the stable," Nicholas said in the world's worst stage whisper. "The two of them have no doubt already done the deed."

"Argh!" Ruddy color filled the captain's face. He waved a hand at Percy. "Who is this sorry excuse of a man?"

The hopeless young man stumbled forward a few steps. "Mr. Percy Marsden, Captain." When he extended a hand, the captain glared, and the appendage fell back to his side.

Both Mia and Nicholas groaned.

"Papa, stop! You're being an ogre." Millie stamped her bare foot. Her dark hair continued its tumble from the remaining pins. "Percy is kind and sweet and attentive."

"Oh, good heavens." Mia blew out a breath. She stormed over to a low sofa, snagged a lightweight wool blanket from the back of that piece of furniture, and then crossed over the floor to the girl. "If you know what's good for you, please remain quiet," she whispered as she wrapped the blanket around the girl's shoulders to shield her body from view. "Eventually, his anger will blow itself out."

She hoped.

"No! I refuse to keep quiet any longer, Miss Hasting." Millie's eyes were huge in her head and brimming with tears that made them luminous. No wonder the young Mr. Marsden had fallen for her. "Percy is wonderful, and I've had to sneak off to meet him or smuggle him into my room because you disapprove of him. You think I'll ruin my life if I'm with him."

Mia crossed her arms beneath her breasts. "Well, a young girl above scandal wouldn't be standing in her father's drawing room in her undergarments, would she?"

A blush stained the girl's cheeks. "We were desperate to see each other."

She narrowed her eyes. "How many times did you smuggle him in?" And where was she that she didn't know about it? A gasp left her throat. "The megrim you said you suffered from."

"Yes." Millie nodded and sent a syrupy grin at Percy. "Yesterday, also."

"Yesterday." It wasn't a question. "I don't—"

"It was why I kissed Lord Wycliffe, so you wouldn't see Percy climb out the window." The sudden silence in the room brewed with shock.

"Why the devil was a young man in your room at all? Did the butler allow him upstairs?" This from the captain, who asked the question Mia herself wanted to know.

"No." Millie cleared her throat and drew the blanket more tightly about her person. "Uh, Percy climbed the ivy at the back of the house. I helped him by fashioning a rope of sorts from my bedsheets." Her blush deepened. "He was so brave! And once he finally came through the window while Miss Hasting waited for tea downstairs, uh, well... I suppose passion overcame us. By the time Lord Wycliffe came through the window we were well on our way to—"

"Stop." Mia held up a hand as the truth lingered in the air. She flicked her gaze to the viscount. "You followed him, saw him from the street and wished to stop him."

"Yes." Nicholas nodded with relief etching his face. "I did try to explain yesterday, but you wouldn't hear it."

Knots pulled in her belly. "I accused you because I believed Millie's lies about you." Why had she not considered the girl was far too accomplished in dissembling? Or was it her way to cause a break between them, to send Nicholas on his way without taking the blame? Her chin trembled. "I was wrong about you, said all those terrible things..."

"If we could return to the task at hand, Miss Hasting?" The captain wasn't best pleased with the side conversation. He fumed with his face like a thundercloud. "The fact of the matter is my girl has been compromised. On your watch. That is outside of enough."

"Oh, I quite agree, Captain. If I hadn't been distracted, if I hadn't trusted her, perhaps none of this would have happened." Her chest ached, for this mess could be firmly laid at her feet. Like a ninny, she'd had her head turned by Nicholas, let him burrow beneath her skin until all she could think about was him. In this, she was no better than Millie.

I am a hypocrite.

"Please don't take the blame, Miss Hasting." Percy joined Millie and dared to slip an arm about her waist, but immediately put space between them when both the captain and Nicholas objected. "Millie and I were quite devious in evading your watch." His face was beet red, but Mia appreciated his candor and courage at speaking up. "We only wished to be together, because we are in love, you see."

Everyone in the room groaned.

"No, hear me out." Quickly, the young man tucked his shirt tails into his breeches. "I have plans, for I wish to become a banker." There was such earnestness in his face Mia was inclined to believe him. "I'm good at numbers, have an aptitude for them. All of that comes easily to me, and I've already turned a few investments that have paid out, have counseled a few lords to do the same."

"One day he wants to open his own accounting house," Millie said with a smile and stars in her eyes as she looked at him.

"You do realize you have nothing to offer anyone at the moment?" Nicholas frowned. "No matter who you marry, you will no doubt need to have a long engagement until you can at least afford to buy a house."

"No!" Once more, Millie's immaturity came through. She again stamped her foot. "I love Percy and refuse to wait."

"Silence!" The captain shoved a hand through his already untidy hair. "This scandal cannot continue. I don't want the gossips to get hold of this story or paint London with it, for then no one will want my daughter." He rubbed a hand along the side of his face, and Mia felt sorry for him in that moment. It must be maddening to know all the plans he had for his daughter had crumbled into dust. Then he turned the full force of his scowl on Percy, and the boy almost fainted before he locked his knees. "There is nothing for it. Mr. Marsden will have to wed my daughter, since they've already bedded each other." Anger flashed in his eyes as he looked at Nicholas. "Unless you'll marry her, Wycliffe?"

Protests erupted into the room.

Captain Featheringham raised a hand for silence. "It would make sense. All of London knows you need to wed an heiress."

Mia couldn't help but glance at the viscount, along with everyone else in the room. Her ears and heart strained to hear the answer he would give, even though she had no right to him.

"Ha!" Nicholas shook his head and eyed the young pair askance. "And run the risk Miss Featheringham is carrying someone else's child I'll be forced to raise as my own? Possibly as an heir?" Shock mixed with annoyance in his voice.

"Oh, Nicholas, that wasn't well done of you," Mia whispered to him as the captain's face grew an alarming shade of purple.

"Why should I marry her and make her life easier? This isn't *my* mess." He blew out a breath. "Not *all* of it, at least. It *is* my fault that I introduced Miss Featheringham to Mr. Marsden, but she had her own free will. This is the path she chose despite the warnings given to them both." With the shake of his head, he retreated a few steps toward the door. "I don't need the coin that much." Though his words were adamant, worry clouded his brow, for they both knew it was a sacrifice and a hardship to turn the girl down.

"I can't say as I blame you," the captain said.

Millie sniffed. "I would never marry someone as old as Lord Wycliffe, especially since his attentions are *clearly* not on me." With a smile at her lover, the girl bounded over the floor to clutch at one of her father's arms. "Dearest Papa, please don't be cross with me. Think back to when you courted Mama. Percy and I are in love. Our union might not be what you wanted for me, but it's what I want for myself. Everything will be right in the end."

"Oddly enough, after watching them together, I agree with Millie." Mia shocked herself by agreeing with the girl. "It's not fair to keep them apart, for he has the potential to be a good man and will do everything in his power to take care of her."

"But not in the way she's become accustomed to," the captain argued.

This time, Nicholas added his own advice. "Probably not for a while, but everyone in this room knows how much you love your daughter, Captain. I'm sure you will help them along where they need it, especially for the sake of possible grandchildren." He offered a tight smile. "Otherwise, you'll antagonize the girl, and she might keep the babes from you. She has quite a temper when spited."

The captain's expression softened. "I suppose…"

"If I may offer a tidbit here, Captain?" Mia interrupted. "While Mr. Marsden is determined to set his own path, he *is* the grandson of an earl, so do bear that in mind when you speak with him." At least that would smooth the poor young man's way and the knowledge should satisfy the captain's requirements of entering the aristocracy.

"Oh, Papa, that's true, and you will take care of me until Percy can properly." Millie clung to her father's arm while holding the blanket in place. "And if you are thinking of sacking Miss Hasting, please reconsider. It's not fair that she lose her position, even though she won't be needed once I wed." The girl smiled at Mia. "Unless you wish to be a governess to my children?"

Ah, the girl never disappointed. Everything was truly about her. Mia couldn't summon the energy to tamp down, pointing her gaze to the ceiling. "I rather think I'm done with the

Featheringham family at this point."

"Miss Hasting failed to perform the tasks her position de-manded."

"Perhaps, but then, even you cannot deny your daughter is far too willful at times." Nicholas stepped in before Mia could defend herself. "Instead of sacking her, would you consider giving her a glowing reference, Captain, so she might find a new position? She *does* need to have a living to get to help her family." When he smiled at her with that slightly crooked smile he sometimes had, flutters went through her belly. "And she *did* try her best to have Millie toe the line."

"Obviously *not* her best," the captain said in a gruff voice.

"Perhaps, but I suppose it's my fault, for if her attention wasn't on me and keeping me from your daughter, she could have steered Millie in a better direction."

"Ha." Mia snorted, for she had to laugh in the situation; otherwise, she would dissolve into tears, and she'd already spent too many hours like that last night. "The girl had no problem finding trouble of her own regardless of where my attention was." But oh, how lovely that distraction had been! She was hard-pressed to feel any regret for that temporary insanity.

For long moments, the captain glanced between them all. Finally, he sighed. "This day has been very disappointing." Though anger still threaded through his robust voice, some of the alarming color left his face as he crossed the room to yank on a brocade bell pull. When the butler appeared, he said, "Please escort Mr. Marsden to my study. We have contracts and terms to discuss."

"Of course, Captain." The butler gestured at Percy, who looked a bit green about the gills as he left the room with the other man.

Then the captain rested his attention on Mia. "As for you, Miss Hasting, I *will* give you a recommendation, pay your wages through the end of the month—"

"And give her a bonus gift for being in the middle of this

mess?" Nicholas asked with a raised eyebrow.

"Fine." The captain waved a hand. "A severance of one hundred pounds if you keep your mouth shut regarding the scandal my girl has made of herself."

"Done."

"Stop, my lord," Mia hissed at him, but in that moment, she lost a piece of her heart to him for his protection and defense. Then she gave the captain her full attention. "Thank you. That is more than generous." She battled back tears of embarrassment, anger, and gratitude. "I shall pack my things and vacate your home by the end of the week." Though where she would go, she had no idea, for going back home wasn't an option if she would snag a new position immediately, but then, she wouldn't need to immediately with the largesse the captain had promised.

"That is acceptable," the captain said in a gruff voice.

"Papa, behave. Miss Hasting can stay for as long as she needs." Millie frowned. She narrowed her eyes on Nicholas. "Don't *you* have something you wish to say to Miss Hasting, Lord Wycliffe?"

"What?" Surprise jumped into his expression. "Why?"

The girl's eyes were sly as she smiled. "I've seen how you look at her, how you act around her, how your face lights up when Miss Hasting is near." Millie shook her head. "Everyone assumes I'm a brainless girl, but I see more than you think. There's *something* between the two of you, and it's been brewing for a while."

Mia bounced her gaze between them. Was that true?

"Uh…" Ruddy color rose up his neck. "Anything I wish to say will be conducted in private and certainly not here."

"Hmph." Millie huffed and readjusted her blanket. "It's a start but not good enough. Though Miss Hasting is dour and no fun, she *has* managed to bring you to heel. I think all of London will be glad of that." Then she transferred her gaze to Mia. "Please stay, at least through the weekend, and come to the Valentine's Day ball Papa is throwing."

The captain snorted. "It'll have to be an engagement ball now." His tones were quite morose. No doubt he saw his chance at seeing his daughter gain a title were slipping away.

The ever-selfish Millie ignored him as she focused on Mia. "Attend as a guest instead of my companion. Please? I..." Her eyes teared. "I've acted horribly, and you didn't deserve such treatment. Now I have Percy, I see that I've been a silly, stupid girl. The world is larger than me and I am *not* the center of it."

"What?" Shock smacked into Mia's chest. Perhaps the chit would turn out well after all. "I would enjoy that very much, Millie. Thank you. However, I'm afraid my gown is suited to a companion instead of a guest."

"Pish posh." The girl rolled her eyes. "As soon as Papa is closeted with Percy, you and I will discuss gowns. We have one day to find you something brilliant that's not as drab as your usual wardrobe." With a grin, she glanced at the viscount. "And you'll come, Lord Wycliffe? As a guest who has no designs on me?"

"I..." He peered at Mia who shrugged. "I wouldn't miss it. After all, it seems the Featheringhams put on quite the show."

Mia struggled to stifle a laugh.

"Brilliant!" Millie clapped her hands. "This will be just perfect!" She beamed at her father, lifted up on her toes, and bussed his cheek. "Don't be cross. Everyone should indulge in romance when it comes their way, and isn't love the best thing any of us can chase?"

The captain's expression completely crumpled. "Go dress, child. I'm going to speak with your intended." As the girl fled the room, he sighed and looked at Mia. "I'm sorry our association has come to this."

"Think nothing of it, Captain. At least your daughter is happy and since Percy is tip over tail for her, he'll treat her well." She winked. "Unless I miss my guess, you'll have a house full of grandchildren in the coming years."

Nicholas nodded his agreement. "Perhaps you can take young

Percy on as your accountant. Then you can be certain he'll do right by your daughter, Captain."

"Indeed. I hadn't thought of it, and I don't have time to do all of that myself." He brightened. "Well, good day to you both. I have business matters to attend."

For the space of a few heartbeats, the silence in the room after such a spectacle was quite deafening. Eventually, Mia turned to fully face Nicholas. All the words she wished to say refused to jump off the tip of her tongue and got all jumbled up in her head, so she focused on the immediate. "I didn't need you to defend me, for I am quite capable of fighting for myself."

"Oh, how well I know it. I'm surprised you didn't slap the captain, since that is your response of choice," he said with the grin that sent mad tingles into her belly and an odd little thump into her heart.

"No matter." She fought off the urge to smile. "However, I do thank you. A hundred pounds will go a long way, especially now that I need to find rooms to let as well as a new position."

"You are the most determined woman I have ever met. You will land on your feet." Silence reigned between them. "I wasn't with Millie like you thought."

"So I heard." What could she say to him when she hadn't had time to sort her own thoughts? "I'm sorry for the words I said to you yesterday."

"I deserved each one." With a shrug, he gave her a wry look. "I should go."

Is that all he would say? Why couldn't she utter the words that she wanted? Instead, Mia nodded. "Will I see you at the ball, then?"

"Absolutely." Then he drifted close, put his lips to the shell of her ear, and whispered, "Wear the stockings, Amelia. I promise to pay correct homage to your legs this time."

Before she had time to revel in his scent or his warmth, he was gone, and she stared at the space he'd just occupied for a long time afterward.

Chapter Sixteen

February 14, 1817
Featheringham House
Mayfair
London, England

"WHY AM I so nervous? I've been in society for years, attended countless balls, yet I feel as if I'll crawl out of my skin."

Since the captain was ostentatious in all parts of his life, his ballroom—because of course his townhouse was on the large size, which meant it could accommodate such a space—was heavily decorated in gilt and crystal. From the frames of the paintings to the grand chandelier to the delicate sconces on the walls, each piece and decoration screamed wealth and the desperation to fit into the aristocracy. And even more gawdy were the red, pink, and gold foil heart and cupid cutout decorations that festooned the doorways and windows. Vases of hothouse roses rested on small tables or short columns strategically placed about the area.

Marcus chuckled as they entered the ballroom. "God, it looks like Cupid's bedchamber exploded in here," he whispered as he threw a glance about the space. Then he looked at Nicholas. "You are nervous because suddenly you've arrived at the point of your life when everything has the potential to change. Where it means something."

"True." Nick scanned the crush of people already in the room, but as of yet he hadn't seen Amelia. "I have had a day to think further upon what to do about Miss Hasting."

"And?"

He sighed. "I'm not entirely certain, but I do know I cannot move forward without either securing her promise or coming to an understanding." Tugging on the bottom of his waistcoat—the gold and silver threads of the brocade fabric were his only concessions to the holiday—he frowned at his friend. "Is that pure folly for only having known her for a week? It doesn't seem possible. In fact, it might be too far-fetched to believe."

Love didn't happen that quickly, did it? And it couldn't be expected to last even if that were so. Was he already setting himself up for failure?

"There are no rules regarding love, my friend." Marcus' eyes were kind even as amusement sparkled in the depths. "At times it takes years to bloom while at others, it comes at you like a runaway carriage and plows straight through your chest. If you know deep in your soul that you are in love with the companion, that you cannot fathom living without her by your side, then you should pursue that with everything you are."

"What if I'm wrong? What if what I'm feeling is pure nonsense driven by lust and my future will be plagued with problems like my parents' union?"

"How many times do I need to tell you that thinking is a man's downfall?" Marcus dropped an encouraging hand on Nick's shoulder and gave him a tiny shake. "Stop fretting and start making strides to build a future you can be proud of. You've learned the lessons from your parents; you aren't them. You know deep down you'll do better."

He nodded. The reassurance went a long way into promoting calm. "Thank you."

"You're welcome, and for what it's worth, I'm happy for you. Miss Hasting seems like a sensible woman who will put you to rights." Marcus dropped his hand and gave him a cheeky grin. "Which is why I can't understand why she might return your affections."

"Do shut up," Nick teased, but he couldn't help his own grin. "That's another fear of mine, though. What if she refuses me?"

"Then she does." His friend shrugged. The string quintet the captain had hired for the event began to tune their instruments. "You have no control over what other people do. The only person you are responsible for is yourself, and if you are content with that, everything else doesn't matter." Then his expression shifted. "I believe your destiny has arrived."

"What?" With excitement buzzing at the base of his spine and anxiety knotting his gut, Nick turned about to see what Marcus referred to, and he caught his breath. "Dear God, she's beautiful."

"Agreed, and you are truly a fortunate man. I'll leave you to it, but expect the whole story at the club tomorrow evening."

Barely aware that his friend had left his side, Nick stared at Amelia as she stood at the opened double doors of the ballroom with Millie at her side. "Please help me to not cock this up," he whispered to no one in particular as he devoured her with his gaze.

While the girl was attired in a white gown with several flounces and lace befitting a young woman in her Come Out year, his attention was drawn to Amelia's silk gown. Made a dark rose color with some sort of gauzy overskirt of pink that also encased the short, puffed sleeves, but it was the low bodice that had his notice dropping to her impressive décolletage. A pearl necklace went around her neck with a cameo broach sitting at her throat, and her incredible blonde hair had been curled and twisted into an elaborate upswept style that made certain she would be noticed. No doubt Millie had given her the loan of a maid, but it was Amelia's eyes he couldn't escape, for as her gaze inspected the room, it crashed into his and he nearly fell into the deep pools of blue. Even from his distance, he wanted to happily drown there.

Before he could convince his feet to carry him across the floor toward her, Captain Featheringham entered the room with Percy in tow. Millie merrily tripped after her beau while Amelia drifted toward the side of the room, not far from Nick's location. They didn't stop until they'd reached the top of the room, where he then called the assemblage to order.

"It is my great honor to announce that not only is it St. Valentine's Day, which is the reason for this ball, but now this event will commemorate the fact that my darling Millie caught the eye of Mr. Marsden—he's the grandson of the Earl of Wexton, you know—and now they are engaged to be married."

Millie beamed as Percy took her hand while polite clapping broke out amidst the crowd. She nodded, and with sparkling eyes said, "We will marry on May Day to incorporate that celebration into our own. Isn't that wonderful?"

"Perhaps she will deliver her first babe on Guy Fawkes Day then in keeping with those holiday pairings." There was no mistaking the sarcasm in Amelia's voice as she came abreast of Nick since he'd been temporarily distracted by the chit's antics. When he met her gaze, she winked. "You know, since they've already gotten up to scandal ahead of their wedding day."

Was there any doubt why he adored her? Nicholas chuckled, for having her near worked to soothe his jangled nerves. "You might not be far off." As the captain told everyone dinner would be served near eleven o'clock that night, then invited everyone to enjoy the opening country reel, Nick escorted Amelia out of the line of traffic as couples assembled on the dance floor. "You are a vision tonight." Just as he'd suspected when he'd first met her, in a gown of fine fabrics and not a few years old, she could easily take the *ton* by storm.

And she was far too good for him. The urge to retch climbed his throat, but he swallowed it down, hoped to hell it could keep that reaction at bay.

"Such gammon you speak, my lord, but I appreciate the compliment all the same." Faint pink stained her cheeks. "You aren't a slouch in the looks department either, and I especially like when you have your valet style your hair like that. It suits you better than the Brutus cut or some of the others men favor."

"Ah." He nodded. "I don't know that I've ever given hairstyles much thought." Thank goodness for Barnes and his knowledge. "You must be proud that Millie has proved such a success. It will certainly help you land future positions." An ache set up around his heart, for if that were to happen, he might lose her forever.

"I'm relieved it's all over. That girl wore me out with worry. Now she's Percy's problem."

Nicholas snorted. "I'm not certain he's aware just how much of an issue his new fiancée will actually prove, but they do seem wildly happy together. Perhaps it is all they shall need." He glanced over his shoulder to where the pair was enjoying the last steps of the reel. "No doubt the captain will be generous with his funding once they do marry." Percy was a fortunate bastard indeed, for he would never need to worry about coin.

"Are you already regretting giving up your pursuit of the girl?" The low question coupled with her gloved hand on his arm brought his attention back to Amelia and the concern in her expression.

"While I won't lie and say I couldn't use the funding, I am acutely relieved it isn't me who is marrying the chit." A shiver moved down his spine. "She is vastly unsuited for me."

"Because you're so ancient?" A snort of laughter followed the teasing.

"Exactly." He gave her a grin as the country reel ended. "I've learned I need a more experienced, older lady by my side in order for me to be happy." When she returned his grin, more of his doubts evaporated. "Amelia." Offering her a hand, he cleared his throat. "I believe the next set is a waltz and would adore it if you might agree to partner me." Bound by the need to appear polite yet formal in her presence due to being in public, he tamped down the words that were fairly wanting to burst from him, but there was nothing for it. Society demanded rules at times, and if he wished to remain an upstanding member for her—for their hoped-for future—he would abide by them.

"That would be lovely. I haven't danced in an age let alone indulged in a waltz." When she slipped her fingers into his palm, faint tingling edged up his arm. She said nothing further as he led her to an empty spot on the highly polished parquet floor, but when they assumed the proper position, a tiny sigh escaped her. "Truth be told, for one terrible moment, I doubted you'd come, Nicholas," she said in a low voice. "After the contretemps in the captain's drawing room the other day, I fully expected you to flee London."

The sound of his given name in her dulcet tones sent ripples of need down his spine. "I considered it, but I wanted to partner with you in a waltz more." When he caught Marcus' eye nearby on the floor as he waited for the dance to start with his partner, the man winked. Clearly, he expected an announcement from Nick tonight. "Besides, I knew from the moment Millie wished to take charge of your wardrobe it would be splendid and a much-needed change from your usual dresses."

A flash of annoyance went through her eyes but vanished the moment he chuckled. "I agree with your assessment. It has also been an age since I had anything new, and though a few alterations had to be made on this gown of Millie's, it is certainly mine now." The brilliant smile she gave him was more than enough reward for his candor. She squeezed his fingers while the hand resting on his shoulder slightly trembled. Was she as anxious as he?

Why?

Then the musicians released the first notes of the piece and Nicholas set them into motion. They chatted about inconsequential things like the weather and the variety of guests in attendance or whether Millie was indeed increasing, but he didn't mind, for he enjoyed listening to her talk, discerning the various inflections of her voice, and he'd missed it since they'd been forced to part after she'd been let go from the captain's staff. Once they'd completed the first turn of the ballroom, something shifted and changed between them.

Changed *for* him.

Or perhaps it had been there all along, but he'd refused to put a name on it until this moment. Nick pulled her closer, as much as he dared while in public. He gave himself over to the simple delight of dancing for dancing's sake. It was an exercise he *did* enjoy—with the right partner. Amelia was exactly that, had been that perfect puzzle piece that had been missing from his life.

Just as Barnes had counseled him two days ago, he would know the answer when he felt content deep into his soul.

With amusement and happiness swirling about him like a comforting blanket, he smiled down into her eyes. When she returned the gesture, the sensation of falling assailed him. Her faint apple blossom scent teased his nose and infiltrated his senses. The gleam of the pearls at her neck drew his notice to the tops of her breasts visible above the low bodice, and he stifled a groan even as his shaft tightened. Yes, he wanted her physically, but a need beyond that had grown exponentially during the short time he'd known her. Everything about the woman in his arms challenged him, provoked him, exasperated him, and alternately made him wish to be a better man; he couldn't wait to discover what she'd do or say next, yearned to know about her family, the sisters she'd spoken of, the dynamics of her siblings, for she kept him in a state of wonderment with her determination for life and her nurturing spirit as evidenced by her urge to help her parents pay their taxes.

The steps of the waltz were effortless as her partner, and the longer he stared, the deeper he fell into her lake blue eyes. He would happily drown there if only she'd smile at him one more time or laugh over something charming he said. Then the startling thought occurred to him that he wouldn't mind waking up with her every morning, or seeing her smile at him over the breakfast table while he read the paper, or walking beside her over his estate in the countryside as well as the dear little cottage in Ireland or hosting dinner parties with her at the opposite end of his table.

Dear God, I'm in love with Amelia Hasting.

Remarkably, that and wishing to marry her wasn't the death knell he'd originally assumed. In fact, hope bloomed further behind his ribcage for he could almost see the future—their future—and he rather liked the thrill of it, welcomed it.

Yet, he was poor, and she was too. How would it even work?

Amelia squeezed her fingers on his shoulder at the next turn. "You have the look of a man who's suddenly figured out the answer to a problem that has plagued him for days."

"I rather think I have." Nick grinned, for suddenly an enormous weight had been lifted from his shoulders and chest. He could breathe again without fear. No matter the obstacles they might face, it would all be well as long as he had her.

If she could find a way to love him despite the muck he'd made of his life.

"That makes me happy to hear." Her smile made him forget reality for a bit. "I hope it means you've come to a decision that might change the course of your life." The answering hope in her own eyes humbled the hell out of him. Would she return his feelings?

"It might indeed, but you and I must talk. There are… things I must say to you that cannot be put off any longer."

"All right." The delicate tendons of her throat worked with a hard swallow.

"Not here." He finally glanced away from her, and it was much like coming out of a dream. His grin widened, for he was in foreign territory. Never in his life had he expected to be here, to want a woman for anything other than bed sport. "I would rather have this conversation privately, and since it is rather too chilly to utilize the shallow terrace…"

"Don't worry yourself, my lord. We can utilize my room. Lord knows that floor should be empty just now."

He snorted. "Unless Millie and her young man have the same idea in mind."

"Oh? That assumes you wish to do more than talk with me." A mischievous light twinkled in her eyes.

Another push of need went through his shaft. "That all depends on the direction of the conversation, but I *am* curious about your stockings," he added in a whisper as he led her off the floor. "Meet me there in fifteen minutes?"

"Well, now I'm intrigued, so of course I'll be there." She winked. "I'll invent a torn hem that will require immediate attention and slip away."

"God, I adore how your mind works." It was also a bit intimidating.

"I must be clever to keep up with you." Then she left his side and spoke briefly to a few people on her way out of the ballroom, no doubt planting the seeds in the event anyone noted her absence.

With nothing else to do, Nicholas made a circuit about the room, talking to a few of his acquaintances, giving his well wishes to Millie and Percy, but then the urge to see Amelia overrode everything else. He excited the ballroom by way of a side door that spilled into a parlor so it would appear he had other plans that ran opposite to hers. Then he quietly sneaked away and when he gained the grand staircase, he took the treads two at a time. He really should declare his intentions and waste no more time, but how to put into words exactly what he was feeling when he didn't fully believe it himself?

I'll have to muddle through or else I'll lose her.

It was an easy endeavor to locate her bedchamber, for she'd left the door slightly open, and once he'd gently closed that panel behind him, turned the lock until he heard that satisfying click, the entirety of his focus rested on the woman standing in the middle of the room near the foot of a four-poster bed dressed in shades of mauve and gold as was typical of the garish decorating style the Featheringhams were known for.

"How can I stand here and converse when you are beauty personified, and the only thing I can think about is removing that gorgeous gown from your person?" It wasn't exactly how he wished to begin this meeting, but there it was. Leopards didn't change their spots, apparently.

A blush stained her cheeks as she slowly removed her gloves. They fell to the mauve Aubusson carpet like dollops of cream. "Did you hear me tell you nay?"

Then he didn't know if he could wait and take the time to rid them both of clothing. An overwhelming urge to join with her filled his being, but more than that, since he'd gone tip over tail, he couldn't wait any longer to empty the contents of his heart. For good or for ill, he wanted to tell the woman he loved her, and what was more, he desired marriage and everything that would entail… if Mia would accept him, flaws and all.

"This has been quite the eye-opening week." It was a lame start to what should be a romantic speech, but then, he was in unknown territory here.

"Agreed." Yet confusion clouded her eyes. "Why would you say that?"

Damn, but she would go straightway to the point. Slowly, he prowled toward her as he tugged off his gloves and tossed them over his shoulder. Perhaps he could embed foreplay with the speech to kill two birds with one stone so to speak. "In the course of one week I have felt as if I've labored in a fog, been held captive in a spell. I've been compelled to chase after a woman who is entirely wrong for me, yet I cannot help what I feel." Easily, he slipped an arm about her, and walked her backward until the bed at her rear stopped the movement. "You have enchanted me, Amelia, utterly and completely until my every thought is about you."

"Oh?" Her chin trembled, and somehow, there was a nearly undetectable waver in that one-word inquiry that nearly had him on his knees.

"Yes." He wrapped his other hand about her nape and dragged her against his body. "For most of my adult life, I have been a rake, a man who cared about nothing or anyone beyond myself and my own desires."

"You are not a rake, Nicholas. It is merely a shield you hide behind because you are afraid of being the man you can be," she whispered, her eyes large and dark in the dim illumination.

"Only you could see that. No one else did." Needing to touch her, requiring that reassurance, he wrapped his arms around her and simply held her, pressed his lips to hers and reveled in how she felt.

"It's a bit of a knack I have… except when it came to Millie." Amelia glided her lips along the side of his neck, just over his cravat, and his whole body tightened. "I'm afraid I failed spectacularly there."

"Not failed. Learned from but one experience, and your strength impresses the hell out of me." He played his hands over her back, following her spine, up and down. The warmth of her seeped into his fingertips. Apparently, she wasn't content with his distracted kisses, for she dragged her lips beneath his jaw. The feel of her kisses on his skin chipped away at his reserve. The dratted woman would sink him beneath a wave of desire if he wasn't careful, and nothing on his heart would be uttered, yet every brush of her lips, each exhalation of her heated breath pushed him closer to that edge.

"In any event, I never thought I would ever feel anything for a woman beyond lust," he whispered as he plucked the pins from her hair. When that blonde waterfall tumbled about her shoulders and back, a sigh shuddered from him. The scent of apple blossoms reached his nose, and he breathed in the sweet floral aroma, for it would always remind him of her.

"I don't believe that has changed, my lord." She wriggled her hips, which worked to further arouse his shaft. Her laugh was a throaty affair that went straight to his stones.

Bloody hell.

"Ah, Amelia." Tangling his fingers in her hair, he framed her head with his hands and then claimed her lips with his. Never had he been more tempted by a woman, more antagonized, more frustrated, more freed, and everything that she did delighted him.

Over and over, he kissed her, tasted her lips, set out to chase away the chill in the air, for her room didn't host a fireplace. With a tiny bit of pressure at his nape, she held him closer, and the second she traced the seam of his mouth with the tip of her tongue, he was lost. His engorged length pressed painfully against the front of his breeches, and damn if he didn't wish to claim her body as he was doing her lips.

He tugged gently on her hair, which encouraged her head backward, and he took advantage by dragging his lips along the column of her slender throat. The silky skin, the tiny sounds of pleasure she made all worked at his undoing, and when she shivered from need, he shoved the importance of his proposal to the back of his mind.

Right now, in this moment, he wanted this woman more.

She tugged at his cravat and once that length of cloth came undone, Amelia pressed kisses to the skin she'd just uncovered, and a shudder of desire went down his spine. "Everything changed the second I met you."

"How well I understand that sentiment." Heated need moved through him, and he shifted to better accommodate his arousal. Needing more from her but also wishing to take control of the seduction, he urged her upward onto the bed with her legs dangling off the edge. "Truth to tell, you have captivated me in every way a woman can," he said as he glided the fingertips of one hand along the bodice of her dress.

"How do you feel about that?" With enough heat in her blue eyes to raise the temperature of the room, she leaned in, took his earlobe between her lips, and then lightly bit that flesh. Need streaked through him. "Hmm?"

Dear God, she would lead him down the devil's own path

and he'd go willingly, even if he had been likened to that deity more than once in his life. "Confused, aroused, enchanted… and oddly enough, emboldened." He followed the edge of her bodice with his lips as he worked the laces at the back of her dress. Once the garment gaped, it was all too easy to tug it downward, and once the shift and stays beneath were dealt with and her breasts were exposed, he groaned at the utter perfection of those pale mounds. "I fought against these feelings, tried to deny them, assumed they would go away if I could but bed you." Wishing to tease her, he brushed the knuckles of one hand over one hardening nipple.

Amelia shivered. She guided his other hand to her breast and held it there. "Obviously, that was a lie." The words were breathless, wispy.

"Indeed, and I kept falling, ever since that day in the carriage. Hell, at this point, that tumble probably started earlier but I wasn't aware of it." Daring much, he gave one of the pink tips a light pinch. A gasp from her was his reward, and her fingers curled into the lapels of his tailcoat.

"What are you trying to say, Nicholas?"

As if he could remember. His shaft pulsed with urgency. God, he wanted her! "I'm in love with you, Amelia." Dear heavens, it felt so good to finally say it aloud. Then fear seized his heart. Would she reject him? Not wishing to give her a chance to immediately respond, he devoted himself to exploring those soft, perfumed breasts. When he took a pebbled tip into his mouth and flicked his tongue over it, her soft gasps and moans urged him onward. Several minutes passed while he explored, and she gave herself over to his attention as if it were the most natural thing in the world.

As if she'd craved him as much as he did her.

It was all too heady. "For days I assumed I was wrong. I denied what is being written on my heart as we speak. But I want you to know, I haven't been a decent man for far too many years." When she surged into him, pressing her lips to his and taking control of the kiss, he couldn't help but grin against her mouth. The woman was naught but a powder keg, and he held the match. Had she even heard his words, understood them? Perhaps it didn't matter. Nicholas kissed her, let her boss his tongue, and then he dominated the embrace, showed her without words how he felt.

And that only served to pour more fuel on the fire burning between them.

"Yet for the last week, you have become a different person. You've curbed your vices, assumed responsibility for Percy, tried to protect Millie." A sigh sailed from her throat, the remaining words lost.

"Perhaps." Easily he delved a hand beneath her skirting, and damn but she was already thoroughly aroused as he stroked his fingers along her heated flesh. She lightly bit his bottom lip when he spread her open and found that swollen nubbin at her center. A moan escaped her the second he rubbed it with varying degrees of friction.

Her fingers dug into his shoulder. "Oh, oh!" Lost in the throes of apparent pleasure, Amelia moved her hips, ground into his hand, which only made him work her over with more determination. "How do you manage to make me wish to fly so quickly?" Her breath came in soft pants. "I... Oh!" A cry of surprise echoed in the silence of the room.

It was such a delight to watch her face as emotions played over it, for she truly enjoyed foreplay. Hell, it was more than that. Over the course of the week, his Amelia responded better to his touches. She wasn't an ice queen at all but instead was an emotional creature who reacted to actions over words. Because he'd been a liar before, had used flattery and charm as a medium with nothing concrete to guarantee those words.

"I am not lying when I say that I have fallen in love with you, Amelia, and I believe the next logical step to our relationship is... That is to say I would like it by half if you would marry me."

As she rode the crest of that quick, shallow release, tears

spilled down her cheeks. They were far more than mere tears brought by finding bliss, and before too long, she was openly sobbing in his arms.

"Why the tears?" Though he was quietly dying to hear her answer, hear her return the sentiment, worry tightened his chest, and he temporarily forgot his throbbing shaft. "I know I'm not the best catch in the world, but I'm not the worst." His attempt at humor fell flat when she only sobbed harder.

Never, for as long as I live, will I understand the female mind.

CHAPTER SEVENTEEN

O*H, DEAR HEAVENS, he loves me!*

Mia shook from the residual waves of bliss he'd given her, but as she clung to him, breathed in his crisp, clean scent, as he let her cry in his arms, she shook from the intensity of her own confusing emotions.

"Is the thought of marrying me so repugnant then?" he asked in a low whisper as he pulled away enough to peer into her face.

"No! Of course not." She wiped at the moisture on her face while shaking her head. "When we met, I would have absolutely been repelled if you had asked me that question."

"And now?" Strain wove through his voice while concern shadowed his dark eyes.

"And now…" A hard swallow into her suddenly dry throat didn't dislodge the ball of emotion lodged there. "I've seen the change in you, I've witnessed the man you are coming to be, and it's wildly attractive." Pressing her lips together, she stared at the loosened knot of his cravat so she wouldn't need to see the disappointment in his eyes. "It's me who is a wrong fit for you, Nicholas. You have made no secret of the fact you need to wed a woman with a sizable dowry, if not a fortune, and I have neither." When he opened his mouth to no doubt protest, she shook her head. "I care for you too much to see all the dreams for your estate fail because I cannot help in that regard."

"Look at me." He put a finger beneath her chin, raised her head until their gazes connected once more. "The coin doesn't matter; the estate doesn't matter. Don't you see?"

"See what?" Being in his presence affected her ability to think clearly.

"I love you. Surely that counts for something, and I would rather have you than full coffers." Nothing except honesty reflected in his face.

"Oh!" Tears again welled in her eyes as she clutched at his shoulders. "Why would you make such a sacrifice? Eventually you would grow to resent me."

He shrugged. "Isn't love worth more than anything else in this world? Millie was correct when she said everyone should strive to chase it."

Was the answer that simple? "I…"

"Sweeting, listen to me." Nicholas cupped her cheeks, brushed the tears from her cheeks with the pads of his thumbs. "I know it's only been a short time. I know it all sounds too fantastical to be true. I know we both doubted the same when Millie and Percy confessed their love for each other, but sometimes, there are things in life that go beyond the known. That doesn't mean they aren't true."

"We cannot both be poor," she whispered as her mind reeled with the incredulity of it all. "I told you that before."

"Do you trust me?"

"Not by half," but she said it with a smile.

He snorted. "If you accept my proposal, we will puzzle out the future together." As he flashed that charming grin of his, flutters moved through her belly. "Who knows? Perhaps we will make having pockets to let acceptable in society."

Despite the gravity of the subject matter, she giggled, fiddled with the folds of his cravat. "Perhaps you should talk with Percy regarding investments and such."

"That's not a bad idea." He dragged the pad of his thumb along her lower lip. "But that isn't all you wished to say to me tonight, is it?" There was a hopeful light at the backs of his eyes that completely broke down the remaining barriers about her heart.

"No, it's not." With a shuddering sigh, another few tears fell to her cheeks. "Like you, I fought against my feelings for I assumed they couldn't possibly be real. A woman like me, falling for a rake?"

"Ah, but you've said all along I'm not that," he reminded her as he glanced feather-weighted kisses to her temple, her chin, the underside of her jaw.

"Mmm." A shiver of need twisted up her spine. Why did every thought in her head vanish the instant he touched her? "You are not. In fact, deep down, you are a good man if you would stop being afraid and let yourself shine." When he brushed a knuckle over one of her nipples and it tightened into a pebbled bud, she gasped. "For years, I accepted my fate, assumed my life was happy and content before, but the moment I met you, everything turned topsyturvy." Doing her best to ignore the delicious things he did to her, she blinked away her tears. "You yanked me from my carefully constructed cocoon of comfort and responsibility, only to thrust me into something new and exciting and brimming with... everything I have always dreamed about."

"Do arrive at the point soon, darling, for I wish to completely ravish you once I've won this argument." The aggravating, annoying, lovely man licked and kissed the side of her neck to the point where she thought she might melt off the bed.

"Perhaps having a slightly wicked husband won't be so bad," she managed to whisper as he'd once more returned to her breast to bedevil that sensitive tip. Pushing herself out of the passionate fog that shrouded her brain, she met his eyes once more. "I don't know how it happened or why, but I can no longer deny the fact that I'm hopelessly in love with you." Another few tears fell to her cheeks. "God help me."

"You love me." It wasn't a question but the shock and awe in his eyes made her both laugh and cry all the harder.

"Yes. I'm a fool, I know, but I cannot imagine my life without you there to bedevil me or challenge me." Her smile felt all too wry as she shrugged. "I want to know everything about you—good and bad—and quite frankly, I cannot wait to build a life with you, even if we both are forced to get our livings like the middle class. At least we'll live honestly."

"Indeed." The grin that curved his sensual lips was far too lovely and charming. "I'm old, though. Just ask Millie."

"And I'm a dried up, unwanted spinster, so I feel we shall suit famously." Needing to reassure herself this wasn't a horrible idea, Mia threw herself into his arms and held him close.

"Ah, dearest, we will have such fun together, the *ton's* gossip mill will be kept quite busy." After he pressed a kiss to her temple, he pulled away to peer into her face. "You are never unwanted." Then he put his lips to the shell of her ear and whispered, "And in a handful of minutes, I'll show you just how wet you can be. Dried up, indeed." As he scoffed in mock outrage, she laughed through her tears, surged up, and kissed him, stifling that sound.

Was there any wonder why she loved him, why she'd fallen for him? No longer did she think him the worst man for her; perhaps she needed a man exactly like him because he was everything she was not, and he would help her grow.

Then the time for words was over, for the viscount claimed her lips with an intensity that stole her breath. All too soon, he encouraged her backward on the bed while her legs dangled over the side, and he followed her down merely to continue plundering her mouth, dueling with her tongue while he teased and bedeviled her breasts and sensitive nipples.

"Before I forget, let me inspect your stockings, hmm?" The viscount slid down her body, then fought his way through layers of skirting, finally bunching them at her waist as he grinned up at her. "You wore them." The delight in his voice played havoc with her heart.

"How could I not, especially when donning them made me think of you, hope you might bed me again?" Was it off-putting to admit that?

"I think you might be a secret vixen, Miss Hasting." Then he gripped her inner thighs and splayed her open. "I knew these silk stockings would suit you." He winked at her as he danced his fingertips along her skin. "The embroidery quite enhances your shapely legs, but the blue ribbons of your garters are a nice touch, and I can't wait until the next time we're together, for we will have more time and I *will* untie them with my teeth."

"Too bad I must wait." Trembles moved through her legs. "I'd hoped to experience your mouth on me." Had she dared to tease him too much?

"Ah, sweeting, you have no idea what it is you've asked." The waft of his warm breath over her sensitive fold sent a shiver of anticipation down her spine as he moved closer.

"If you're supposed to be the devil, let us hope I'm the one who will eventually win in this game you've made me play." How much did she adore teasing him? She buried the fingers of one hand into his hair, urging him closer.

"It is only satisfying if both opponents are well matched." Then he touched his mouth to her button, and she nearly launched off the bed.

"Ah!" Certainly, she was not ready for that. Had no idea what such a thing would feel like.

He chuckled. The vibrations sent her into another level of wonder. "You'll enjoy this." And he began the next stage of his seduction even though he'd already well and truly caught her.

"Merciful heavens." From the moment he employed his lips and hot tongue to her most sensitive, private parts, Amelia slowly lost the last vestiges of her sanity. "This... You..." She couldn't catch her breath, for with each nibble, every nip, all the swipes and strokes of his tongue, she was hurled higher and higher into a realm of pleasure where she'd never gone before.

Wild sensation coursed through her body. She shook from it. Tears unashamedly fell to her cheeks for the feelings were too big, too much, too overwhelming, but she craved so much more.

Never once did Nicholas shy away from his work. He was a man bent on throwing her over the edge, and she hovered there, trapped, waiting with held breath and a hammering heart for him to release her into that dark void.

But he didn't. Oh, no.

The wicked man kept her poised on the razor's edge, pinning her there with every stroke of his tongue, each calculated nibble, every new torment of suction on that swollen button until she squirmed and gasped for breath. She curled her hand into his hair alternately to shove him away and cease the exquisite torment but also to hold him to her tighter exactly where she needed him.

When she attempted to buck him off, he gripped her thighs that much tighter. Mia shook as tears of pleasure rolled down her cheeks. Her back arched, which put her deeper into his care, and his head bobbed between her thighs as the dratted man hummed his approval.

"I'm nearly there." The rushed whisper was filled with blatant pleading. "Nicholas, I need—Ah!"

The dam holding back the mounting pressure within broke. She shattered in spectacular fashion, fell into that black void full of the most wonderful bliss as her inner walls convulsed with a violent release. Throwing back her head, a half-stifled scream escaped her throat, and she hoped none of the servants would come to investigate.

The viscount glanced up, but she was barely aware. "Tell me again how you are a dried up and unwanted spinster."

Oh, she despised how smug he was, but she couldn't help her grin. "So arrogant. Perhaps I'll change my mind about marrying you."

Slight panic flitted over his face. "It is your decision." He came over her body once more. "And one I will abide by."

"Hush, Nicholas. Nothing could tear me away from you." Such a dear. She reached between them and quickly manipulated his frontfalls until his rampant length sprang out. "However, I will torture you a bit. It's only fair." When her palm brushed the head of his member, his muscles went taut.

"Bloody hell."

"Not so arrogant now that you're the one at my mercy, hmm?" While he claimed her lips and rolled one of her nipples, Mia drew a finger up and down his hardened shaft. She adored that his body tensed, waiting for action. Yes, indeed, they would have such fun together, though she largely suspected he would work her into a state of exhaustion most times. Shoving the thought from her mind, she gently wrapped her fingers around his member, slid them up and down, grinning when he moaned. In the mood to explore, when she traced her fingertips over his stones, the poor man shivered with apparent need. "Too much?"

"I'm still alive," he managed to say but there was heavy strain in his voice.

"Good." Enjoying herself, Mia fondled his stones, then leaned upward to kiss his chin, his cheek, then his mouth. It was a rather awkward position, but she made it work, for this was the most scandalous fun she'd ever had in her life. "Shall I continue?"

"Yes. Dear God, yes."

"Mmm, you feel so lovely," she whispered as she caressed his equipage, rubbed a fingertip along the skin between his stones and his anus that Millie had told her would drive a man wild. It must have been true, for a tortured sound somewhere between a howl and a groan left Nicholas' throat, and he yanked her hand from his person.

"Enough." In a thrice he had her once more on her back, and he settled between her splayed legs. "I need to be inside you." He buried his face between her breasts, kissed each one before sucking a nipple into his mouth and fitting the wide head of his shaft to her opening. When she arched her back and he rolled the other nipple with his fingers, he flexed his hips and penetrated her with a powerful thrust.

Mia gasped. "I adore this moment."

"As do I." Holding himself slightly over her while still stand-ing, he stroked into her with slow and lazy strokes.

She canted her hips, twined her legs around his to meet each new thrust, and was nearly separated from reality. Joining with him was like a dream, made her lost in the raw heat of his body, the strong feel of him as she clutched at his forearms, his shoulders, slid a hand down to squeeze a tight buttock.

"Ah, sweeting, you are the only one I ever want." He pulled out of her body with a grin, but as she protested, he winked. "Steady." Repositioning her, he settled between her raised legs while her bum hung off the edge.

"Why have you stopped?" But the new position excited her, and she couldn't wait to learn all he would teach her.

"Pardon the delay." With a grin that caused her heart to skip a beat, he gripped her hips and thrust hard into her body, going as deep as he could.

"Oh, dear lord!" The sensations crashing over her were so exquisite she felt them in every point of her body.

"Agreed." Over and over, he pumped into her, harder, faster. He worked her body as well as his until they were both panting, gasping for breath, their moans mingling in the heavy silence.

Pressure built and stacked inside her core. Surely, she would break from it and soon. "Hurry, Nicholas. I cannot last." Mingled moans became more frantic, and her noises of encouragement grew louder as he once more worried her swollen nubbin with his thumb but never slowed in his rhythm. "Oh, please…" She curled her hands into the bedding. Seeking a surcease of the wild feelings throbbing through her body, she drew her legs closer to her chest, and the viscount went ever deeper. That was all it took, for a strangled sort of scream left her throat, and she was tossed over the edge into the most perfect bliss she'd ever known.

"Mia!" He fell over the edge after her, grinding his pelvis against hers to prolong the wicked sensations. "I'd suspect you're trying to kill me if I didn't think you enjoy this sort of thing so much." He collapsed onto her body, his breathing as ragged as hers.

"You dratted man, don't you know if I were going to kill you,

I'd use poison? It's less messy." Amelia chuckled as she clung to him, held him close, and as his delighted laughter tickled through her chest, she pressed her lips to the side of his neck. "As odd or as surprising as it seems, I do love you."

"I love you, adore you, will worship at your feet if you so desire it." He crawled onto the bed and collapsed. "If this is how it is between us after a week, what will it be like after ten years, twenty?"

Amelia giggled. It was so freeing to be with this man. No, he hadn't solved any of her problems, and neither had she done the same for him, but they would meet them all together, and that was already better than she had before. Exhausted and sated, she came up the bed to lie next to him, put a palm to the side of his face. "We should be so fortunate as to have a love that burns hot through the years."

"Is it possible? I mean, after all, you've already slapped me three times." The teasing in his voice and eyes was adorable.

"You deserved it, but yes, it's possible. I know because I've seen it in my parents." If her heart grew any fuller, it would burst.

"What if as time goes on, you aren't enamored with the man I truly am?"

"That is always a risk, I suppose, but then, I am not perfect either." She gave him a tired smile. "You might fall out of love with me at that point, or perhaps you'll despise my family. There are many unknowns."

"Yet you wish to go ahead with this relationship?"

"Absolutely. I have faith, and fate hasn't steered me wrong yet.

His smile could light up the room. "Shall we wed immediately, or do you wish for the banns to be read?"

"Honestly? I want my family to be a part of it. Now that I'm without a position, would you mind terribly much if we traveled to Landover Manor in Bedfordshire to tell my parents? The banns can then be read, and we can marry by Easter."

"For you I would do just about anything as long as I can keep you happy." His eyes shone with gratitude. "After all, I won you. That's the only thing I need."

"Me, married before Millie." Amelia snorted and shook with laughter. "I never would have dreamed something like this would happen."

"Oh, I knew I'd bed you," Nicholas said in a low whisper as he pulled her against his body. "Falling for you is an unexpected but most welcome gift. Thank you for keeping me from Millie. I would have been singularly unhappy in that union."

"She would have thrown a vase or a perfume bottle at your head multiple times, for you can be quite aggravating at times." But she snickered to temper the words.

"I have the scars from when other women have done the same."

"Ooh, something new to explore, and I haven't seen you naked…"

"There is that." He kissed her and for long moments there was no talking at all.

Then Amelia stirred, pulled back to peer into his eyes the best she could in the shadowy darkness of the room. "We should return downstairs. Dinner will be served soon, and I've worked up an appetite." She drew a hand down between their bodies to let her fingers brush along his flaccid length. "Unless you want another round?"

"Ah, dearest, give me a few hours, and once I'm back to full strength, there is nowhere you can hide that I won't find you." He pinched her arse cheek for emphasis.

At her squeal, they both laughed. "I cannot wait to see what becomes of our lives." There were no guarantees this was true, but she knew they would turn out right in the end, and sometimes a lady just had to take a chance… even on a devil.

None of it would have been possible without Captain Featheringham needing a companion for his willful daughter as she tried to burst her way into the English *ton*, which she did in spectacular fashion.

Life certainly had a way of being surprising.

EPILOGUE

April 20, 1820
Wycliffe House
Mayfair
London, England

AMELIA HARCOURT—VISCOUNTESS OF Wycliffe—smiled as she peered at her two-year-old son in the nursery. Never did she think that being a mother would be a part of her life, but fate had proved her wrong. The boy was perfect in every way, with her golden hair and blue eyes, while the rest of him was purely Nicholas.

She laid a hand on her swollen belly and sighed. There were three more months with this current pregnancy, but already she was as big as a house and twice as tired as she was when she carried little Gideon.

"He'll sleep for a long time yet, my lady," the nursery maid said in a whisper as she passed through the room with an armful of clean linens. "Best go put your feet up while you can."

"Perhaps you are right. I am behind on my reading." With a smile and a nod at the young lady, Mia left the nursery suite, went slowly down the corridor, and then entered the suite of rooms she shared with her husband.

"Where have you been? You should be resting." The concern in Nicholas' voice made her smile. "I worry."

"Perhaps too much." There was no point in arguing with him, for he would have his way… at least in this, so she let him guide her to a chair in their adjoining sitting room. "I'm not an invalid," she said as she sat down.

Immediately, he grabbed a footstool, brought it to her chair, and placed her feet on the embroidered cushion. "No, but if my suspicions are correct, you're carrying twins, and I refuse to risk the babes coming too early."

A sigh escaped her. "Is everything in readiness for travel?" In two days' time, they would journey to Moss Cottage in Ireland, the property his father had left to him that had been built by his grandfather. Since they married three years before and had spent a glorious honeymoon there, they made an effort to travel there every year at this time, weather permitting. It was where she would have the new babe—or babies if that was what fate would give them.

"It is. The staff has been informed. By and large, everyone is ready for the adventure." The dear man sat at her feet with a hand on her knee. As always when he was near, butterflies chased through her belly. "You're certain you wish to give birth there?"

"I am. It means so much to you and your history. Our Gideon was born at my father's manor so it makes sense the new little one will be born in Ireland. I want them to be proud of all their roots." Last year she'd lost her father due to his deteriorating mental state, and since her mother was too frail to travel, it was only natural she'd go to where it was most tranquil. Most of her sisters had scattered around England or even farther, but there was talk of getting together for the Christmastide holidays this year. "Besides, I'll have everyone I need to attend me, and we'll return to London in mid-autumn."

"Right." Nicholas nodded. "I have an important vote in the Lords on the second of June, but then I'm all yours once more." He slipped his hand up to her thigh. "I'm beyond excited to meet the new young one."

"So am I." She took his hand and placed it on her belly. "After this one, though, I would like to begin using sheaths and other methods for preventing pregnancy, for I don't wish to spend the next ten years of my life pregnant or birthing children." Her chin trembled, for it was a delicate topic. "Since I didn't marry until later in my life, I'd like to enjoy the little ones as well as you while I still can."

"That's understandable." With a grin, he surged to his knees, brought her hand to his lips, and placed a kiss on its back. "I'll do whatever you want, for fewer children means more time to spend with you."

"Good."

"Oh, I had a letter from Percy this morning." He waggled his eyebrows. "Some of the investments I originally made with him have matured and doubled once more. The repairs on the hall should be complete this summer, and should the new babe be a girl, there will be more than enough for a sizable dowry. She'll never need to take a paid position as a companion."

"As if that is such a bad thing." Without that, they would never have met. Mia squeezed his fingers. "I'm so glad Percy is a successful banker." His investment strategies were sound and solid, which had allowed Nicholas the freedom to put forth his ideas for farming and reform with a bit left over to pay the rest of their bills and obligations while still living comfortably but modestly. It also left the tenant farmers happy as well as the poor in the viscount's parish looked after. "He's proved a valuable asset." Additionally, Millie wrote faithfully to her every month. She had two children around Gideon's age and was pregnant with her third child. And since Percy was the nephew of Nicholas' best friend, they saw Mr. Chapman on a regular basis as well.

"Who would have thought it possible?" The viscount scrambled to his feet only to press his lips to her forehead. "Never have I been as content, as happy, as you have made me."

"Such gammon. You made yourself that way when you decided to be the man you truly are instead of the man you wished to hide behind." But she smiled, for there wasn't a day that went by where she didn't thank God for him.

Oh, they had arguments over the years, and a couple of them had been serious enough to temporarily separate them to different residences, but there was always a compromise in the offing as well as forgiveness and above all love to bridge the gaps and heal the wounds. As long as they remembered why they'd entered into their wedding vows and what was at the core of their relationship, they would always land on their feet.

"Because of you." When he grinned, the skin at the corners of his eyes crinkled. "I'm going to order tea. Would you like anything else?"

"Nothing except you sitting with me, enjoying the afternoon before the hectic days of travel are before us." She waved him away while he left the room, and she closed her eyes.

Life was what a person made of it. Unless they were content with their lot as it was, they wouldn't find that if they married, and being wed didn't guarantee instant or long-lasting happiness unless the couple worked for it and took nothing for granted. But that was exactly what made one's existence exciting, and the milestones one passed during the journey oftentimes brought the sweetest joys.

It was all in how one looked at things.

The End

About the Author

Sandra Sookoo is a *USA Today* bestselling author who firmly believes every person deserves acceptance and a happy ending. Most days you can find her creating scandal and mischief in the Regency-era, serendipity and happenstance in Victorian America or snarky, sweet humor in the contemporary world. Most recently she's moved into infusing her books with mystery and intrigue. Reading is a lot like eating fine chocolates—you can't just have one. Good thing books don't have calories!

When she's not wearing out computer keyboards, Sandra spends time with her real-life Prince Charming in central Indiana where she's been known to goof off and make moments count because the key to life is laughter. A Disney fan since the age of ten, when her soul gets bogged down and her imagination flags, a trip to Walt Disney World is in order. Nothing fuels her dreams more than the land of eternal happy endings, hope and love stories.

Stay in Touch

Sign up for Sandra's bi-monthly newsletter and you'll be given exclusive excerpts, cover reveals before the general public as well as opportunities to enter contests you won't find anywhere else.

Just send an email to sandrasookoo@yahoo.com with SUBSCRIBE in the subject line.

Or follow/friend her on social media:
Facebook: facebook.com/sandra.sookoo
Facebook Author Page: facebook.com/sandrasookooauthor
Pinterest: pinterest.com/sandrasookoo
Instagram: instagram.com/sandrasookoo
BookBub Page: bookbub.com/authors/sandra-sookoo

www.ingramcontent.com/pod-product-compliance
Lightning Source LLC
Chambersburg PA
CBHW060402310726
48976CB00003B/918